BEHROUZ
GETS LUCKY

BEHROUZ
GETS LUCKY

A NOVEL

AVERY CASSELL

CLEIS
PRESS

Published in the United States by Cleis Press, an imprint of Start Midnight, LLC, 101 Hudson Street, 37th Floor, Suite 3705, Jersey City, NJ 07302.

Printed in the United States.
Cover design: Scott Idleman/Blink
Cover photograph: Shutterstock
Text design: Frank Wiedemann
First Edition.
10 9 8 7 6 5 4 3 2 1

Trade paper ISBN: 978-1-62778-170-1
E-book ISBN: 978-1-62778-171-8

This is a work of fiction. All characters and events portrayed in this novel are fictitious and not intended to represent real people.

CONTENTS

OF CLITS AND COCKS

L et's take the time to tell all. Behrouz and Lucky are older queer rascals, our favorite curmudgeonly, tenderhearted gay uncles rolled with a sweet coating of hedonism and snark. When we start off our story, Behrouz is sixty and Lucky is forty-nine years old. Although they both are easily settled into their gender identities, their preferred pronouns and the words they use for their various naughty bits are not apparent to our fine readers. After all, this is just a smutty little love story, so we can safely lay it all out on the line without worrying about asking rude, politically incorrect, or insensitive questions.

Behrouz identifies as a transgender genderqueer, and Lucky identifies as a butch dyke. Both Behrouz and Lucky were born female, and both often pass as male. Behrouz started taking testosterone late in life, at age fifty-five. Lucky never has taken testosterone and is not tempted to start.

If we were to ask Behrouz which pronouns they prefer, they would toss one fey wrist into the air and say, "Whatever you're comfortable with!" That's a lie. Behrouz prefers they/them or he/him. If we were to ask Lucky which pronouns she prefers, she would say she/her.

Unless Lucky was topping and in the mood for honorifics, in which case she would prefer the more masculine "sir," rather than the more feminine "ma'am."

Behrouz and Lucky both call their clitoris their cock, flesh cock, or clit, but usually just their cock. They call the whole package their cunt. They own a ridiculous variety of expensive silicone dildos in many sizes, which they also call their cocks. Lucky has a favorite silicone cock, which is seven inches long, one-point-eight inches in girth, curved, and black. Lucky likes to say that black is classic and goes with everything. We concur with her good taste. Lucky and Behrouz both still have breasts. Behrouz binds to appear flat-chested and so that their shirts fit better. Lucky usually wears a sports bra. They will talk about both their breasts or their chest, and it means the same thing. As we all know, everyone has an asshole and assholes have no gender.

I wrote this book because I wanted to see more people like myself represented in smut and romance. I wanted to see older genderqueer and butch masculine-masculine couples having hot sex and BDSM shenanigans. I wanted to read about people with full lives, lives that included adult children, grandchildren, parents, books, marvelous food, over-the-top drag, and cuddly cats along with lots and lots of hot fucking. I wanted reality, with heartburn, forgetfulness, and aching joints. I also wanted protagonists that cared about San Francisco and were activists, in their own quirky way. And finally, I spent most of my childhood in Iran and love Iran as my other home. I wanted to include a little bit of that amazing and beauteous country in this tale so that my readers could get the chance to love the country too.

CHAPTER ONE

LUCKY

I was sixty, and long past the age of hope, young lust, love, and bewilderment. I was sixty, using my senior discount to buy oatmeal, black tea, and ginseng at Rainbow Co-op, and silk neckties at Goodwill. I was a time-traveling, part-Persian expatriate. I had been an outsider all my life, and felt insulated that way. Insulation is protection, but it is also isolation. Even though I lived in San Francisco, that bastion of sexual and gender freedom, I lived outside of the galaxies of the butch, FTM, genderqueer, and leather communities. I'd hitchhiked across the country, been a streetwalker, smoked opium with princes, raised children, been fisted on Twin Peaks, sung in punk bands, grown up in Iran, had threesomes with bikers and members of British Parliament, and followed family tradition to become a librarian. I'd buried one daughter and two lovers, spent decades in the Midwest, kneaded bread, gotten sober, been homeless, pretended to be a boy wanting to be a girl, driven across town in a blizzard at 5:00 a.m. to slap a gigolo who was wearing pleated black silk panties, taught preschool, attended PTA meetings, and tickled grandchildren. It's-a-long-story was my middle name.

At sixty, and in my considerable dotage, I spent my evenings wearing a quilted, charcoal velvet smoking jacket with a foulard silk cravat, and worn, cuffed flannels while delicately sipping English Breakfast tea with my cat, Francy, strewn across my lap, a pile of tattered paperback Dorothy Sayers mysteries at hand, and vacillating between wanting to manifest a lover and relishing each delicious second alone. Between chapters, and inspired by Lord Peter Whimsey and his paramour Harriet Vane, I imagined a lover, a you. If I could manifest you at 6:00 a.m. when I was lolling between the sheets distractedly having my morning prework come, or on Sunday afternoon when I was settling in for a leisurely fuck session with myself, my two biggest silicone dildos, nipple clamps, my S-curved metal dildo, a metal sound, a stainless steel butt plug, Eartha Kitt wafting from the stereo, a fountain of lube, dim lights, and a cushion of towels and rubberized sheeting to soak up the spillage…I would imagine a you.

Sometimes I craved you when I came home, tired from a day of advising patrons, giving restroom directions, problem-solving minor computer issues, and searching for copies of the latest bestselling romance. Sometimes I craved that moment of perfect domesticity when I'd open my door to the oregano- and tomato-scented smells of minestrone soup wafting from the kitchen, and you in the rust velvet armchair in the living room. I'd fall to my knees on the rough wool of our Tabrizi carpet, start to crawl across the red and gold fibers, imagining that moment when I could unbutton your fly and fill myself with your cock as an appetizer. Your pipe would be smoldering in the ashtray, filling the air with the sultry sweet aroma of tobacco and cherry. You'd lean back and spread your denim-clad legs, rubbing your cunt as I approached on my knees, the workday rolling off me the closer I got. Reaching your cunt, I'd rest for a minute, my lips caressing the bulge in your crotch, as grateful for your hand on the back of my neck and your packed jeans as I was for salt. I'd growl softly, nipping at the thick blue fabric, damp from my spit and slightly threadbare from past administrations. You would unbutton your fly slowly, each button releasing a soft pop. I'd cover your cock with my mouth until it reached my throat, then ease up and lick the shaft, lost in your smell and your palm firmly pushing my head into your cunt. Your cock would shove the outside world aside, erasing demanding supervisors, aching joints, and crowded MUNI buses until all that was left was your cock in my throat.

I had a shallow, translucent blue glass bowl on the dining room table that I filled with garnet-colored pomegranates, dusty plums, phallic bananas, and tart green apples, and sometimes I longed to see your house keys on the table next to the bowl of fruit. Did I want this complication to interfere with my quiet life? Did I really want someone to know my quirks and fears? To discover that I sometimes ate cheddar cheese, figs, and cookies for dinner, to twist her hand into my silver-haired cunt, to be privy to my mood swings and self-doubt, to be content to live with my need for solitude? I'm Middle Eastern to my part-American core, and as such have a deep belief in fate. At a jaded and indecisive sixty, I decided to leave love and lust to fate.

How did we meet? How does fate decide to roll her dice? Was it at the park, commiserating over fawn-colored pigeons fighting for brioche crumbs at our feet, while the ginkgo trees shed golden, fan-shaped leaves on the park bench? Was it in an airport while listening to the murky flight update announcements, wondering if we should grab an overpriced stale croissant and latte before our flight, and finally reaching for our lattes at the same time, our fingers touching over scattered copies of USA Today? Maybe it was at work, sighing and rolling our eyes over gum-snapping coworkers, discovering mutual tastes in movies and politics in the lunchroom, meeting outside the office on the sly, and texting filthy thoughts to each other across the table during meetings.

In reality, we met prosaically. Lacking a noisy yet accurate village matchmaker, we filled out our profiles on OKCupid, rolled our mutual eyes at the idiocy of naming the five things one could never do without, and updated our profiles earnestly and regularly. I worried about whether I sounded too shallow, and you fretted about sounding too serious. I mentioned that I had an Isherwood haircut, lank thinning

3

brown hair, hazel eyes, a husky build, and a pale DAR complexion. We both were annoyed at OKCupid's lack of queer identity choices. I changed my sex from male to female and back again monthly, while she identified as bisexual so as not to leave out possible FTM matches. I mentioned that I was a daddy in the streets and a strumpet in the sheets. Although I took testosterone, I was not a man or even FTM. She put up an out-of-focus picture of her repotting plants, said she spoke French, ironed and starched her sheets, had olive skin, dimples, and a graying pompadour. She didn't mention her sexual proclivities at all. I mentioned flagging red, gray, black, and navy right in the first paragraph, said that I cooked Persian food and collected bird skulls, put up a photo of myself half-dressed and playing an accordion, and said that only butch dykes need apply. She was eleven years younger than I, a rough-hewn-looking butch who gave me five stars, which made my heart flutter and my cunt get wet in anticipation. I rated her five stars back, and nervously sent her a short, overly edited but carefully flirtatious email suggesting that we meet for tea and conversation. Then I heard nothing for five months. In the interlude I went on a series of fruitless first dates, but I had not forgotten her. In spring she finally wrote back, suggesting that we meet for coffee. Her name was not Amber or Dixie or Tyler, but Lucky. And I wrote to Lucky, signing my name *Behrouz,* which means lucky in Farsi.

We met at Café Flore, the classic rendezvous for queer blind dating in the Castro. Public transportation was two steps away, so it was easy to flee from the date if it was awful. Café Flore was loud, and gay as fuck, with mediocre food and sweet servers. We were both on time. I wore pleated gray flannel pants, a white shirt with a Campbell clan wool necktie, my tattered gray Brooks Brothers jacket, purple silk socks with striped garters, horn-rims, my hair slicked to one side, and my favorite butterscotch-colored brogues. Lucky wore a stately pompadour, a red-ribbed wool sweater with frayed cuffs over a white oxford shirt, black 501 button-fly jeans, three gold rings on her right hand, and harness boots. She was stocky and muscular, a little shorter than my five-eight, had deep-brown hair threaded with gray, small breasts, olive skin, a chipped front tooth, hazel eyes, a large aristocratic nose with tiny nostrils, black-framed glasses, and a beguiling swagger. She drank black coffee, and I sipped sticky-sweet soy chai latte.

I was immediately turned on by Lucky, trying not to look too eager as I glanced at her rough gardener's hands, evaluating them for size and dexterity. I was nervous and unsure if she liked me back. I was never good at reading signs, and knew that my reserve was often read as disinterest. I wanted to feel her hand in my cunt. We started slowly. We talked about our cats, the general state of classism and disrepair in San Francisco, our jobs, food, and our upbringings. Lucky's tuxedo cat, Elmer, had died two months ago, after living a long and productive life of catching mice, napping in her oval, vintage, pink porcelain bathroom sink, and skulking on bookshelves. My ginger cat, Francy, had one bronze eye, a puffed-out tail that was longer than her body, and liked to pee with me when I came home from work. I told her about my love of books, organization, and social service, which led to the good fortune of a job at the San Francisco Public Library. After studying biology, Lucky had fallen into gardening, and spent her days planning gardens and fondling manure and plants. We agreed that the recent invasion of stealthy, gleaming-white Google buses with black-tinted windows that transported entitled tech workers from their cubicle penthouses in San Francisco to their jobs in Mountain View were shark like, and wondered why they hadn't been violently defaced yet. We mourned the loss of Plant It Earth, Osento bathhouse, Faerie Queene Chocolates, the dimly lit Mediterranean place on Valencia with Fat Chance belly dancers swiveling sensuously around the tables, The Red Vic Movie House, and Marlene's drag bar on Hayes Street, and then we sighed like curmudgeonly old farts wondering where the past had disappeared.

Lucky was raised Jewish in Columbus, Ohio, a hotbed of Republican ideology and Christian intolerance, graduated a year early from Bexley School for Girls, then fled to UC Berkeley for sexual and intellectual freedom. Her dad was an insurance adjuster and her mom worked part-time in the ladies' undergarments section of Lazarus

5

department store. Her father worked late hours and fancied himself a suave businessman, leaving the house each morning awash in citrusy Spanish cologne and cigarette smoke, and sporting a flashy gold Rolex wristwatch won while playing cards. Her mom was bitter around the corners and sentimental in the middle. She was a brunette in turquoise double-knit pants suits and the sweetly floral scent of Chanel No 22. Lucky told me about coming home to find her mom drinking endless goblets of chardonnay while listening half-cocked for the metallic sound of her father's key in the front door, and the sneaky shuffle that announced his belated presence home. Lucky was an only child, but lived in the same Tudor-style home in the same quiet middle-class neighborhood her entire childhood, with the oak-lined streets, and her aunts, uncles, cousins, and friends with their families protecting and loving her even when Lucky's folks were distracted.

Since our family had moved every two years from state to state, country to country, and continent to continent, I found Lucky's childhood geographic stability both exotic and enviable. At age seven, Lucky decided she wanted to be a boy. Each night she'd stare dreamily out her bedroom window while stroking the faint down on her upper lip to wish a mustache into existence. Wryly, Lucky told me that it didn't work, but now she was content with her hard-earned butchness. As a child, Lucky escaped into books, and spent hours in the Bexley Public Library, scouring the shelves for anything related to sexuality and gender, which wasn't much in the 1960s. Lucky's curiosity and scholastic diligence paid off with a full university scholarship and an early release from Ohio. I'd also grown up immersed in books, hiding in odd corners at home with a stack of books and a pocket full of raisins. I related to the escapism that they provided to desperate kids like us, junior outsiders and renegades.

After three hours of exchanging stories and too much coffee and chai, we started to talk about sex and desire. Our drinks cooled as the temperature heated. We both lived in San Francisco, home to sexual freedom and excess, with everything from International Ms. Leather, to the Eagle, Mr. S, the 15 Association, the Exiles, regular play parties for every identity and orientation, BDSM coffee houses, and more. One-time hookups, public play, and casual sex were easily obtainable, but I was embarrassed to admit to Lucky that in my mid-fifties I'd grown out of the ability to do casual play and sex. It didn't work for me anymore, and although I missed the immediacy and physical relief of instant sex, I needed lovers, continuity, and intimacy. Lucky commiserated, and said that she'd felt the same ever since turning forty-three. Even though we agreed that we both wanted love and deeper intimacy, everything felt dangerous and forbidding—as if we were getting ready to foolishly leap off an emotional cliff, our hearts potentially shattered on the shoals below.

I flushed as our eyes met. We both stopped breathing for a second, unsure if we wanted to continue. Finally, Lucky inhaled, leaned forward, pierced me in my eye with the future, and murmured, "Tell me. What do you want? What do you need?"

I blushed, my eyes widening and quickly looking down, and my cunt tingling. I admitted to wearing my hankies on the right, and a proclivity for getting fisted, giving head, ass-fucking, bondage, and getting beaten. Lucky reached across the table and held my hand, my palm facing up and her calloused hand beneath mine, leaving me feeling exposed, trapped, and cradled all at once. I swooned a little at her touch. Lucky smiled a lopsided, sweetly sly smirk, and I imagined one pointed incisor sharply peeking through her lips, her teeth hard against my neck and biting my flesh. She told me she was a top and a sadist, and had been that way since she was a baby dyke in plaid flannel shirts, Frye boots, and Carhartts. I blushed again, and felt my nipples harden painfully in the tight confines of my binder, as I whispered through dry lips that although there was no accounting for chemistry, thus far we seemed to have chemistry just fine. I told Lucky that I had simple tastes really, all I wanted was to suck her off, then be beaten, and fisted until we were swimming in a pool of come.

Lucky asked, "And what do you call your top? Daddy or Sir?"

And I answered, "I call my top, *baby*."

Lucky looked at me with her hazel eyes turning green as polished sea glass. She leaned closer, took my hand, and bit the side of my palm while looking into my eyes. As she bit harder, my hips lifted, and I groaned. I wanted Lucky's teeth on my neck, my breast, my ass. There is a vulnerability to a hand's underbelly. It is my favorite place to be bitten, so tender and so blatant—I melted. I wanted her to read my desire with her mouth, hurting me because she needed to, and me letting the sharp sensations course through my flesh, forming a loop of desire between us.

"Baby," Lucky said, managing to draw the word out like we'd already taken our clothes off and were lying hip to hip. She didn't huff up in toppish indignation, wasn't quizzical or offended, but understood that "baby" was my code for hotness, tenderness, and love.

After four hours at Café Flore, Lucky murmured, "Let's go."

Lucky stumbled lightly over the shallow steps leading down to the sidewalk, exclaiming that her new bifocals were a bear to get accustomed to, then leaned in to kiss me on the sidewalk in front of a gaggle of Sisters of Perpetual Indulgence and next to the organic stone-fruit stand at the farmers market. "It's Raining Men" was playing tinnily through Café Flore's speakers. She kissed exactly correctly…and if that sounds dry, it isn't meant to be so. Her lips were firm and pliant, and fit mine like a T-shirt on a teenager. She'd mastered the art of the tender lower-lip bite, and as I delicately licked the corners of her lips, we quickly became breathless. We pulled away a quarter of an inch to prolong the anticipation, and fell onto each other after five seconds. I pulled Lucky closer as a Sister with a violet Marie Antoinette wig wolf-whistled in our direction. Lucky slipped one muscular thigh between my legs as my cunt melted and throbbed. I moaned into her mouth as her wide palm smoothed my back under my jacket, and I whispered that I wanted her hand inside of me. Now. Lucky growled—a low nip from deep in the back of her throat. The Sister with the lime-green boa passed us a fistful of condoms. I was starry-eyed and damp as we stumbled to my apartment in nearby Hayes Valley.

It was dusk, that magical time when the day ends and night begins, when responsibilities dissipate, and mystery and longing fill our hearts.

The evening air smelled of jasmine, anticipation, and piss, the violent and sweet scents circling us as we walked. The moon was rising as bright as a streetlight, and the sidewalks were full of early evening dog-walkers, with their pups tarrying by trees and potted plants while the owners peered into their palms at their phones. We barely talked. We'd talked through an entire afternoon. Words mean something, but I needed to know how Lucky tasted, how she touched, how we smelled together as we heated up. All I could think of in that fifteen-minute walk was Lucky's hand in my cunt, her gardener's fingers entering one by one, packing me full of her. Anything else was gravy on the cake. You know.

By the time I unlocked the door to my flat, it was dark and the full moon watched us. The streetlights had followed us home, each lighting one by one as night fell and we were closer to my apartment. I unlocked the top bolt, then struggled with the pesky bottom one, trying to make the stuck key turn. As I jiggled the lock in the dark hallway, Lucky pressed her body against mine from behind, rubbing her cock against my ass, and reached around to untuck my shirt and run her hands up toward my nipples. I moaned, humping the doorknob with my clit and almost dropping the key. Finally the brass key turned, and the door flew open under our weight. Lucky pushed me suddenly through the dim foyer, down the hallway, and into the sandalwood-scented living room, then to the floor. I wasn't expecting the quickness, and fell to the Persian carpet, my jacket still on and my shirt half-untucked. She stood over me, unbuckled her black leather belt, threw off her sweater, unbuttoned her jeans, pulled out her dick, and started stroking it with her hips insolently cocked forward.

"On your knees. I want you to suck my cock. Now."

I crawled over, leaned forward and opened my mouth. I loved filling my mouth with stuff, whether it was cock, chains, or fingers. My cunt was soaked, my dick was throbbing, and I wanted nothing more than to suck Lucky's cock. I wrapped my lips around the black silicone and took it to the hilt while looking up greedily at her. Lucky thrust her hips forward, then drew away, teasing me with just the head

9

until she roughly pushed it all the way in again, banging my throat rudely. I could smell her cunt heating up, and sucked her cock, pushing it hard against her cunt, then letting up, and then pushing it in again. I was lost in the rhythm, smells, and sounds of cocksucking, feeling my cunt muscles spasm the more turned on I became by Lucky's moans and growls, and the feeling of my mouth being stuffed.

Lucky grabbed my head, shoving me harder into her groin while letting loose with a stream of fuck noises and words. "I'm gonna fuck your mouth until I come. Suck me, my little invert."

I was slobbering with drool running down the sides of my mouth as I made slurping and snorting noises while she pulled my hair and fucked my mouth. I desperately wanted to jack off, but even more desperately wanted to suck her dry. I wanted Lucky to come down my throat and out my asshole, her heat burrowing into my body. I wanted her to come like lightning through my cunt. I fucked her cock harder with my hot mouth, until with a tremendous series of guttural grunts Lucky came, my swollen lips wrapped around her big black cock.

Lucky's hand loosened on my hair for a minute, then she pushed me backward on the rug. I fell awkwardly on my back, supported by my elbows and looking up at her dazedly. She kneeled over me, her pompadour sexily disheveled, her cheeks flushed, her eyes half-closed and blazing, then took my face between her calloused hands and we kissed, a long luxurious smooch, full of promise. I shrugged off my jacket as Lucky did the same. As I was unknotting my necktie, I heard the swooshing sound of her leather belt being jerked rapidly through her belt loops and looked up to see that she'd doubled it up and was grinning at me evilly.

Lucky shoved me sideways growling, "Bend over the ottoman."

I kneeled over the high, Moroccan-leather ottoman, as she yanked my flannel trousers and my briefs down to my knees. Lucky's hand reached between my thighs, cupping my cunt, then withdrawing slowly, her fingers separating my labia and running from my cock to my cunt to my asshole. I could feel salty sweet precome drip down my thighs. I moaned and pushed back, trying to draw her inside of me.

I didn't care where, I just needed her fingers inside of me pumping and rolling and fucking…filling my hungry holes. Instead, she stood up, hovering over me, letting the heat between us build. Suddenly she drew back and let at me with her belt against my ass. The first hit was a kiss. My cunt was slammed into the ottoman and my ass reached up for Lucky. She hit me harder the second and third times. I still wanted to jerk off, but didn't want to come yet, so I shoved my clit into the side of the leather, forgetting about the belt and spreading my legs to expose my cunt to her touch, then closing them rapidly as I remembered what was coming and the leather flew through the air. The next hits were harder and faster, and I could feel Lucky's grin and her hard-on behind each swoop of the belt as it thumped my ass. I was making whimpering noises, and each time her belt hit me, it drove my chest forward, pushing the air out of my lungs with a whoosh. My ass was on fire and my cunt felt hollow. Suddenly, I heard the snap of latex. Lucky dropped to her knees and started grabbing my burning ass, twisting my newly bruised, tender flesh. I moaned at the fresh pain. Then there was a cold slurp of lube and one finger circling my hole. I was frantic for her hand and bucked, trying to suck her in, but she slapped my ass with her free hand.

"Impatient, are we?"

One finger, a second finger, and finally a third slipped into me, with her thumb rubbing against the side of my engorged, stiffened clit.

"Please fuck me. Please! I need your hand inside my cunt," I begged.

Lucky groaned but pulled out, prolonging my agony as she teased my cunt by barely dipping her fingers inside of me. I sobbed as she finally started pushing four fingers into my cunt while biting my shoulder with her pointy teeth. By now I was inarticulate with wanting to get fucked. The world had shrunken to Lucky's hand in my cunt and her breath on my neck. Then she was twisting her hand inside, I opened up to Lucky, pushing back, and we were fucking—her gardener's hand in my cunt, the wettest nest, everything swollen and rippling. Lucky's mouth. My cunt. Lucky's cunt. My cock, my clit. Lucky's cock. I was

11

fucking her back and she was growling. I was making noises that said, "Fuck me fast and hard." I could feel my orgasm start in my belly—a heavy roll undulating from my chest down to my cunt as I shot out a gush of come, my cock swelling and my cunt clenching around her fist. Lucky was shouting as I sputtered hoarsely, my salty come squirting out a second time, soaking us both.

I slid off the ottoman to the carpet, panting, my pants tangled around my calves and come dripping down to my knees. Lucky fell down to the floor and we held each other close until our breathing slowed down. We were still mostly dressed, our clothing soaked with sex and sweat. I tried to get up, and my knees creaked as I stumbled over my twisted and damp trousers. I tipped over onto the floor laughing. Lucky was in better shape, but her wrist joint ached, her shirt was wet up to the armhole with my come, and her cock was listing perilously to the left. I sat Lucky down on the olive mohair sofa, put Eartha Kitt crooning "C'est Si Bon" on the stereo, poured her a snifter of cognac, and hung up our jackets. Woozily, I staggered into my bedroom, fetched Lucky a fresh shirt from my cedar-lined wardrobe, changed into a dry pair of pants, and made my way to the kitchen to fix us a postcoital snack of a simple omelet, à la Alice B. Toklas.

In the kitchen, I turned on Marlene Dietrich dramatically singing "Black Market" and swung my well-oiled hips. I let the warmth of the afterfuck flow through me lazily as I vigorously beat the eggs, water, cheese, and a hearty sprinkle of coarsely ground black pepper with a fork, then slid them into the hot skillet. Soon the omelet was bubbly and I plopped bread into the toaster, singing along with cabaret singer Marlene's racy wartime entreatments from *A Foreign Affair*.

I could hear Eartha Kitt's husky voice as I strolled back into the living room carrying a silver tray with plates of hot omelet and crisp buttered toast. As I walked through the French doors into the living room, Lucky was humming to Eartha while rubbing her wrist. I cleared the low, Persian, engraved copper-tray coffee table of leather-bound books, dime-store mysteries, a prickly tomato pincushion, and a clutch of fountain pens and put down the tray, then sat down next to Lucky, massaging her wrist and hand, pressing my thumbs into her over-fucked joints. We ate, denim knee to flannel knee, devouring the steaming eggs quietly.

Eggs and toast finished, I suddenly became nervous and insecure. Was this just a queer, kinky, senior-citizen version of the one-night stand? Did I want this invasion of heat and conversation in my midst, winding its way through my apartment and life? It was easy to know what I wanted when my legs were spread—my cunt and Lucky's hand conversed fine. What the fuck was I doing? I must have jolted in panic, because Lucky removed my empty plate from my lap, leaned over, and snuggled me against her shoulder.

Lucky said softly, "Hey, you."

I said, "Hey, you too," back. And this is how it all started.

CHAPTER TWO

SOMETIMES

I don't like romance stories and here I am, hoisted by my own petard. Does this story exist to tell the narrative of love between Lucky and Behrouz? Is that all there is? Or am I so trite that a twisted nipple will get me to follow someone anywhere, down whatever tired old lane that person chooses? Two people meet cute, fuck, fuck some more, shack up, have some minor adventures—all this a leaky raft on which love floats. Boring as fuck unless you're the one whose heart is thumping like a cat with fleas scratching its ear, its furry leg thudding upon the floor. Is not being able to get out of bed with each other a good enough reason to shack up together? Is that all I have?

I think about the last scene in Djuna Barnes's *Nightwood,* with poor Robin crawling in circles, the hapless dog nipping at her in horror. I ask, is that me? Are you the tender dog, circling in feral misery? It is not love, is it? We're not unhappy. Me, I'm crawling at your feet, my tits dangling, sore nipples brushing the coarse carpet. Tender. Everything is tender now.

But here I am, getting ahead of myself. Of course, there were moments between Café Flore and scuttling down the darkened hallway with your tail between my legs. This is how it was—we fucked, then we ate an omelet by the cool light of the silvery moon. I asked you to leave because I was suddenly schoolgirl-shy or maybe I just needed to be alone. The truth is that I was used to being alone and did it well. There was a red-hot second of tenderness. Between us.

You said softly, "Hey, you."

I said "Hey, you too" back. "That was great, but I need to get up early tomorrow and am no good at sleeping with people."

You recognized a hint when you heard one. We kissed tenderly before you left, promising to meet up again soon. Maybe the next weekend even. I needed to be alone to think about the explosion of us that had just occurred in my living room. Your hand inside of me, your cock between my tender lips, balancing plates of food on our knees afterward, you in my borrowed starched shirt, the white oxford sleeves dangling past your worn knuckles, not sated yet. I could hear you whistling "Walkin' After Midnight" as you walked home down my street.

I lied. The next day was Sunday and I didn't have to work. I had no plans other than a lazy outing to Arizmendi Bakery for a sticky pecan roll and a stroll to Golden Gate Park's Arboretum to write, feed the squirrels, nap in the meadow, and take pictures of plants and flowers. And now I could add, to brood about possibilities and bravery. I hadn't expected anything to come of this date. Masculine-masculine pairings were not common, particularly in my age bracket. Our sexual, emotional, intellectual, and kink chemistry took me by surprise. Over the past few years, I'd gone on a spectacular number of fun three-hour dates that had not led to anything except new friends. Which isn't bad, but doesn't keep you warm at night.

I woke up alone, luxuriously stretching across my full-sized bed. Stretching from corner to corner, rolling my sore body on the soft saffron-colored sheets and reveling in the pain of fresh bruises, I got up, slipped into my brown corduroy dressing gown, made a pot of smoky sweet tea and a plate of Plugra buttered rye toast, took my turmeric and niacin supplements, then retired to the living room with the curtains open, the brilliant morning sun streaming through the wavy glass in the bay windows, and Francy sprawled on her back inside a pale oval of sunlight on the Tabrizi carpet, with her green eyes half-closed and bunny paws up. The room still reeked of come and sweat, with a light dusting of sandalwood. I put on Eartha Kitt again, remembering how Lucky had said, "Suck me, my little invert." I'd liked that. A lot. It was the invert part that made my cock stand up. Anyone who could use that popular Jazz Age, Radclyffe Hall-esque term while cock-sucking had my complete respect and attention. I sighed, finished my tea, licked my greasy fingers clean of salty butter, and hopped into the shower, letting the hot water steam my doubts and aches away. I got dressed in overalls, an orange-plaid Pendleton flannel shirt, and brown Frye lace-up ankle boots, grabbed my rucksack with my latest scarf-knitting project, my black-and-white composition notebook and fountain pen, and headed out for MUNI. It was a breezy, cool sixty-two degrees outside with swirls of fog icing the tops of buildings, perfect for a morning's deliberations in the park.

I texted Lucky from the N-Judah, *Good morning my little invert. I hope to see you again soon. I loved fucking last night!*

I heard back right away, *Me too! Gotta go. My mom is in town and I'm squiring her about. Meet up maybe next Friday night? Invertly yrs.*

Yes! Have a delightful time with your mom. Later.

After getting off with all the other Sunday park-goers at 9th and Irving in the Inner Sunset, I walked two blocks to the bakery, bought a sticky pecan roll and a ginger shortbread, ducked into Green Apple Books and picked up a copy of *Cha-Ching!* by Ali Liebegott, then set out for the three-block stroll to the Arboretum. I walked through the seven-foot-high, navy-metal-gated park entrance, showed the guards my San Francisco ID for free admittance, and made a beeline past picnickers, nappers, slow-walking strollers, and wobbly toddlers for my favorite bench in the Fragrance Garden under a gnarled magnolia tree. Birdsong was in the air.

Settling in, I opened my bag of sweetness and my book, staring at the rosemary bush opposite me, and promptly forgot to read. This was a fine conundrum! I had found the potential for heartbreak on an OKCupid date. It wasn't exactly irony, but it sure wasn't what I'd expected. I sighed, put down *Cha-Ching!*, got out my notebook and pen, and wrote a poem.

This kettle of fish,
is not fine,
as much as dubious.

I will hold OKCupid
fully responsible
for my future heartbreak.

I delicately ate my sticky pecan roll, picking up loose pecans as they fell off onto my lap and popping them into my mouth. I could worry myself into a stupor if I had the time, and I had the time right now. I restlessly got out my phone and texted my daughter in Ohio: *Hey kiddo! How are things?* We texted back and forth for a while. I was starting to unwind a little. It was hard to be clearheaded about Lucky. As I'd aged, I'd developed the ability to be more present and open-hearted in life, and that included the difficult parts along with the pleasant parts. Breaking up was so painful, and the older I'd gotten the more painful it had become. Was I willing to invite potential heartbreak into my life in the form of a smooth-talking, olive-skinned, filthy-minded gardener with talented hands? "Where is my sense of adventure?" battled with "Where is my sense of self-preservation?" What the fuck was my problem, with all this dillydallying, willy-nilly indecision? I was a waffling Libra, but I needed to get a grip. Now.

Hands. That's right, I'd almost forgotten. Lucky had hands with delicate ribbons of earth under each crescent-shaped fingernail and fingers that already knew how to reach inside my cunt to yank out strings of orgasms like one would pull yarn from a skein. Oh fuck! I was getting wet while sitting on a park bench in the shade, surrounded

17

by French tourists snapping photos of bushes and a tottering couple walking propped up by carved wooden canes. My nipples were hardening inside my binder and my shorts were damp. I wondered if it would be in poor taste to find a deserted shady pathway to fondle myself. Just for a minute to relieve the ache. I rolled my eyes at myself. You'd think that one's hormones would have wilted by age sixty, but I was more randy and responsive now than I'd ever been in my twenties and as I'd aged, I knew even more so what to do with it.

I got up, brushed off a few stray pecans, then meandered out of the Fragrance Garden, turning right toward the Ancient Plant Garden and Waterfowl Pond. Past excited turtle-watching kids, flocks of vaguely belligerent geese, and gangs of stroller-pushing parents, to the plants of Australia. I remembered there was a secluded stone wall surrounded by trees in that area of the park, and I found it. The tall trees and bushes made it even cooler, so I pulled my gray hoodie out of my rucksack, put it on, then sat back waiting for the armies of tame squirrels to find me and amuse me with their antics.

I was happily feeding the squirrels sticky bun crumbs when I heard a voice: "Hey, you!"

I looked up as the bushy-tailed rodents scattered. "Lucky!"

There stood Lucky in her red buffalo-check shirt, black newsboy cap, 501s, and boots with a beaming elderly woman beside her. "This is my mom, Betty. Mom, this is Behrouz. Remember, I told you about them? They're a librarian and a writer."

Lucky's mom was tiny, around five feet tall with short, thick, curly white hair, oval, gold, metal-framed glasses, brown eyes, a deep tan, an expansive lush build, and wearing a deep purple cotton turtleneck sweater, white knit pants, a long, flowing, brightly flowered wool challis scarf, a chunky turquoise necklace, and red walking shoes. I could smell a light whiff of elegant and spicy Cristalle by Chanel.

"You must be that nice person that Lucky told me about! I'm always happy to meet one of Lucky's friends."

Betty and I shook hands, "Pleased to meet you. I hope you're enjoying your visit to San Francisco."

18

"Oh, yes. Lucky has worn me out traveling all over the city, but I'm flying back to Florida tomorrow morning. We're getting ready to walk over to the Japanese Tea Garden. Would you care to join us?" she asked effusively.

I agreed. Lucky looked pleased but a little abashed at the turn of events, as we meandered through the park to the Japanese Tea Garden.

Once there, we sat at an oak table under the shingled awning and ordered pots of savory Genmaicha and flowery jasmine tea along with a plate of teahouse cookies and an order of dorayaki, red-bean-paste-filled cakes. Lucky's mom was exuberant, filling me in on her life at the retirement community in Florida. The community was known for its freewheeling ways, and she told me proudly that she enjoyed the freedom that came with being single. She ate Milano cookies for dinner and green power shakes for breakfast, woke up at 5:00 a.m. to read and meditate, had learned how to play tennis, and was a member of a women's reading group, an international cooking group, and a bridge group. Betty had read *Tantric Orgasms for Women Over 60* in her women's reading group a year ago, and it had changed her life.

She confided, "I have two gentleman callers and experience sexual ecstasy daily! Now Lucky, it was never like this with your father, bless his heart. Of course, he drank some and his diabetes didn't help. You two should try some of this tantric sex. You never know, you might like it!" Betty chortled.

I blinked in astonishment. Lucky turned a becoming shade of apricot, and I turned hot strawberry pink.

"Did Lucky tell you that I'm turning eighty on Wednesday? Lucky flew me out here as a birthday present, and we have eaten cake every single day I've been in San Francisco! One bakery after the other: Stella's, Tartine, B Patisserie, Golden Gate Bakery, Dianda's. Well, you can see where Lucky got her sweet tooth." Betty patted Lucky's arm lovingly and beamed even more brightly.

I could see where Lucky got a lot of her personality. Betty was a delightful handful of hedonistic little old lady.

Eventually, the sun started going down and we parted ways, Lucky and Betty headed back to Lucky's so that Betty could pack for her flight home, and me home to do my Sunday evening chores.

I got home, fed Francy, and laid out my shoe-shining kit, scuffed shoes and boots, shirts, and my bottle of homemade amber-scented spray starch. Every Sunday evening I liked to take a shower, get into a pair of Liberty of London paisley cotton pajamas, turn up the music, then shine my work shoes and boots, and iron and starch my dress shirts for the upcoming week. I loved the smell of shoe wax, steamed cotton, and amber, and the Sunday evening ritual made me feel satisfied, sexy, and complete. I was onto my third shirt, when my phone chirped. It was Lucky texting and wanting to know if I'd like to get together during the week. Perhaps Wednesday would work?

I felt more relaxed about seeing Lucky again now that I'd met her in the park. Seeing her with her clothes on and interacting with her mom made her more real and less a porntastic figure of my imagination. She was no longer Lucky-the-gardener-with-talented-hands-and-a-sly-smile, but Lucky-the-person. I texted back, *Wednesday is swell!* Then I hesitated. Was it too soon to send her dirty texts? Would she think I was being forward? Obviously, given the chance, I could and would worry about anything, including whether it was proper to sext someone who the night before had been wrist deep in my grateful cunt. And really, I wanted to be witty and suave…a combination of Djuna Barnes, Phil Sparrow, and Oscar Wilde, but all I could come up with was a plaintive, *I want your hand inside of me. Now.* I hoped that Lucky could hear my tone in my text. I was begging her, my knees to the floor and my cock hard.

In half an hour. Be ready. Signed, your invert, was the somewhat terse text from Lucky.

I hurriedly put away the metal ironing board, my laundry, boots, and shoe-shine kit, then took a fast whore's bath, washing my pits and cunt and brushing my teeth. I undressed, then put on my silk robe and a black rubber jockstrap. The special robe, the 1930s burnt-orange silk one with the black shawl collar.

Twenty-seven minutes later my doorbell rang and I buzzed Lucky up. I opened my apartment door. Lucky stood there and we stared at each other. We didn't say a word. I pulled the cord of my robe, letting it fall open, then reached over to unzip Lucky's brown-leather jacket. With a growl, Lucky grabbed my hair, shoving me to the carpeted floor and shutting the door with her boot. I fell to my knees, not caring for anything except that I was on the floor and Lucky was towering over me—me looking up, and her looking down. She kicked me forward with her black-leather harness boots as I half crawled and half rolled to the center of the hallway. She wasn't kicking me very hard, just hard enough to let me know that she was in charge, that for now, she controlled my body. I heard the snap of a glove. Lucky fell to the floor, parted my legs, and started fucking me quickly with three fingers, then four fingers, then her entire hand. Each time she added another finger she grunted, while I grunted right back. I skidded forward with the force of her fucking, my knees burning against the carpet and my cheek chaffing on the coarse wool. I'd been ready for her all day, wet and throbbing, and as soon as I'd heard Lucky ring my bell I'd flooded again. With a howl that started in my gut, I started coming, my sensitive tits rubbing against the scratchy carpet, Lucky's right hand pistoning in and out of my desperate cunt, and her left hand squeezing the bruises on my ass from the belt beating the night before. Lucky was fucking the past three years of celibacy out of me, and those lonely years were shooting from my body. Lucky and I had traveled from the middle of the hallway to the corner at the end, where I had a Victorian oak wooden library stand holding my mother's copy of the two-volume *Compact Oxford English Dictionary*. My head banged against the library stand as Lucky and I fucked. For one minute, I wondered if I was going to get brained by the *OED*, then all thoughts fled. I came, yelling as loud as I could, coming over and over, my come squirting out, soaking the carpet.

"Oh my god. Thank you, thank you, thank you," I babbled, as Lucky and I lay panting on the hallway floor.

"No, thank you," Lucky murmured, petting my head.

We stood up shakily and I led Lucky into the living room where we sat quietly on the sofa for a minute. I held Lucky's hand, kneading her fingers. "What about your mom? Don't you need to go back home?"

"I needed to pick up coffee, half-and-half, and yogurt at the corner store. I told Mom I'd be right back."

"You snuck out to fuck! What are you, like fifteen?" I giggled. "Let's talk later this week. I really like you. I'm sorry. I just, you know."

"I do know. And I really like you too. Let's get together later on this week. Not Wednesday, but Friday. Are you free Friday night?" Lucky asked.

"Yes. I'll text later." I walked Lucky to the door, kissed her good-bye, and she left.

Monday through Friday was spent in a haze of lust. All I could think of was what shenanigans Lucky and I could cook up if we had a few hours of time and a good night's rest. I woke up at 5:00 a.m. each morning, my hand between my legs, wishing that Lucky's cock was behind me pushing forward, the tip against my ass and her fingers twisting and stretching my tender nipples until I cried out. It was difficult to leave for work in the morning, to stop touching myself and put on clothing. I'd stir my morning oatmeal naked, my left hand holding the wooden spoon and my right holding my tit, pulling my nipple until I'd cry out in pleasure, hunched over a pot of bubbling oats. Sometimes I'd spank my breasts with the spoon before stirring, beating my chest, my nipples swelling and engorged. And as I bent over the stove, I'd again imagine Lucky behind me, squeezing my breasts while rudely plunging into my cunt, my ass. Fucking me into the stove while I held on to the over-head stove hood to keep my balance. Riding the F streetcar to work, I knitted, dropping stitches in my distraction, my scarf decreasing from thirty-two stitches on Monday to twenty-four by Thursday, a wobbly testament to my desire for Lucky. I daydreamed at the library, sitting in long afternoon library meetings while imagining Lucky's grubby gardener's hands touching me. I loved those vestiges of earth beneath her nails, the calluses on her stubby fingers, the softness of her palm. I wanted to fuck Lucky in a pile of dirt, sinking into the rich soil with her, the smell of plants and dank rising, enveloping us.

22

Tuesday night, I came home, opening my front door to my darkened hallway. I remembered our quickie on Sunday night. I flicked the light switch revealing honey-colored walls, the library stand with the *OED,* and the rough maroon-and-brown Persian carpet runner. I wanted a repeat, but more, always more. I wanted to crawl down the carpeted hallway, my rump swinging from side to side. An invitation to Lucky, to have her way with me, beat my ass, my thighs. Take great handfuls of my flesh and twist them, squeezing the bruises clean as I howl. My howls caught in my throat, and I longed for the look on her face as she hit me, so fiendishly delighted.

I texted Lucky on Wednesday, channeling e. e. cummings, if only he had texted. *The bruises on my ass are gone, but knee rug burns remain. Look forward to your lips and your sweet etc.*

I heard back within minutes, *No wartime, but thinking of your smile yes knees and of your etc.* I liked a gal who got the poetic gist.

On Thursday, I came home from the library, staggered down the hallway in a sexual frenzy, and threw off my corduroy sports coat, tweed trousers, oxford shirt, and Scottish tartan necktie as if they were on fire. I retrieved my rope, tit clamps, a handful of clothespins, my largest cock, a stainless-steel sound, a bottle of lube, my njoy, a hand towel, a waterproof pad, and my Hitachi wand, tossed them on the bed and settled in for a one-person fuckfest.

Francy fled the bedroom. She knew what I was up to. I turned my blankets and sheets back, then laid out the waterproof pad and towel. I bound my breasts in a figure eight, wrapping the rope around my chest, then around each breast, tweaking my nipples into hard points when I was done, then applying my tit clamps. The tight clench of rope around my chest and digging into my soft breasts, and the sharp pain of the clamps on my nipples made me gasp, my cunt swelling, wet, and hard. I'd been thinking about Lucky all day at work between recommending books to patrons, helping them with their computers, and processing holds. I lubed up my cock, sliding it into my asshole slowly, feeling myself open up eagerly until it was all in but the last inch, then sat on it, shoving the remainder in. I groaned in relief at being so filled, and started jerking off my clit, my cock. Testosterone had filled me out, the way hormones fill out the chest of an adolescent girl. My clit's legs that traveled from my clit to my cunt opening had grown, so when I became excited both my clit and its legs became erect, hard, and swollen. I fucked my asshole, imagining Lucky grinding into me with her cock. I wanted everything filled, so I greased up my sound, felt for my pisshole with my index finger, and slipped the cold sound in slowly, fucking my pisshole gently while I sat on my cock. I was filled up twice over now. I caught the chain between my tit clamps in between my teeth and yanked, causing the clamps to pull and twist my nipples with pain and pleasure. The sound felt soft and raspy in my pisshole, so close to my G-spot that it made my legs shake with excitement. I needed my cunt and mouth filled too. What if Lucky were there, dangling a heavy metal chain over my mouth? I'd open wide to swallow the chain, the taste of steel on my tongue, filling my mouth. I twirled the sound in my pisshole and snorted in pleasure, then slid it out, lubed up the large end of the stainless-steel njoy and slid it into my dripping cunt. The fat cock in my ass bulged into my cunt, taking up space, making the njoy difficult to insert, but I wiggled the metal toy and finally got it past the bulge the cock made and inside my wet hole. I started fucking myself, sliding up and down on my cock and pressing into my g-spot with the njoy. I was coming in small waves, my come showering over my hand as I fucked myself.

It wasn't enough, but it never is enough. I removed the njoy, took eight clothespins and pinned four to each nipple flanking the clamps. Then I grabbed my silicone paddle from the bedside table drawer and started whacking my thighs, each whack a sting that made my nipples harder and more engorged, making the clamps and pins more painful. I started fucking myself with the njoy again, coming harder, soaking the towel, begging for more, my hips thrusting. I wanted a bigger cock in my ass, I wanted two cocks in my ass, I wanted three cocks in my ass, I wanted to be filled up until all I was were holes filled with sensation. I was cramming as much of the cock into my ass as possible, grunting with need. I turned on the Hitachi and started rubbing my clit. I spasmed as I yelled with my last orgasm, then fell back panting, my throat sore and my muscles tender. I couldn't move, so I lay there for a few minutes in postcoital relaxation. Then I slowly dismantled. I untied my breasts, removed the cock from my ass, the pins and clamps from my breasts, and the njoy from my cunt and hobbled into the bathroom to wash up my toys and my cunt.

I'd felt like an insatiable one-man band, every part of me stimulating another part. Riding the cock in my ass, my teeth pulling on the tit-clamp chain like a bit, one hand fucking my pisshole with the thick sound, and the other hand forcing jet after jet of come from my cunt with the njoy. This was the disadvantage to fucking oneself. It was difficult to roughly overtake oneself. I was hoping Lucky would change things.

I learned the word *insatiable* when I was four from a picture book that my mother would read to me. I clearly remember her pointing to the picture of a little boy and reading excitedly, "'More, more!' he cried. He was insatiable!" I loved the word *insatiable* so much, and clearly took it to heart.

I spent most of Friday in a state of panic. Would Lucky be turned on by my insatiable urge to fill my holes? For that matter, would I be enough for Lucky? Was I kinky enough? Could I give her what she wanted? I had forty-five years of BDSM notched into my bedpost, was incapable of being vanilla for any sustained length of time, yet I worried. Much of my experience was acquired outside of the leather community and Lucky had considerably more experience within the leather community. Suppose I was actually a BDSM dilettante, but didn't know it? That everything I did was merely a dalliance... nothing. I hated my internal whining and insecurity, even as I knew that unsureness when starting an affair was normal. I dressed carefully on Friday. A Liberty of London orange floral paisley shirt, black wool vest, an olive-green velvet bow tie, pleated rust herringbone wool trousers, a tweed blazer, and olive-green captoe oxfords.

I called my best pal Tov while I was at lunch. "What if Lucky doesn't like me? What if she thinks I'm boring in bed?"

"What are you talking about?"

"Lucky has all this experience. Probably more than I do. Suppose I'm too vanilla?"

Tov laughed at me, "Nervousness is such a turn-on for us tops. We love hearing bottoms get all off balance. And I know that you're as kinky as they come."

"That's easy for you to say. You're the top! What if they come with a toy bag stuffed with needles and singletails, neither of which I have much experience with and both of which frighten me?"

Tov started humming "You're the Top," then said, "That is what negotiations are for."

"Oh fuck. I'm doomed." I sighed dramatically. "Thanks for listening. I've got to go. We have a departmental meeting in two minutes. Love you. I'll call you tomorrow."

"Good luck with tonight. We'll talk later. Bye." Tov hung up laughing. At me, not with me. At least I'm pretty sure of that.

After work, I caught BART to Mission and 16th, then walked up 16th to Big Lantern to meet Lucky. I grabbed one of the tables near the front window. It offered some privacy. Big Lantern was cheap, unpretentious, and close by. It was ideal for a second date and as a place to flirtily negotiate our play. Lucky arrived a few minutes after I'd taken off my Harris tweed blazer. She was wearing a worn brown leather jacket, a black cable-knit turtleneck sweater, black 501s, baby-blue suede chukkas, a wide, studded, brown leather cuff, and a smile. My nipples got hard immediately, and I was thankful that I'd thought to wear a lined black wool vest over my shirt. I needed all the layers I could get between my nipples and the world if I hoped to get through dinner without advertising my desire to rip my clothing off, climb onto the glass-topped table, and spread my legs open to Lucky's fist. We ordered taro vegetable puffs, turnip cakes, pork siu mai, steamed BBQ pork buns, vegetable turnip buns, shrimp dumplings, vegetable dumplings, and a pot of tea.

"It seems a little weird to see you when I have all my clothes on," I said.

"We can fix that later," Lucky said, grinning.

The waiter brought our dim sum, and we spread out happily. I adored the creamy turnip cakes dipped in hot mustard sauce, while Lucky hogged the steamed BBQ pork buns. We were temporarily quiet until about halfway into dinner, when we both took a deep breath at the same time and started talking.

"How was your week?" Lucky and I asked simultaneously.

I wanted to be an adult and tell her that someone set a fire in historical romances, at one point all the toilets were out of commission for two hours, and Arial Gore gave a talk on memoir writing during our Writers Talk Writing series. But all I could think about was Lucky and me fucking. Instead I blushed and admitted to Lucky that I'd spent the week jerking off and thinking about our two all-too-brief interludes.

Then I cursed myself internally for sounding like a character from *Downton Abbey* crossed with a twenty-first-century, peevish, queer slut, so I told her about the fire in historical romances, clogged commodes on three floors, and meeting famous writers. I immediately felt more mature. Lucky was suave, yet she oozed vulnerability and was tender with her mother. Could it be that she was a bad boy who had actually grown up? Or maybe that was my hopeful heart.

"Let's go back to my place and fuck," I said. I'd never been good at being subtle and would cut to the chase given a moment. I also hated processing and Lucky was looking serious, or maybe it was sexy. I was so nervous I couldn't tell the difference.

"Wait. I want to know more." Lucky reached across the table with her greasy fingers and held mine, twining them together. "Tell me your limits. What you want?"

"Didn't we do this already? At Café Flore? Remember?" I asked querulously.

Lucky raised one bushy graying eyebrow at my tone, lowered her voice, and increased her pressure on my fingers by squeezing them hard. "Please answer my questions. I want to know more."

I blushed at Lucky's sudden change and her demanding tone of voice, then decided to follow instructions. "If you want to be called

'Sir,' I'm fine with that, but not 'Daddy.'" I thought back to my conversation with Tov earlier that day and kissed Lucky's forefinger. "I've never done needles and have done singletails only a few times. Not enough to count or form an opinion. I like canes and floggers and being tied up. And assfucking. Also being fisted and sucking cock, but you already knew that part. I don't like being gone down on unless I'm wearing a cock. My tits are supersensitive. I'll try most things at least once. I'm pretty simple, really."

"I usually don't use honorifics like 'Sir,' but I do like it sometimes. I'll let you know when. I liked it when you called me 'baby' the other night. What is your safeword?" Lucky asked, as she fed me a nibble of turnip cake.

I sighed and felt my fingers in Lucky's grow restless. I was always worried when we got to this part during negotiation. It was not sexy, and I felt too vulnerable. "I don't use safewords. It isn't that I don't believe in them, but I didn't grow up with them. I learned S/M outside of the leather community and we just plowed ahead. If it worked it worked, and if it didn't work, we wouldn't do it again."

Lucky looked at me oddly, almost calculatingly, and stroked my fingers softly. "Okay, no safewords for you then. Should I stop if you cry?"

"Oh god, no. Please continue. I like to cry. Not every time, but sometimes," I said with longing and reverence. I licked a spot of mustard sauce from Lucky's forefinger.

"Water sports?"

"Yes, but I've never swallowed. So to speak." I giggled.

"Boot stomping?" Lucky asked menacingly, her eyebrows wiggling like Groucho Marx's and her dimples deepening.

I felt pressure on my foot, and Lucky's chukka was pressing down on my oxfords oh so casually. I gasped, "Yes, but it's scary. And I need aftercare."

"Do you usually need aftercare?" Lucky asked, surprised, her ankle boot riding up my leg slowly.

"No. I take it back. My idea of aftercare is being on my knees sucking your cock! Seriously, if I'm collapsing in a puddle of come with bruises and marks up and down my body, it's all good. What about you? Do you need aftercare?" I was trying not to sink under the table. All I wanted to do was crawl under the dim sum-littered table to Lucky's lap, unbutton her jeans, take out her cock, and suck. I licked my lips.

Lucky caught my lip licking and grinned, stroking my palm with her fingernail. "Sometimes. All that swinging, tying, and pistoning can be tiring. A little chocolate or cheese. A hand massage helps." Lucky held my wrist with her other hand. "Do you have any physical limitations?"

I groaned softly at Lucky's grip on my wrist, the touch of her finger on my sensitive palm, and her boot on my leg. My erect nipples throbbed painfully in my tight binder, and I was squirmy and damp. Breathlessly, I answered, "I have a slightly prolapsed uterus from childbirth and a misdiagnosed thyroid condition. Fisting helps. Fisting is practically medicinal for me." I snickered. "I can't get up from kneeling easily anymore, I have chronic pain in my legs that I treat with turmeric, and my stamina for some bondage positions is limited. I'm fucking sixty and my body lets that fact be known in uncomfortable ways. And you?"

"I have mild arthritis in my hands and knees and gardener's elbow. It sucks, but acupuncture and pot salve helps." Lucky leaned forward, holding each of my wrists down on the table firmly, my left wrist next to the leftover pork siu mai, and my right wrist next to the remnants of the shrimp dumplings.

Between five days of anticipation, dim sum bondage, and Lucky's climb up my leg, I was done in. I glanced at Lucky's precious hands with some alarm. "Can we go now?" I whined. This negotiation process had felt a little demanding in a good way, a little processy in a demanding way, a little flirty in a hot way, and although I loved the hot parts and the demanding parts, I was ready for it to be over with ten minutes ago. Lucky just laughed at me.

We got the bill, split it, and meandered to my place, bumping

29

shoulders. It was another beautiful night in San Francisco. It was in the fifties, cool enough to make our jackets useful. It was a short thirty-minute walk to my place and we got there quickly, happy for privacy.

Once inside, Lucky asked for tea. I hung up our jackets and Lucky's leather satchel on the Eastlake coatrack, and started some hot water in the red metal kettle for tea. I liked that Lucky was guiding the fuck. However, if I'd had my way we'd be naked by now. Or at least I would be naked, but it was cozy in the kitchen with Lucky. She admired my collection of vintage velvet paintings, paint-by-number paintings, and 1970s porn movie posters. She scanned my two shelves of cookbooks as I got out my Brown Betty teapot, turquoise Fiesta mugs, sugar, and Ceylon tea. Lucky left to use the bathroom while I puttered in the kitchen, laying out tea and sandy digestive biscuits on my metal Queen Elizabeth coronation commemorative tray.

We had tea in the living room, Francy sleeping on the Moroccan-leather ottoman, the tea tray on the Persian coffee table, and ourselves sitting side by side on the olive mohair sofa with the velvet drapes keeping out the sounds of traffic. Lucky leaned in for a kiss. It was the most delicate kiss, a sweet exchange of air between us. Lucky's breath felt like an electrical current. Our lips touched lightly, then we drew back. I licked the corners of Lucky's mouth with the tip of my tongue, stiff and wet, slowly tracing an arc from one side of her mouth to the other. Our breath traveled between us, generating sexual energy until I swooned, falling toward her. Lucky caught me by my wrists and tightened her grip as she bit my lower lip, first delicately, then harder. I groaned with need as Lucky pulled me up from the sofa, restraining my wrists behind my back while walking behind me down the hallway and into my bedroom. I blearily saw her snag her satchel on the way into the bedroom.

I had just enough time to turn on the bedside lamp before Lucky shoved me backward against the walnut wardrobe. "Undress."

I was paralyzed for a second as my cunt flooded and my clit hardened more, then I shakily unbuttoned my vest, untied my velvet bow tie, and unbuttoned my shirt revealing my chest in its binder. I struggled to get out of my oxfords, socks, and slacks, carefully draping my clothing on the valet stand. I'd worn my new shorts, the navy knit ones with the white contrasting piping and tiny white buttons. I eyed Lucky's oversized satchel nervously and expectantly. Lucky took off her turtleneck sweater and opened her 1950s black-leather doctor's satchel. I averted my eyes from the open bag, however I caught a glimpse of what I thought was a cane.

Lucky slapped my face lightly, and said, "All of it off."

I stepped out of my shorts clumsily and struggled to take my tight binder off over my head.

"I'm 'Sir' tonight."

"Yes, Sir," I responded, keeping my eyes to the carpet, my nipples painfully tight and hard in the cool night air. Lucky spun me around, then fastened my wrists behind my back with padded leather cuffs.

"Thank you, Sir," I gasped, as Lucky clasped tit clamps around my sensitive erect nipples and they started to burn, sending a current to my cock. "Thank you, Sir!" I thanked Lucky once more. I was awash with thankfulness.

Lucky pushed me over to my tall mahogany bed by my manacled wrists, then hissed menacingly while hoisting me up on the bed by my crotch, "Lean over the side. Up and at 'em!"

I fell onto the quilted bed, a pouf of lavender from the bedclothes rising as my chest hit the mattress. Lucky gripped me tightly by the back of my neck with one hand and knocked my legs apart with her booted foot. I rested with my head turned sideways, my cheek against my worn handmade quilt. I could glimpse a square of purple Japanese hopping bunny fabric, next to a square of blue William Morris Liberty cotton lawn and I focused on those two prints. Lucky rested full length along my back, pressing into me, one part comfort, one part promise, and one part threat. I could feel the softness of her breasts with their hard nipples under her white T-shirt against my mid-back, her warm breath against my neck, and her stiff cock against my ass. I lay as still as I could, trying desperately not to rear back against her cock with my hips. I wanted her to learn the shape of my outstretched naked self, to soak it up with her body until she could read each flush, twitch, and moan. And I wanted to learn her desires, to sniff out her needs before she knew them and offer them to her on the platter of my flesh and my heart. We lay together carefully, adjusting to each other's bodies and desires, the room deepening with anticipation. The room was starting to heat up. I couldn't easily see, but I could feel Lucky's presence beside me like a generator, a conductor of pleasure.

Lucky bit the nape of my neck, sending a sharp pain through me, then pushed herself up, digging her hips into mine as she straightened up. She caressed my ass gently with her rough palm, swooping down to dip into my pulsing cunt with two fingers, then back up lightly over my asshole. I sensed a swing behind me, then felt the sting of the cane against my ass, driving my hips into the bedside. I clenched the quilt loosely, then more tightly as she continued to beat my cheeks with the cane. She beat me methodically, three strikes to each cheek over and over, the stinging pain driving me forward. She had not asked me to keep count, and had not mentioned needing this ritual, so I lost myself in the giddy delight of handing it over and giving it up to Lucky. At one point Lucky paused to run her hand through the river between my thighs.

I said, "Thank you, Sir," pushing my clamped tits into the mattress, squirming to release more pain. My cunt was clasping in pleasure, the muscles tightening and swelling.

I heard the pop of 501 fly buttons, the tear of a condom being opened, and felt a cold dribble of lube against my asshole. Lucky's thick cock worked its way between my burning asscheeks, sinking into my ass like a missile looking for its target. I moaned as she started fucking me, drawing out so the tip of her cock rested in my asshole, before diving in deliberately, the contact of her hard rubber harness irritating my bruised ass. She teased me with her cock, drawing out slowly, stopping, then sinking in up to the hilt and repeating this intolerably slow half-speed fuck.

"Hold still," she commanded, while choking me lightly by holding me down by the back of my neck. Lucky fucked me snail-like while I forced myself to not move, my clit growing larger and rubbing against the quilt. It became a meditative fuck, with Lucky chortling as she pistoned leisurely into my asshole with her cock, squeezing my sore asscheeks with her hands and twisting them painfully. I could feel drops of precome dripping down my thighs as I shuddered from containing my need. I was getting a feel for what Lucky wanted, learning what turned her on. She liked desperation and obedience, and I aspired to give her these.

"Please, please, Sir!" I begged. What was I begging for? I was so delirious that I almost no longer knew what I pleaded for. I wanted to come, but my pleas were for something greater than a string of orgasms. I wanted to give myself to Lucky and I wanted Lucky to take me, to devour me with her greed and her needs.

Lucky reached around to my tender nipples, twisting and pulling the clamped, swollen, reddened flesh as she sped up. "Now," she grunted, and started fucking me deeply and quickly, slamming into my bruised ass in her hurry to come. With a drawn-out groan, Lucky came, balls deep in my black-and-blue ass. I whimpered. I'd been holding back so long that I had not come yet and couldn't. Lucky rested a minute, popped her cock out, and lightly stroked my back with her hand, dipping in between my legs, then drawing her hand out, painting my thighs with my juices. I lay there panting, half sobbing in need.

I felt a whoosh by my feet, then the confining metallic click of padded ankle cuffs around my ankles. "Alley-up! On your belly." Lucky then rolled me onto my belly like a tumbleweed and hogtied me, fastening my ankles to my wrists behind my back.

I lay there helpless as she stood back and laughed. "It looks like my little invert is stuck for the night," she said, then reached over to pull off the tit clamps. She pinched my tender nipples cruelly, teasing them until they were diamond cutters, crinkled all hard and yearning and desperate.

I felt a cold metal plug going into my ass, then Lucky's fingers lightly stroking my cunt from my cock to my hole, leaving me twitching, my clit engorged and slippery. She started fucking my cunt deliberately, adding fingers one after the other. First just one delicate forefinger, then two fingers barely filling me, then three curved digits, my cunt pulsing and pleading, then four fingers as my cunt grabbed her hand begging for the remainder. "Please fuck me…oh god, I need you! Sir!" Then Lucky's hand slid into me, my flesh opening up for her, the most tender cave. Lucky's fist twisted inside me, as my cunt caught fire, everything gripping and contracting and holding. Me holding her with my cunt muscles as I fucked her back, her words spilling over my back. "Fuck me! Fuck me! Fuck me!" Lucky shouted, and I came with a deluge of salty come spraying over and over and over, pumping out come as if it would never run out. My ears were buzzing and I was shaking, but I could hear Lucky very faintly. She shouted triumphantly, "Yes!" as we came together. Lucky unfastened the cuffs, then we collapsed in each other's arms in giggling exhaustion.

We snuggled, Lucky nibbling on the fancy-schmancy chocolate I'd put in my bedside table drawer for her and me soothing my raspy throat with gulps of ice water. As we were drifting off to sleep, Lucky asked me if Francy slept with me in the bed. Just then, there was a soft thud, and Francy leapt onto the covers, carefully arranging herself in a furry ball between our knees for the night.

We spent the weekend undressed, spittle and come flying, taking breaks only for quick meals on the lam and hot showers. Sunday evening found me tender, striped, marked, and bruised. We had not left the apartment once. We did not wander in the tiny urban park a quarter block from my apartment, we did not step out for coffee and chai at Ritual Coffee, I did not meet Tov for our regular Sunday midafternoon writing date at Café Flore, and Lucky missed her Sunday early evening meditation at Rainbow Retreat with her best friend, Poppy. Sunday at 7:00 p.m. found me laying out my dress shirts for the week, setting up the ironing board in the living room, and fetching my shoes and shoe-care kit. It felt like a fairy tale. The weekend shimmered phantasm-like. I needed to be alone. Some of my desire for solitude was due to being overwhelmed at the intensity of our sexual and emotional connection, but some was due to my age and habits. I needed space to settle. Lucky seemed more inclined to linger past the magic witching hour of Sunday night preparations for the work week, and I hoped that I wasn't hurting her feelings by shooing her out of the apartment.

As I ironed my shirts for the week I brooded. I pressed my aqua-and-brown-striped button-down shirt thinking of the limitations and quality of time. Was I able to be Lucky's friend? Her confidant? Fucking was easy with Lucky, and through fucking and play we built intimacy. I was sixty. My rose-patterned Liberty shirt started me mulling about time. How much time did I have left? The older you get, the faster the finish line speeds toward you. While starching my purple-checked shirt, I contemplated expanding our emotional and intellectual intimacy. Did I want it, and for that matter, was I capable of it? Maybe I was like the fellow in the Adult Children of Alcoholics meeting lead that I heard thirty years ago. He said that he had a point with intimacy that he was incapable of traveling beyond. In each relationship he would pull out his troupe of intimacy tricks, with the relationship staggering along until he ran out of tricks. Then the relationship would peter away sadly. Was that me? By the time I'd reached my white oxford shirt, I wondered. Was I stunted, doomed to repeat each relationship Groundhog Day–like, until I keeled over, lonely and unloved? The dramatic, depressive temperament of the artist. I guessed we might as well find out.

I felt a tinge of hopefulness, but I felt mostly doomed. As a child, my parents nicknamed me the Voice of Doom and I re-earned that moniker daily. I wanted to pull away. That is the truth. I called Tov and whined that Lucky texted me every day. I yearned for those texts, yet they stifled me. I became the king of mixed messages, even to myself. I started carrying my phone in my chest pocket, the buzzing of each new text from Lucky vibrating my heart into panic and my cunt into action. We could not keep our hands off each other. And that is also the truth.

The next three months were a whirlwind courtship. We fucked almost daily. I had to buy a new stack of trick towels to keep up with my prodigious amount of come. I didn't have the time and lost the inclination to shop for household goods, so I started getting groceries delivered, even Francy's cat food and kitty litter. My apartment reeked with a combination of come, sweat, and pheromones. With regular lunchtime quickies, I had to buy new underwear just to make it through the week. Epsom salt baths became my friend, soaking away my muscle aches. I discovered that Lucky had a weakness for San Pellegrino and sandalwood soap, so I set my Amazon Prime Subscribe and Save account to deliver sparkling water, Caswell-Massey sandal-wood soap, nitrate gloves, condoms, and lube weekly. I cleared out my nightstand top drawer and filled it with sour gummies, chocolate, and licorice from Miette down the street, in case of energy depletion emergencies. Lucky developed a violet bruise around her wrist like a bracelet from fisting me every day, and one glorious Saturday after-noon we broke two slats in the bed, and three silicone dildos clean off at the base. My nipples became tender and sore. Lucky discovered how sensitive they were and delighted in torturing them at every chance, pulling, twisting, squeezing, and clamping them. She would torment my tits while I was cooking, the smell of sautéed sweet onions and butter rising as Lucky came up from behind me to hurt me, reaching around and slipping her hands beneath my shirt to grasp them. Once my poor nipples were swollen and aching, she would command me to crawl down the hallway, my tender nipples rubbing against the rough Persian runner. I sobbed as she sauntered behind me, beating my ass and my thighs, occasionally taking great handfuls of my flesh and twisting them, squeezing the bruises clean as I howled and she laughed.

For three months, we stayed in to fuck. From May to June, we missed festivals and events. The Sisters of Perpetual Indulgence Easter Hunky Jesus Contest in Dolores Park, the San Francisco International Film Festival, the Sing-Along *West Side Story* at the Castro Theater, the Cinco de Mayo parade in the Mission, the annual AIDS Candlelight Memorial in the Castro, watching the Bay to Breakers costumed foot race, listening to queer punk Pansy Division at El Rio, the San Fran-cisco Silent Film Festival, and the always cruise-worthy Dyke March and Trans March. We were fisting as the Dykes on Bikes zoomed down Market Street during Sunday's Pride Parade.

We spent most weekends and many weeknights at my place. I stayed the night at Lucky's a couple of times and ate dinner there once. There was more room at my apartment, and besides I had Francy to watch over, pet, feed, and otherwise wait upon. Lucky lived alone in a beautiful third-floor studio apartment in the Mission. She was still mourning Elmer's death and said that her tiny sun-filled apartment reminded her of him. She couldn't brush her teeth at her pink oval sink without seeing his white paws draped elegantly over the nickel faucets. His presence lurked in the seat of her Mid-Century leather reading chair. She claimed to be happy spending the majority of her free time with Francy and me, however I fretted that she missed her home.

Lucky installed a pole in my closet in the beginning of May to store the clothing that was following her to my apartment like wayward lambs. One Saturday we went to the hardware store on Mission near Van Ness, the huge one with a lumberyard in the back. The store smelled like machine oil, freshly cut lumber, and Wrigley's spearmint gum. Motown hits played through the loudspeakers: "Baby, baby, where did our love go?" Diana Ross sang huskily. It was full of people buying items for their weekend projects, home renovators roaming the isles and examining each nail, power tool, and tub of tile grout seriously. I eyeballed Lucky appreciatively, admiring her walk, her style, and her all-over hotness as she sauntered down the aisles in her denim 501s, white T-shirt, Mr. S hoodie, black bandana in her left pocket, and brown lace-up boots. In the rope and chain aisle, a lithe leather boi flagging a gray bandana on the right gave Lucky a sideways wink, while a plump, sweet, high-heeled femme asked her for help deciding how much rope to buy, laying her manicured hand over Lucky's rough hand to eloquently make her point. Lucky flirted like others breathe, with a bouncy innocence and delight. I liked the bubble of sexual heat that surrounded Lucky, drawing others into her orbit. How could I resist being charmed?

We meandered through the store, discovering that it appealed to our shared fetish for domestic pleasure. At one point we ended up in the home appliance section among the refrigerators, stoves, dishwashers, washers, and dryers. We both sighed over a humongous, gleaming, stainless-steel-and-black Viking six-burner, two-oven stove, caressing the metal top greedily while thinking of all the delicious stews and cakes that it could create if we owned it.

"Peach khoresh and cardamom pistachio shortbread," I said enticingly.

"Lemon-roasted chicken and sour cherry pie," Lucky murmured back, biting the side of my neck.

"Spicy rugelach and tarragon goat cheese tarts," I retorted, groaning.

"Salted mocha brownies and garlicky eggplant patties." Lucky pressed her groin against my ass from behind, leaning over my shoulder as a pretext for examining the burners. "I want to suck your cock while you're leaning up against this monster. Take it way down, letting you fuck my throat until I need to ream you from behind. Turn you over like a pancake, pull down your pants and fuck you. The pound cake baking in the oven, everything smelling of vanilla and sex, with you bent over, my cock sliding up your cunt. Fucking you until we both come against the stove, the oven handle hard against your clit."

"Then the timer goes off as we come, you with a yell. We fetch the cake from the oven, and eat it in bed," I whispered back to Lucky hoarsely.

We took the long way through the rope and fasteners aisles before finding ourselves in front of a box of wooden closet poles, talking to a portly middle-aged Latino man with faded nautical tattoos.

"Can I help you, sir?" he asked Lucky.

"I need a five foot pole to put into my boyfriend's closet," Lucky replied.

I pretended a sudden interest in metal closet flanges in order not to burst into unseemly giggles. A pole in my closet indeed! Metaphorically, Lucky had been putting her various poles into my various closets for the past two months. My asshole still tingled from Lucky's vigorous pole-reaming that very morning and I was wearing a thin rope harness

38

tightly around my chest and under my binder. The rope was rough and itchy. It dug into my skin; just its proximity to my breasts made my nipples throb with anticipation.

We got a pole and flanges, along with a length of new red rope and a set of bits. There was a key duplicator next to customer service. I looked at Lucky, then I looked at the pole, then I looked at the key machine. "Hell, if you're putting your pole in my closet, maybe you should have a key."

Lucky threw in a set of silicone critter key caps, and we took off for home. After all, it was Saturday and Saturdays were for fucking.

Sex and sensual pleasure infused every moment together. The nail in my bachelor coffin might have been the morning I found Lucky in her button-front red-plaid boxers and a wife-beater ironing an aqua linen shirt, spray starch in hand, while singing along to Etta James's "You Can Leave Your Hat On." I swooned on the spot.

Perhaps it was when I spied Lucky's key on the dining table next to my blue glass bowl filled with fruit, or when I heard the soft clang of keys on the tablecloth-covered wood as she walked into the living room. Her keys sat there until morning when we went to work, right next to my keys. They looked so friendly and hopeful together, Lucky's raccoon keys nestled next to my red-leather-clad keys. My heart jumped inside my chest. What were we doing?

Or maybe it was the morning I came out of the shower in my red-plaid Pendleton robe to find Lucky seated on the side of the made bed in a still-warm white button-down shirt, her black cocksucking cock strapped on, and wearing her Dehner dress-patrol boots. Lucky stroked her cock with a smile on her lips, then nodded to me for service her. I fell to the kilim carpet, my mouth open and greedy as Lucky's hips tilted forward, her hazel eyes gleaming.

Or it could have been the nights spent talking and snuggling on the sofa, Francy curled up between us, the fog outside and torch songs inside. We'd often find ourselves in the kitchen at 8:00 p.m. cooking, stirring butter and sugar for a cake, sautéing shallots for a crustless goat cheese quiche, or mixing a batch of overnight-yeasted waffles to bake the following morning. Lucky would dice while I stirred, bumping elbows companionably in the tiny kitchen. Then, after eating and fucking, we'd trade stories in bed until we'd drift off to sleep.

After three months of our seclusion, our best pals Tov and Poppy became querulous, demanding something more from us than brief texts in between bouts of fucking. One Sunday morning I woke up at 7:30 a.m., turned to Lucky, who was reading and drinking a large mug of black coffee while snuggled in a nest of gold-colored cotton sateen pillows, and said decisively, "I need leeks."

Lucky put down *The Trials of Radclyffe Hall,* took a fortifying gulp of black coffee, raised one bushy eyebrow, and asked, "Do you need them this very minute?"

"What I mean is this: we have been fucking for three months. That's all we've been doing," I said, drawing the sheet up over my chest to cover my tender nipples. I didn't want to be distracted by any sexual shenanigans. "We need to get out and do normal things too... or at least I do."

I felt all stumbly and clumsy and claustrophobic. This feeling had been brewing for a week or so, and now that I'd started, I continued speaking nervously. "I miss Tov. I miss the infamous conjoined poly trio James, Laura, and Nona. I miss my writing group. I even miss grocery shopping!"

"Are we processing?" Lucky asked with trepidation.

"No, we're getting dressed and going to Rainbow Co-op."

Lucky uncovered one of my breasts, fondling my nipple with her calloused fingers then leaning over to suckle and nibble it until it was a hard ball. I pushed her away, "I mean it! We can fuck later. I want leeks now!"

Lucky started laughing at me. I knew I sounded like a petulant three-year-old that had just had their cupcake taken away. I started laughing at myself too. "Pouting aside, I've got to leave the apartment. Now. You can come with me or you can stay here and keep Francy company. Your choice, kiddo." I kissed Lucky's forehead and got out of bed, tossing the sheets aside dramatically.

My knees ached, so I downed another turmeric capsule with a glass of orange juice, then got into a steaming shower, lathering up with Mistral Amber soap, luxuriating in the deep spicy scent. It was always like this with me. I would brood silently for weeks until I figured it out, not stewing exactly, but just a wiggle of discomfort beneath the surface. Once I knew what direction to take, I wanted to move quickly. I got out, threw on a rust ombre Pendleton shirt, my overalls, and a pair of Frye harness boots.

Lucky was in the kitchen eating a bowl of Greek yogurt with blueberries when I went in to pick up my knapsack. "Wait up. I'll come with you to Rainbow. There are a few things I need too, but not leeks." Lucky grinned and grabbed a canvas shopping bag and we took off for Rainbow.

Going to Rainbow for the first time together felt curiously solemn and momentous, as if we were hatching, breaking out of a secret cocoon of fucking and orgasms to be in the so-called real world. I blinked once we hit the midday sunshine, stunned that there were people walking about, drinking lattes, pushing strollers, waiting for buses. I'd spent the past twelve weekends indoors fucking, lost in our world of cunts and cocks and bruises and kisses. It struck me that I'd hardly ever even seen Lucky in the daylight, outdoors. She was wearing a red long-sleeved waffle T-shirt, a Mr. S hoodie, black 501s, Wescos, and green-tinted aviator sunglasses. She looked like the kind of dyke that I'd walk into a lamppost cruising, so distracted by her hotness that I never saw the post coming.

As we walked down Folsom Street, Lucky groped my ass. "You're so hot. Wanna cruise the salt section at Rainbow with me? Then we can snag free cheese and fruit samples."

I squeezed Lucky's meaty ass, her flesh so tender beneath my palm, "Baby, I've got a senior discount at Rainbow and Goodwill. Stick with me and you'll be set for life!"

Rainbow was crowded with its usual weekend hordes of pony-tailed sensitive New Age guys scowling at Spanish cheeses, frail-looking vegans in blue Mohawks comparing flavored seitan, middle-

41

aged lesbian couples wearing sensible shoes with carts full of herbal supplements and soy milk, and young tattooed queers lurking over the sauerkraut. These were my people and it made me happy to be amongst them. We joined the flock, both of us piling our handbaskets high. I stocked up on Taylor's Scottish tea, bulk raisins, bulk oatmeal, bulk walnuts, Oscar Wilde sharp cheddar cheese, leeks, expensive free-range eggs, turmeric, ginko, and ginseng. Lucky bought coconut oil, beeswax, vitamin E oil, goat cheese, and a tub of fresh mozzarella. We split up so Lucky could pick up spices and I could get toiletries as they were on the opposite ends of the store.

As usual, I was drawn to the hand soap aisle like a toddler to a mud puddle. My downfall was Rainbow's humongous selection of imported and locally made soaps. I had a stash of at least a dozen bars at home at any given moment. I soon became lost in sniffing the bars, admiring the packaging and colors. I'd added a square bar of sea salt in a nautical-themed package, a local bar of piney cedar wood, a French bar of peony pink grapefruit, and was contemplating a bar of very pricey Spanish amber when Lucky interrupted me.

"I'm glad to see that you understand the importance of cleanliness!" She grinned.

"It's true. Smelly things are my weakness." I giggled, winked, then looked down at Lucky's red plastic grocery basket. Right on top were a handful of white paper spice packets, each carefully labeled in Lucky's meticulous angular handwriting. "Rosemary salt, truffle salt, gray salt, pink Himalayan salt, and fleur de sel. "Someone has quite the salt habit, I see!"

I leaned over to smooch her.

"Behrouz!" a perky but nasal voice exclaimed.

I looked up from our clench to see Adrian. I'd met Adrian while waiting to get into a movie at Frameline, the local GLBTQ annual film festival. Adrian volunteered with them each year, corralling flirtatious and rambunctious queers, lesbians, gay men, dykes, bisexuals, FTMs, and MTFs, etc., into tidy lines. I thought of it as the GLBTQRSVP film festival, but never to Adrian's face. Adrian was very serious and very sensitive. He was a transdude who was sensitive to most scents, all cats, pineapple, tobacco, pot, gluten, chocolate, hemp, and silicone. He had three pet ferrets and two spouses. He was also prone to being triggered by life, that is, racism, incest, foul language, violence, sexism, fatphobia, transphobia, homophobia, Christianity, and classism. I'm sure that I've left something out. His delicacy fluctuated from month to month. As a result, he would go into a snit at the drop of a word, and we'd often go for weeks without talking. He annoyed me most of the time, but charmed me some of the time. I found him good-hearted if awkward, and was grateful that I was more shallow and less touchy than Adrian, as it allowed me to be more comfortable in the world.

"So this is where you've been hiding yourself!" Adrian chided me. He carried a basket piled with mango juice, cherry pie, caramel sauce, strawberry sauce, and several pints of ice cream. He put the basket down and cocked his hip at Lucky. Apparently Lucky's legendary charm was already taking effect. Adrian was wearing fuchsia nylon hot pants, black Doc Martins, a pink ribbed tank top embellished with TRANS MARCH 2012 in chipped silver metallic script across the chest, and a black-and-white buffalo-checked flannel shirt. He fanned himself with his left hand, swooning. Lucky had that effect.

"Hiding at Rainbow Co-op? Hardly. Adrian, meet Lucky. Lucky, meet Adrian." I tried not to roll my eyes.

Adrian shook Lucky's hand damply and tittered, "You'll have to come to the unicorn hunt and play party that I'm hosting next week! We'll have a posse of rainbow unicorn pets plus a griffin or two! You'll get to see my new tail!" Adrian giggled again, simpering at Lucky and turning a delicate shade of seashell pink. As his eyelashes fluttered flirtatiously, a flock of silver glitter spilled down, freckling his chubby cheeks.

Lucky responded sweetly, "We'd love to, but we're hosting a little shindig that weekend. We figured it's about time to come out of hiding. We'd love to have you."

"I'll email you an invite." I tugged on Lucky's hand. "Gotta go now. See you later!"

Once out of Rainbow I asked Lucky what that was about. We hadn't made plans together, certainly not to throw a party. We'd spent the past three months fucking and friendships had fallen by the wayside.

"I figure it's time we met each other's friends. Are you okay with throwing a party at your apartment? I'm sorry I didn't ask first, but I didn't want to go to Adrian's unicorn hunt and it seemed like great timing." Lucky smiled at me beguilingly.

Lucky was right. I'd been fielding increasingly frantic and irritable texts and calls from my friends wanting to know if I was all right. I'd told them that I was busy getting beaten and fucked, but this was wearing thin. I reminded them that I was making up for years of nonconsensual celibacy, but they whined that I was acting like a straight sixteen-year-old girl with her first boyfriend. And truthfully, I missed them too.

Each new manifestation of intimacy frightened me. I would recoil, worried that either it was a trap or that one of us would stumble, bringing both of us flailing to the ground. Then, I would settle. The word baggage was so coolly polite for this bone-chilling fear. Spending more than three nights together in a row, meeting Lucky's mom, daily texts, Lucky's toothbrush in my bathroom, Lucky cooking me chicken soup when I caught a cold, shopping at Rainbow together, me ironing Lucky's shirt in the morning, sharing Pendleton flannel shirts, making house keys for each other—the list grew and grew, one act piled upon the other, never toppling over. Would I ever grow confident enough to live without doubt? My childhood nickname continued to be an apt moniker.

I took a steadying breath. "Okay. When?" And with that, we started planning our first dinner party of many, although we didn't know that at the time.

Once back at my place with our bounty, we spread out in the living room with cookbooks and Post-It stickers, reading recipes out loud, dissecting them, and picking potential dishes for the party. An hour into our food wallow, our energy started fading, so Lucky put on water for tea. We settled in with a platter, Southern pimento cheese sandwiches made from a simple spread from the Georgia Masters Golf Tournament recipe and cut unto dainty triangles, and a pot of mango black tea. Lucky decided on baking an onion tart with mustard and fennel and a pound cake, and I decided upon peach khoresh with rice, tadig, David Lebovitz's gluten-free brownies, and a traditional Persian appetizer of lavish, Bulgarian feta cheese, and fresh mint.

Food daydreaming and cooking had become favorite pastimes of Lucky and me, right behind fucking. Lucky's copy of *The Moosewood Cookbook* and *Jerusalem: A Cookbook* had migrated into my apartment just the week before. I liked cooking with Lucky even though we had different preparation habits. She used a garlic press, while I minced garlic with a knife. I preferred to clean as I cooked, while Lucky wrecked the kitchen and then cleaned after eating. Lucky whipped cream with a whisk, while I used an electric mixer. I threw dinners onto plates willy-nilly, while Lucky plated with fussy precision. Despite our culinary differences, we'd learned to relax into camaraderie in the kitchen.

After our first trip to Rainbow together, our relationship shifted. It was plain that we had gone beyond tricks. We started nesting, our mutual fetish for cozy domesticity leading us to reading together, playing Scrabble, cooking, writing together, and playing gin rummy. I introduced Lucky to the lazy joys of checking out library ebooks online at midnight, while she insisted that we also visit the Main Library near Civic Center when we went to the nearby Sunday farmers market. We discovered that we both craved consistency and had missed our friends terribly, so Lucky resumed attending Buddhist meditations at Rainbow Retreat on Sunday afternoons, while I resumed meeting Tov at Café Flore for our Sunday writing date. Lucky happily went back to puttering twice a month with the San Francisco League of Urban Gardeners, and I returned to answering the crisis line at San Francisco Suicide Prevention. We read together on my cushy sofa with my handmade, wool-suiting patchwork quilt wrapped around us and our sock-clad feet intertwined, Francy sleeping contentedly between us. Then we tottered off to bed for a round of fisting, cocksucking, and orgasms before sleeping the sleep of the well loved and the well fed.

We added more permanent bondage to the bed by tying rope to the bed legs. I gave Lucky a space in my toy drawer for her favorite floggers, dildos, and butt plugs, and we bought an antique glossy moss-green McCoy pottery umbrella stand for Lucky's canes. We discovered that although we both loved sleeping with Francy curled between us, we did not agree on sharing showers. Lucky thought showers were sexy excuses to soap each other up, slipping hands and cocks through the bubbles and suds, then letting the hot water wash everything clean again. Showers were meditative for me. They were precious time for me to be alone, renew myself, and ground myself to earth and pleasure. Lucky was more outgoing and gregarious, while I was more introverted and craved time alone. We both were stubborn in our needs—mine for solitude and Lucky's for company. However we also had equally strong desires for intimacy. We were finding that we were well matched and that our areas of possible compromise complemented each other's.

Lucky was spending more and more time at my place. By the time the weekend of our coming out party and potluck rolled around, it was clear that it was time to have another talk. I wanted to wait until after the party though, in case things blew up in my face. We did not need verbal fisticuffs before our first cohosted party. I expected the party to be a fishbowl of judgment, with both of us being examined by our friends for approval or disapproval. Was I good enough for Lucky, and was Lucky good enough for me? As Lucky hand-penned tabletop ingredient placards for the dishes, we took turns predicting our friends' reactions to one another.

"Poppy will worry that you're encouraging my tendency toward butter and deviancy," Lucky muttered as she labeled her onion tart *Vegetarian,* the peach khoresh *Has Meat & Gluten Free,* the rice *Vegetarian & Gluten Free,* the brownies *Gluten Free with Nuts,* and the pound cake *Butter & More Butter.*

"Oh fuck, we don't have any gluten-free, vegan main dishes! I wonder if Adrian will come. I can't remember if he's talking to me this week," I said as I poured ice cubes into a vintage iridescent cut-glass bowl.

"How many people are coming now?"

"Between the two of us, Poppy and Tiny, Tov, Birdie and Tamera, the Nona-James-Laura trio, Ian, Maxwell, Ebony and Faye, and perhaps Adrian and his latest trick. Or his spouses or maybe a unicorn. Who the hell can tell with him! I think Adrian already thinks you're a player and will break my heart."

"Can we designate the apartment a glitter-free zone? Please!" Lucky begged as she set out the black cloth napkins.

"I wish. You can't stop the glitter." I fetched a stack of glasses from the kitchen as the doorbell rang with an early guest.

It was Ian Stecher, the elderly and notorious gay leather fetish photographer and baker par excellance. Ian stood huddled next to my doorstep, holding a glass platter with a blue plastic lid under his leather jacket. "It's about time!" It must have started raining a little bit ago, and it was pouring now. We were in the midst of a several-years-long drought, so this unaccustomed shower was an immense relief. The air smelled wet and fresh, and great wafts of gray clouds rolled overhead ominously.

"Oh, no! Come on up." I dragged Ian upstairs, while Lucky carried Ian's strawberry tart into the living room, and then I dried him off in the bathroom like a baby, rubbing his bald head until it shone.

After Ian, the rest straggled in over the course of the next thirty minutes, damp from the rainstorm, bearing dishes, and curious about whatever had distracted their friends so thoroughly the past few months.

Ebony and Faye were exes who, after breaking up, managed to remain friends and roommates. They came in a flurry of Christian Dior Eau Sauvage and Miss Dior. Ebony was a muscular black German Brony and Faye was exactly what she sounded like, the most delicate and fairy-like blonde transgirl possible. Ebony wore leather overalls, a tight red waffle-weave top, and boots, while Faye wore a vintage lavender silk blouse, skintight white leather pants, and white iridescent patent-leather high-heeled boots. They brought a rosewater-scented golden Persian saffron-rice pudding topped with crumpled green pistachios in a beautiful clear iridescent Carnival glass serving dish. Faye planted her slender six-two self in front of me. "Let me take a look at what has made my little Lucky so starry-eyed!"

Poppy and Tiny were androgynous twinsies, and Poppy was Lucky's best friend from the Rainbow Retreat Buddhist group. Poppy was from an old Georgia United Daughters of the Confederacy family, and Tiny was second-generation Chinese and grew up in San Francisco's Chinatown. They were sweet middle-aged dykes in their forties and both wore flannel shirts, jeans, chain wallets, and Vans. Poppy wore an antique blue ombre flannel and Tiny wore a barn-red and black buffalo-checked flannel. They were into urban foraging and carried a huge bamboo bowl of salad made partially with greens that they had personally harvested from around town. Tiny later surreptitiously read my palm while softly but pointedly grilling me about my job, my relationship with my family, my exes, and my intentions.

The ever-dapper Birdie wore a spiffy red western shirt embroidered with giant black roses on the yoke, worn jeans, and black pointy-toed cowboy boots, while her femme girlfriend Tamera wore a tight black tank top, excess cleavage, love-that-cherry red lipstick, a full 1950s sequined floral skirt, and red cowboy boots. They brought baked chicken seasoned with mustard and sweet paprika, along with a basket of still-warm Southern biscuits, dense and flakey. "I used lard for you 'specially," Birdie drawled into my ear. "You two look great together!"

The Nona-James-Laura trio had just flown in from New York where Laura had been giving a lecture on polyamory and responsible nonmonogamy, so they were a little bemused, disheveled, and tired. Nona was a glittering fashion kaleidoscope in shades of purple leather, satin, mohair, and tulle topped with a fuchsia Mohawk. James was stately as always, wearing worn leather jeans, an orange tweed waistcoat, a gray-plaid flannel shirt, boots, and his giant Barbara Bush pearls. Laura wore a knee-length silvery knit wrap dress, gray lace tights, and tiny silver kitten heels topped with leather bows. They plopped several bottles of wine from their tote bag onto the table and collapsed in a heap on the sofa, each entwined with the other in an entangled mass of jet-lagged polyamory triad.

Maxwell, a seventy-year-old, randy, leather–Daddy sweet-tongued devil, brought a new trick, a sweet little cub barely learning to walk named Jay. Maxwell came in full leather regalia, with the trick on a short leash, attentive to a state of adoration, and carrying a cobalt-blue Fiestaware platter of still-warm chocolate chip cookies. "I figured everyone likes chocolate chip cookies. The boy made them right before we came and right after he blacked my boots. Useful little bugger!" He tousled Jay's short blond hair.

Maxwell looked long at Lucky and me, Lucky in her 501s, aqua linen button-down shirt, mustard-and-aqua windowpane wool waistcoat, and Wescos, and I in my black pleated pants, pink-and-gray floral shirt, dark-gray knitted necktie, and black-and-red cowboy boots.

"You both look great! And look at that spread," he said, as he had his boy set down the plate of cookies. Then he said sotto voce to Lucky and me, "I thought all butches went for high femmes with glossy red manicures, seamed stockings, fuck-me heels, and long black hair. And most of the transdudes I know end up becoming gay men. I'm surprised that you two hooked up at all. Isn't this a little strange? I mean, how does it work? And who's the top?"

"We manage." Lucky and I smirked in unison, rolling our eyes as we poured glasses of wine and sparkling water for Maxwell and Jay.

Nina interjected warmly, "There's nothing wrong with a little boi-on-boi action!"

I'd forgotten about how judgmental people could be, particularly when others start coloring outside of the lines. Masculine-masculine couples were not common in the dyke and queer community, and many folks saw masculine pairings as distasteful, taboo, and unnatural. Or only good for tricks, something to relieve the itch if there wasn't a femme around. There were a smattering of dyke and genderqueer Daddy-boi couples in the kink community, but they were mostly people under the age of forty. Dykes, queers, and transmen over the age of forty were pretty strongly invested in butch-femme or FTM–gay men dynamics. There was even the Butch-Femme Social Group, and TM4M Cruising Night at Eros for transdudes and gay men. Before I'd met Lucky, the only people I'd found to date were either twenty years younger than me, or butches that were on the down-low and deeply confused and ashamed about their unexpected masculine attraction. I'd met one other butch dyke who was turned on by masculine people, but that relationship was brief and fiery.

Tov came late, his new boyfriend, Mikail, in tow. He'd had a difficult time finding a parking space. Tov was my best friend. He was a philosophy professor who wrote and grew orchids as hobbies. This was the first time I'd met Mikail. He'd met Mikail on GROWLr, which was one step up from SCRUFF and three steps over from Recon. Mikail was from Turkey, in his forties, and owned a cookbook store in the Inner Sunset called Little Spoon. Tov shrugged off his Mr. S hoodie, removed his wet boots, then held Lucky's hands with both of his, staring intently into her eyes. "I'm so glad to finally meet the person who is making Behrouz so," he paused mischievously, "glowing!"

Adrian texted that he couldn't make it. He'd had an allergic reaction to the shampoo that his latest play partner used. He'd broken out in an itchy, scaling pink rash and had a migraine. He threatened to come by if he recovered in time.

It was a great party. Birdie brought her guitar and performed a tune that she and Tamera had written about a couple that fucked so much they forgot to eat and sleep and destroyed their apartment with their antics, while Tov nudged me chortling. I said, "Hey George Jones already sang that song!" and we broke into an impromptu rendition of "Leaving Love All Over the Place."

Tiny discovered that she knew Birdie from the past. They had dated for a couple of months twenty years ago. They'd met at Black and Blue, the tattoo parlor where Birdie apprenticed briefly before getting a job with the city. Tamera drew herself up huffily once she caught on to Birdie and Tiny's decades-old dalliance, glaring and all but baring her love-that-pink nails.

I was in the kitchen fetching more ice when Poppy strolled in to grab some more pita bread for the hummus. As she sliced the bread rounds into eighths she gave me a tight pious smile. "I wanted to talk to you about something. I'm concerned and don't want to see either of you hurt. You know, Lucky usually dates femmes. You're not her type at all."

I stared at Poppy, aghast at her rudeness. "Things change," I replied dryly.

"I wish you two all the luck and all, but don't you think it's a little weird? I mean two masculine-of-center folks dating each other? Butches usually date femmes, you know. I mean, it's okay for fucking, but not for romance," Poppy said huffily.

I didn't want to insult Lucky's best friend, but I was horrified. Was she trying to make me feel insecure, or was she just being petty and closed-minded? I tried to rearrange my face into a neutral expression. "We're happy together."

"Whatever, but I don't see it working out in the long run. It just isn't natural," and Poppy started to breeze out of the kitchen with the turquoise Fiestaware plate of freshly sliced-up pita bread.

I stopped her. "Have you ever heard that expression about eating one's own? Passing judgment is fucked up and hurts us all in the end."

Poppy huffed off to the living room as I gritted my teeth, dumped fresh ice cubes into a metal serving bowl, and returned to the party.

Beth Ditto of the Gossip's paean to untrustworthy backstabbers, "Listen Up," was playing as I walked down the hallway to the party. It seemed fitting.

By 9:30 Maxwell had Jay kneeling in the center of the room, whistling show tunes and shining everyone's boots while we feasted on tarts, cookies, salads, chicken, and biscuits, gossiping avidly as torch songs played in the background. I don't know if our friends were reassured, but at least now there were names to know and faces to remember.

The party lasted until midnight, when we shooed Maxwell and Jay out the door. It had stopped raining. The moon was high and shining white, with trails of clouds hurriedly flying past. We waved the crowd off, standing in front of the wrought-iron gateway, our arms around each other's shoulders and happy to be alone again.

The next night we dissected the party while polishing shoes and ironing shirts for the upcoming workweek. I almost didn't tell Lucky about Poppy's kitchen ambush, but decided to after talking about Maxwell's unexpected catty comments.

"Poppy corned me in the kitchen and scolded me for corrupting you with my hidden deviant masculine desires."

"What?" Lucky looked horrified and annoyed.

"She gave me a dressing down about the unsuitability of butch people hooking up with one another."

"Do you want me to talk to her? She may be my best friend, but that's no excuse for mean-spirited comments! First Maxwell then Poppy! I expected flack from strangers, but not from our friends!" Lucky said angrily.

"No, please don't say anything to her. Remember, you two have been best friends for years," I pleaded. Lucky was steaming by now.

"But I want to say something. Our relationship is none of her business, and her attitude is narrow-minded!"

"Look, I took care of it. Besides, I'm hoping that over time she'll adjust. I think that once Maxwell and Poppy settle and get used to us, they'll be fine. They're both good people, just set in their ways."

"Whatever." Lucky grabbed a pair of brown Frye boots and started cleaning and polishing them gruffly. "Let me know if you change your mind. I won't have that kind of bullying, even from Poppy."

We'd spent the past few months holed up together, blissfully letting our community's negative judgments about gender identity, socialization and orientation fade from our consciousness. Tonight had been a reminder. It was always something. I knew some transdudes that dated dyke femmes and were alarmed when they were perceived of as a straight couple in public. The repulsion for butch-butch couples had been around since the 1940s, and although I understood the dynamic had relaxed some in the past decade, I'd seen little evidence of change. I felt very fortunate that Lucky and I had found each other.

CHAPTER THREE

TENDER

W e were getting serious. We'd met each other's friends, had keys to each other's apartment, and had weathered colds and crankiness, in addition to afternoons of fucking and cake. It was obvious that we were going to keep on seeing each other.

One Wednesday night after a dinner of steamy, spicy sesame rice noodles with tender asparagus, meaty shiitake mushrooms, and spinach, I approached Lucky as we washed the dishes together. Well-fed bellies tolerated processing vastly better than empty or poorly fed ones. I was quieter than Lucky and detested drawn-out processing, but it was obvious that we were headed toward more commitment with capital letters, no glitter. When we talked about monogamy and polyamory during our first date at Café Flore, it was frivolously. How were we to know that we'd still be fucking, fisting, and flirting three months later? That we'd have exchanged household keys, nursed each other through colds, read Hergé's *Tintin in Tibet* aloud on Friday nights, minced innumerable onions side by side, traded neckties, and remained enamored?

"We need to talk," I announced gloomily while cleaning the metal cooking spoon with a soapy green scrubber.

I think that by now Lucky was accustomed to my sudden pronouncements, the periodic flare-up of the Voice of Doom that overtook me, resulting in short, fatalistic, blunt conversations. "What is the problem?" she asked, as she dried the spoon on a red-striped cotton tea towel.

"Are we monogamous or what? I think we should talk about it and decide. It would suck if we got waylaid by a trick or something," I announced decisively.

"I'm happy the way things are right now. It's working for me." Lucky looked at me curiously, took a gray tea-pottery mug from me, dried it, and put it in the drainer.

"I know that neither of us is seeing anyone else, but what if we want to? What if one of us ends up in an unexpected clench during Queer Leather Hour at the Eagle? And you've always had a passel of tricks trailing behind you. Well?" I pushed onward stubbornly. I hated this pigheaded urge in myself to push conversations, but felt powerless to stop. This was important. I'd been in successful monogamous relationships and successful polyamorous relationships. I'd also been in both where there'd been cheating, lying, and hurt feelings.

"Do you want someone else? Is that what this is about?" Lucky asked.

"No. I just want to be prepared. How about you? Do you want someone else?" I asked Lucky as I cleaned our dinner plates in the hot, soapy dishwater.

"No. At least not right now. I'd rather take this as it comes, just do it organically."

I raised my eyebrows. "No. And I mean really, no. As far as I'm concerned, 'Organically' is code for fucked up. Let's decide what we are, then change it if we need to, and not after the fact! I'm leaning toward polyamory so that you can see new people. Me, I don't have enough time for someone else and barely have enough time for every-thing I want to do!" As soon I said this I realized that I was partially whining about time, and my lack of it.

"You are little Mr. Bossypants aren't you!" Lucky exclaimed. "How about we're monogamous for now and we revisit it in a year. I'm not seeing anyone else right now and I'm not looking." Lucky dried each plate and stacked it with the others in the cupboard.

I felt chagrined. I'd been whining and pushy, yet still had managed not to tell Lucky what was really bothering me because I didn't know what it was until that very moment while washing dishes in the kitchen. Sometimes my lack of self-awareness annoyed me. One would hope that at age sixty, you could figure these things out, but apparently I was mistaken.

"Lucky, I'm sorry. It's more than just the monogamous–poly kerfuffle. I need more time alone. I haven't been able to write as much as I want to, and I prefer writing alone. This is my bigger issue. Oh fuck!" I was embarrassed.

"Oh! This is really about time management?" Lucky looked bemused. Fortunately, she also looked amused. "How about we take a couple regular nights away from each other. Maybe every Monday and Tuesday? No communication. No texts, no emails, no dinner. Nothing. Then by Wednesday, we'll be chomping at the bit to see each other again. I have plenty to occupy myself while you're writing, carousing, and jerking off."

"Yes! That is perfect. You don't mind?" I was incredibly relieved that Lucky understood that my need for solitude was not in conflict with my need for Lucky. And I was also grateful that she was so even-keeled. Was it her study of Buddhism and meditation, or did Lucky just have a fabulously calm nature? I didn't know, nor did I care. I just knew we balanced each other out. And I needed solitude in order to need Lucky.

I pulled the plug, letting the dirty dishwater drain. I took down two red pottery bowls and scooped us bowls of creamy Three Twins cardamom vanilla ice cream topped by hefty spoonfuls of sea salt caramel sauce. "Baby, I love you!"

Lucky left for the living room as I scooped out the ice cream, and I thought about what I'd just said. I'd just told Lucky that I loved her. I wasn't the type of person to blurt out "I love you" during sex, and I'd never said these words to Lucky before. I knew that I had a crush on Lucky, but love? I didn't fall in love easily or quickly. Did I love Lucky? As I stood in the cool light of the open-doored, battered white Frigidaire, in my tiny orange kitchen, I realized that after three months, I was in love with Lucky. A gleaming new moon crescent shone through the kitchen window. I filled Francy's blue pottery IKEA water dish with fresh water from the tap as I thought about this new information, then I made my way down the darkened hallway with our ice cream to the living room to join Lucky.

Lucky was already reading *Season of the Witch: Enchantment, Terror, and Deliverance in the City of Love,* her glasses sliding down her nose, graying pompadour mussed, and totally engrossed in true tales of San Francisco history from the 1960s to the 1980s. Francy had staked out her feet and was sprawled across both of them, belly overhanging Lucky's red ribbed socks and purring loudly. I looked at Lucky fondly. I was in love. With Lucky. What a strange life it was.

During the next few months, our lives calmed down some and we became more familiar with each other's regular routines. As our individual daily lives started becoming our coupled daily life, we did more and more couple things together. We both read at the Queer Open Mic at Modern Times Bookstore in the Mission, and at Smack Dab at Magnet in the Castro. We shopped at the Civic Center farmers market on Sunday mornings, meandering among the freshly hatched techbros, Asian and Russian families, Tenderloin residents, jugglers, musicians, and beggars to find the cheapest and freshest organic fruits and vegetables, sniffing and poking the spinach, new green garlic, purple plums, and tender berries, then stuffing our knapsacks with our bounty.

Lucky went from perimenopause into menopause. She woke up each night at 3:30 sharp the way old people do, her periods finally stopped completely, and she had some faint bleeding when I fucked her that would evolve into a weeks-long vaginal irritation. She started going to Circle Community Acupuncture for the sleeplessness, and decided to stop getting fucked in her cunt until she could figure out a solution to the bleeding and atrophy. I'd had the same issue a few years before and used a topical estrogen cream for a while. It had helped, so Lucky made an appointment with Kaiser to see if she could get a prescription.

We started throwing monthly potluck salons, inviting our circle of friends over to share food and witticisms. Birdie and Tamera always brought a guitar and played a song, Ian brought his tablet and showed us his latest photography of handsome men in fetish gear, Mikail recited filthy poetry, and Ebony read to us from her memoir in progress. Maxwell and Poppy loosened up about gender identity and butch coupling, and one night under the influence of several homemade blackberry cordial and champagne cocktails, Poppy even drunkenly apologized for her unkind words and bad behavior at our first potluck. Fueled by too many Gene Kelly movies, Lucky and I started taking tap dancing lessons together, envisioning nighttime twirls around lampposts in the park. Lucky finally admitted that the candy I'd been buying her from Miette's fancy candy boutique was wasted on her, and that she vastly preferred the more plebeian California See's Chocolates, particularly anything with milk chocolate and nuts, although her favorite was the old-fashioned milk buttercream.

We both dreamt of flying, although we flew differently. I jumped up and left the ground like a slow-moving rocket, arms by my side and effortlessly airborne. Lucky flapped her arms like a bird, soaring in elegant circles. I discovered that Lucky liked to sing "I Enjoy Being a Girl" in the shower, and she discovered that my favorite dinner when I was blue was macaroni and cheese, applesauce, and green peas, and that I liked to mix them together into a monster mash on my plate. In short, the honeymoon phase was over but it still felt like a honeymoon. Learning about Lucky was like being on the most fascinating archeological excavation in the world. I'd uncover something new, brush it off carefully to avoid any damage, then admire it with delight, and Lucky seemed to feel the same about me.

It felt comfortable, even though it was unexpected. I remembered being single and throwing a potluck where everyone except for Tov and I were coupled, and how annoying they were, each couple in their cocoon of shared experiences and mutual domesticity. They finished one another's sentences and completed one another's thoughts, two people becoming one. If there was a disagreement, you could hear the repetitive structure of their argument as they explained their differences, something that they had carefully honed over the months and years until the disagreement was a calm recital of facts, all the sting removed. One's legs started where the other one's legs stopped. I was so put off by the experience that I didn't throw another party for eight months. Were we one of these interlocked couples now, or had our enforced two days without communication slipped us over the hump from a couple that was possibly codependently living in each other's pockets, into a couple composed of two individuals who adored each other?

With Monday and Tuesday free, I started back to work on the book I'd been writing. Lucky was right, by the time Wednesday rolled around, we were so eager for each other that we were fucking in the hallway. I'd be distracted all Wednesday afternoon, texting Lucky filthy texts about where I wanted her hands, daydreaming during meetings, and squirming in my office chair. I'd leave work, get home, and wait for Lucky's key in the door. Francy heard Lucky before she arrived, and would scamper to the door eagerly, fluffy tail held high with the orange feathered tip swishing rapidly. Lucky would walk in the door, drop her knapsack, kiss me, and grasp my hair, forcing me to the carpeted hallway floor. Her pants fly would be already undone and she'd be packing, waiting for my eager mouth to envelop her cock. I'd breathe in the night air on her jeans and the musky scent of her cunt as I'd lick the head. I'd peek up to see her looking down at me, watching my lips, my open mouth. It was hard to resist swallowing more of Lucky's cock immediately. I'd hold out for thirty seconds before I'd quickly deep-throat her cock, my lips pressed against Lucky's shorts as her cock hit the back of my throat and Lucky possessed my mouth, fucking me with quick hard jabs. Then Lucky would yank down my overalls, throw me facedown, and fist me, her hand burrowing deep inside of me, as surely as her key had slid into the keyhole just minutes before. My cunt clenched her hand back as we fucked, both of us grunting and yelling our desire as we came. We'd collapse briefly on the Persian hall runner, dust off, then rise to begin the next few days together.

One Saturday evening in August, Lucky taught me how to make marijuana salve to relieve the pain of aching joints. She'd discovered the miracle of pot salve at Poppy's fifty-eighth birthday party in Oakland. Most of the people at the party were lesbians and dykes of a certain age, all over fifty. A long conversation on using marijuana salve to help with painfully arthritic joints was interspersed with gossip about who'd broken up with whom, new girlfriends, lesbian drama, new homes, new pets, new jobs, and bad health. Lawyers traded marijuana dispensary recommendations with social workers, while librarians traded salve recipes and directions with nurses, and truck drivers traded medical marijuana doctors' names and numbers with bartenders. Many of the women at the party were sober and had been for decades, so using marijuana for its pain-relieving properties while avoiding getting high was important. With the Indigo Girls singing "Closer to Fine" and over a table laden with hummus, gluten-free carrot cake, lentil salad, kale chips, and deviled eggs, they discussed coconut oil, buds and stems, beeswax, and vitamin E oil.

Lucky told me about the party as we arranged our ingredients in my tiny kitchen, Lesbians on Ecstasy's "Summer Luv" blaring from the tiny countertop speakers. Lucky had been cooking the coconut oil and marijuana together in a Crock-Pot at her place for two days, and had brought it over for our medicinal craft experiment. We drained the savory swamp-colored liquid through a cheesecloth funnel, then added the beeswax, vitamin E oil, and a few drops of ginger and vanilla essential oils. We decanted it into Victorian cut-crystal dresser jars with sterling silver engraved lids. It was pea green goop by the time we were done, but Lucky swore that it was the only thing that had brought any relief to her sore hands and knees. I was excited, skeptical, and eager to try it on my knees. Giggling, we rushed into the bathroom, I rolled up my pant leg, and Lucky rubbed green gobs into my knobby pale knees and her swollen knuckles.

We inadvertently started traditions. Were we making a family?

That was what chosen family did. They created themselves from dust and dreams. And isn't that how traditions start? One minute you're eating a coconut tart at Tartine's, and the next minute you're seriously reviewing a list of San Francisco bakeries and pastry shops, trying to decide which one to explore next, and planning on visiting one every first Saturday of the month. Lucky and I shared a sweet tooth, not that there was only one tooth between us. We decided that we would tour the sweets of San Francisco, neighborhood by neighborhood, and cake by cake. Stella's in North Beach was great for cannoli and sidewalk people-watching, B Patisserie in Pacific Heights for exquisite traditional Viennese pastries, Golden Gate Bakery in Chinatown for their rich yellow egg custard tarts and rowdy crowds, Devil's Teeth in the Outer Sunset for their over-the-top cinnamon sticky rolls and proximity to the beach, and The Ice Cream Bar in Cole Valley for their herbal-infused ice-cream floats and flirty smart soda jerks. We had our sticky work cut out for us and threw ourselves into this project with enthusiasm.

Many of those adages about getting old are true, and one that was truest was the one about waking earlier and earlier until I was waking at hours that used to be my bedtime. I remembered crashing at 5:00 a.m. after nights of drinking white Russians, making out with punk girls on the dance floor, and picking fights with straight rockabilly guys. Now I woke each morning between 5:00 and 6:00 a.m. Lucky and I both slept naked. I loved looking at her warm olive skin next to my pale freckled flesh. I woke each morning with Lucky curled behind me, her tiny hands draped over my chest until her fingers came alive, half asleep and reaching for my nipples, twisting them and resetting the current that ran between my nipples and my cunt. She would twist and pull those tender knobs of flesh until I'd whimper, my ass pressing backward against her cunt, my asshole twitching, opening. Lucky thrusting her hips, grinding into my ass. I'd get up to piss, and when I came back to our bed Lucky would have put on her cock. I'd crawl under the warm cotton sheets and quilts, rubbing my ass against her cock, with her hands pulling my nipples and then pinching them with her fingernails. My nipples were always tender these days. It was our mission to keep them hard, expectant, sore, waiting. I'd feel her cock at the entrance of my asshole, resting, barely pushing in, and my asshole would open, urging Lucky's cock to slide in. Lucky would slide in an inch slowly then slide an inch out slowly, then slide in two inches and slide out two inches, until all seven inches of her cock was buried in my ass. She would bite my neck, an anchor as we fucked. All I wanted was to be filled by Lucky, her pumping deep inside of my ass, her hands now grabbing my breasts and squashing them tightly, renewing bruises left over from days before, as we fucked each other into another day. The smells of sex, freshly laundered sheets, our bodies fucking, and Lucky's sweat made a cave that overtook me, until I came with a wail and Lucky came with a forceful thrust and a growl.

Afterward, we'd lie in bed, the quilts in disarray as we talked and dozed. I'd turn down the lamp and turn on the bedside radio to keep us company as we chatted about the books we were reading, our projects, our wishes, and our days. We were slowly building a life.

Were U-Hauls in our immediate future? The old dyke adage was that lesbians moved in together on the second date. Of course, dykes were also supposed to get a toaster every time they recruited a straight woman into their midst. If that had been the case, Lucky, who was a reformed playboy, would have had a kitchen crammed full of toasters from floor to ceiling like a wayward art project. As it was, she had one beat-up but elegant vintage 1930s rounded-top stainless steel Sunbeam toaster on her tiny kitchenette's white-tiled countertop.

A month after our coming out party, Lucky approached me with nervousness and excitement. We'd just finished preparing and devouring a dinner of a corn, zucchini, goat cheese, and fresh mozzarella quiche, with a spinach and avocado salad, and were curled up on opposite ends of the sofa together covered with a woolen men's-suiting patchwork quilt, Francy sleeping between us. Lucky was wearing an olive-green vintage lightweight quilted wool smoking jacket and black woolen lounging pants, while I was wearing floral Liberty of London cotton lawn pajamas. We enjoyed dressing up in elegant lounging wear for evenings at home, even if we disrobed once we went to bed.

"Behrouz, the Petersons are moving out of state. She got a teaching job at the University of Pennsylvania and he's going with her. Their roommate is moving in with her girlfriend in Oakland," Lucky said meaningfully.

Lucky had inherited a three-bedroom Edwardian flat in the Inner Sunset from her close friend Henry Bennett, who'd died of AIDS ten years ago. Lucky had rented the apartment out for income, staying put in the rent-controlled studio apartment in the Mission that she'd lived in for twenty years, and now the renters, the Petersons, were moving to Pennsylvania, leaving the apartment vacant.

"I guess you'll need to find new tenants. That shouldn't be hard with the market the way it is right now. Or are you thinking of selling? I wouldn't recommend that though. That apartment is a great investment," I said.

"Maybe I can find another use for the apartment." Lucky held up her book in front of her face, *Birthright: Murder, Greed, and Power in the U-Haul Family Dynasty,* and pointed at the book's title. She wiggled her eyebrows and dimpled her dimples.

I'm gullible, bad at getting jokes, and was never very good at poker. I have the kind of face that gives everything away. On the other hand, my emotive expressive features make me an exciting bed partner. I tilted my head in puzzlement and asked, "What do you mean?"

Lucky started giggling, "Look at the book I'm reading! *U-Haul and...*" she paused expectedly.

"And murder? Who got murdered?"

"No, silly. U-Haul and lesbians and apartments..."

"I'm still on murdered. What are you trying to say? Is everything okay? Is Betty all right?" I looked at Lucky intently, trying to decipher her message by reading her facial expression.

"Oh fuck. You'd suck at charades. Do you want to move into my giant apartment together?" Lucky asked me, laughing.

I was stunned. We were getting along marvelously, I was in love, and I thought that Lucky was in love too, although she had not said those words yet. I'd never considered living with another person again. I'd had roommates, lived in collectives, lived with husbands, lived with girlfriends, and was now living alone. I had a rent-controlled one-bedroom Victorian apartment in a trendy, centrally located, safe neighborhood and had anticipated living in this apartment until I died. Or until I instigated the formation of my imaginary collective for elderly queer perverts, which would most likely never happen. In my head, the gang of us lived in a manor with a live-in masseuse and a burly butch dyke gardener, a bit like Lucky actually. We'd eat and cook together, get old and cantankerous together, read and write smut together. And raise chickens, so I could feed them cracked corn at sunrise, scattering dried corn and singing Doris Day tunes.

I never imagined living with a lover again. It was chancy to give up a rent-controlled apartment, especially in San Francisco where the average one-bedroom apartment cost as much as three quarters of my annual salary.

"Oh, I don't know," I replied skittishly. "We'd be living together. All the time. In the same apartment. Sharing a bathroom. Sharing closets." The Voice of Doom was on a rampage.

Lucky cocked her head quizzically, then stood up. "I'm making us a pot of tea." She left to give me time to brood.

I thought about it. We'd be living in the same apartment. Lucky would have to give up her place in the Mission and I'd have to give up my place in Hayes Valley. Suppose it didn't work out and we hated living with each other, then what? We'd be fucked, or rather I'd be fucked. There is no way I'd find a new affordable apartment in San Francisco. Hell, not even in Oakland. I'd have to move back to Ohio. If I moved to Ohio, I'd have to become a Buckeyes football fan. I'd definitely never get laid again and I'd probably get gay bashed. Or something. I'd start wearing sweatshirts and eating at fast-food restaurants. And I wouldn't have health insurance so I'd have to stop taking T, so then I'd be just an old fat balding dyke. Lucky and I would despise each other. We'd break up and I'd never get laid again. Fuck. My brain

63

jammed, stuck in a tailspin on the possibilities. Then I remembered "the song of mehitabel," always a guide in times of self-doubt, which is often the only kind of doubt worth mentioning, "Oh, wotthehell, wotthell," I muttered, "there's might be a dance in the old dame yet."

Lucky came back into the living room and set the Queen Elizabeth tray on the engraved copper tray coffee table. She poured us each a mug of ginger tea, and passed my mug over to me, along with a couple of anise cookies. "Well?"

I felt pale and was glad that the lights were turned down low. I didn't want Lucky to see how frightened I was, and mistake my self-doubt about living together for self-doubt about my love for her. "Okay. But we need to talk." I was starting to feel giddy, but this was how I often made big life decisions, by jumping off the cliff, eyes closed and fingers crossed. If I didn't just fecklessly jump, I'd be in a quandary of doubt for years. Besides, I needed to turn my brain off about Ohio.

"Yay! It's a huge apartment with three bedrooms. They're moving out next weekend, then we can go in, pick out paint colors, hire painters and cleaners, and move in," Lucky enthused cheerfully.

"Do you want to get a roommate? I mean, it's big enough but I'd rather not. It's going to be enough of an adjustment just to live together without throwing another person into the pot. How much is the mortgage?" When confronted with change, I often switched into high fix-it-and-control-it gear, and I was on a roll. "Do you own the entire house of just the second floor? What are the utilities like? Do you know the downstairs neighbors? Is the stove gas or electric? Is there a washer and dryer? Is there a yard? A balcony?" I poured another mug of tea. "When can we look at it? Do you want to share a bedroom or do you want separate bedrooms? I can see the advantages of both. Romaine Brooks and Natalie Barney built two side-by-side houses with a shared living room. Everything else was separate. Of course, we're not Natalie and Romaine." I took a deep breath.

"Are you done yet?"

"For now." I dunked an anise cookie into my tea until it was soggy and ate it. Lucky handed me another cookie.

"No roommate, just us. And Francy. I was thinking of getting another cat. We have enough room to share a bedroom or not. Your call. I own the second floor, not the rest of the house. The mortgage will be paid off next year. I'd really like to make one of the bedrooms into a library with floor-to-ceiling bookshelves and armchairs in front of the fireplace. We can go over any time. I'll need to call John and Autumn first, but they're usually pretty relaxed about my stopping over. I think Daphne has already moved out."

I was excited about shacking up with Lucky but had a hard time showing it. It was like my capacity for outward fun had been buried years and years ago. I'd unpack it, shake it out, look at it dubiously, but the Voice of Doom was strong. I wanted to put on my party hat, shake noisemakers, throw confetti, but felt flummoxed. Lucky, on the other hand, was already maniacally scrolling through images of built-in library bookshelves, debating whether to get something made or to find a set of antique shelves. We balanced each other. Part of me just wanted to give up, take a hot bath by myself, and let the steam, scented soap, and candlelight untwist my thoughts, but I didn't get up. A larger part of me wanted to leave the Voice of Doom baggage, dump that suitcase by the side of the road. Maybe I'd never throw confetti, but I could learn not to run away.

I thought about our styles. We both felt strongly about the beauty of our surroundings. Lucky leaned toward Mid-Century and modern, and I toward Victorian and the Arts and Crafts movement. Between us we had two love seats, one sofa, one antique wooden bed frame and one brushed steel bed frame, numerous armchairs, one 1940s chrome-and-Formica dinette set, four bedside tables, at least eight rugs, and two large clothing armoires. The only saving grace was that Lucky lived in a studio apartment, thus she owned fewer furnishings. I was a packrat, and decorated through overkill. Lucky was more spartan, but far from a minimalist. The truth was, we were two decorating tops looking to move in together.

"Maybe a set of Mission oak Gustav Stickley shelves in the library?" I said.

"I was thinking teak Danish Modern built-ins," Lucky replied.

"A leather-covered William Morris armchair would be perfect in the parlor," I sniffed haughtily.

"Of course, a Ray and Charles Eames leather lounging chair and ottoman!" Lucky retorted, trying not to laugh.

"We'd be remiss if our dining room lacked a low, sleek Paul McCobb étagère," I said.

"The better to fuck you over," Lucky growled.

"Oy! This is how it's going to be for the entire next month isn't it! Potato and potahto all the way," I laughed.

And we burst into a verse from Gershwin's "Let's Call the Whole Thing Off," making Francy pounce off in a huff at our caterwauling.

The next day, we planned an outing to our new apartment, Arizmendi Bakery, and the beach. The Petersons were out at a going-away brunch. It was foggy and cool, perfect weather for huddling at the beach with hot tea and sticky pecan rolls. We filled a green metal Stanley thermos with sweetened mango black tea, and packed our rucksack with a blanket, notebook, and tape measure. We intended to measure rooms in order to plan furniture arrangements, and windows in order to plan curtains. We both dressed warmly, wearing T-shirts with plaid flannel shirts over them, and hoodies, then set off on the N-Judah train to the Inner Sunset and Lucky's Edwardian apartment, soon to be our Edwardian apartment.

We stopped off at the bakery first, buying a white paper bag of ginger shortbread cookies, two humongous pecan rolls, and a loaf of light rye bread for later. Sauntering to the apartment was odd. This would be our neighborhood. Arizmendi, our local bakery. Green Apple, our local bookstore. Golden Gate Park, our local park. Progress Hardware, our local hardware store. Instead of eating spaghetti at Chow on Church Street in the Castro, we'd go to the Chow on 9th near the park. Goodbye to Dolores Park in the Mission with wall-to-wall, littering, champagne-guzzling techbros. Goodbye to itsy bitsy Patricia's Green Park in Hayes Valley with its designer each-scoop-individually-made-at-six-dollars-a-scoop ice cream. Hello to Golden

Gate Park with its buffalos, Stow Lake, the de Young art museum, the windmills, and the Arboretum.

The apartment building was a classic two-story Edwardian, painted in glorious shades of fey purple with charcoal-gray trim and gold metallic accents, the entrance flanked by two potted rosemary plants in tall red ceramic vases. A dozen gray marble steps led to the front doors. Lucky's apartment was on the second floor; the door was unfinished and had its original beveled and leaded decorative glass panes. I was immediately enamored with the cast-iron Art Deco doorbell with its graceful swooping lines and bossy instructions. It said PRESS in the round center buzzer. Another family lived on the first floor. Lucky had only met them a few times, but said that she understood from the Petersons that they were quiet.

We opened the front door and climbed up the steep carpeted steps while holding on to the polished wooden bannister. There was a window at the top of the stairway that was set with stained glass in an Art Nouveau design of three deep-pink roses with green leaves on an amber background. The steps led to a small square foyer that was paneled with original wainscoting. Lucky and I stood together looking down the long hallway with doors on either side leading to as yet unseen rooms. There were three doors to the left, and four doors to the right. The Petersons' belongings were already boxed up and shoved to the side. We wandered through the rooms on the right-hand side. First was a parlor with a large bay window overlooking Golden Gate Park. French doors led into a dining room with a smaller bay window, then into the kitchen, which had a small tidy combination pantry and laundry room in the back; lastly, there was a half toilet that opened onto the hallway. Leaving the kitchen and crossing the hallway, there was the library with a working fireplace, a bedroom, and then another bedroom with a connecting master bath.

Fortunately, most of the woodwork, including the flooring, had been left natural and was in relatively good shape. My apartment in Hayes Valley had ugly, cheap, ubiquitous oatmeal-colored low-pile carpeting, so I was gratified to see the gleaming hardwood floors.

"Lucky, my Persian carpets will look amazing on these floors," I whispered. I wasn't sure why I was whispering except that the apartment was twice as big as both of our apartments combined, and a million times more glamorous. I felt a little like an imposter, the poor wee prince who has been suddenly lifted up into a royal lifestyle and now wanders about drooling with confused delight and wonderment.

On closer inspection, the kitchen proved to be a large square room with a double window along one wall. It had an awesome vintage 1950s white-enamel forty-inch Wedgewood stove with two ovens, a small battered vintage white Frigidaire with a rounded top, dark-gray soapstone countertops, matte charcoal-gray rectangular slate tile flooring, a huge vintage white farmhouse double sink, and warm caramel-colored oak cabinets glowing with a deep patina and adorned with bronze cup-pull handles. The kitchen walls had matching oak wainscoting, giving it a 1930s bungalow feel. There was a separate small shelf-lined pantry off the kitchen with a stacking washer dryer. It was very cozy, and I was already imagining wildflowers on the kitchen table, the red teakettle whistling, white curtains adorned with pom-pom trim fluttering in the cool breeze, and a cardamom pound cake baking in the oven.

The room that Lucky wanted to turn into a library had a stunning, unpainted, antique Art Nouveau wood fireplace mantel that was festooned with elegant carved trees and two mantelpiece mirrors. Both the tentative library and the bedroom next door had large closets, and the main bedroom had a closet that stretched the length of the room. Aside from the bathrooms, the entire apartment was painted with dingy cream paint, but that was easily remedied. All the rooms in the apartment had beautifully curved coved ceilings with picture rails. Except for where Henry had renovated with antique stained glass, all the windows had their original beautifully blemished wavy glass panes.

The bathroom off of the main bedroom had charcoal gray wainscoting topped by olive-green, gray, and peony-pink swirling Art Nouveau William Morris wallpaper, a white claw-foot tub, white and gray hexagonal floor tiles with dark-gray grout, and a white pedestal sink. The small high window was inlaid with more beveled and leaded decorative glass panes, similar to the ones in the front door.

The small toilet near the kitchen was also lavishly decorated. It was papered with William Morris Strawberry Thief wallpaper in sage greens and deep peony pinks, and had small white hexagonal floor tiles with dark-gray grout and a deep-rose ceramic pedestal sink and toilet. There was one narrow rectangular window set with clear beveled and leaded panes.

The dining room had a lovely rectangular stained-glass transom over the center bay window. It was a graceful design with a beautiful Art Nouveau stylized sensuous curved floral motif, a clear background, and rose, sea-foam-green, and sky-blue rondels scattered throughout the design. It reminded me a little of some of the Liberty of London cotton paisley fabrics that Lucky and I had admired a few weeks before, thinking they would make dandy dress shirts.

Lucky got out her phone. "Let me show you the Mid-Century dining room table and chairs that I've been eyeballing," Lucky began scrolling through her phone looking intently for a picture of the dining room set.

I was suddenly mesmerized by Lucky's forefinger as it moved on the phone screen. Her calloused finger traveled from the top of the screen to the bottom of the screen, then she picked it up and moved it again from top to bottom, and a third time from top to bottom, stroking the glass screen as she searched for the dining room set. I blushed. All I could think of was Lucky's finger stroking inside my cunt, burrowing its way inside, curled up like a fiddlehead only to unfurl inside of me, hard and searching. Her sensitive fingertips searching for each tender swollen spot, wet and eager. Her finger, the sweetest scavenger. So, yes, I blushed imagining her finger slipping inside of me.

Lucky looked up from her phone. "Are you okay?" Comprehension lit her eyes as she recognized my blushing muddle for what it was and ran her hand over my chest, fondling my breasts. She ran her hand along the waistband of my jeans, slipping her thumb under the denim, and teasing me. "What do you want?"

"Your fingers!" I gasped. "Inside!" Articulateness had fallen by the wayside. I leaned into Lucky's grip. "Please!"

"Do you think we should?" Lucky asked lasciviously and eagerly. "Suppose Autumn and John return? What then?" she asked as she unbuttoned my jeans slowly. "Are"—one button popped out of its buttonhole. "You"—a second button popped out of its buttonhole. "Sure?"—and a third button popped out of its buttonhole.

I wiggled, trying to get my pants down and Lucky's hand closer. "Oh yes," I panted.

Lucky pushed me over to the dining room table that had been shoved against the wall, ready to be taken away by the movers. It was covered with a paint-splattered navy-blue cotton tarp. "Bend over."

I bent over, placing my palms on the tabletop. Lucky stood behind me. She pulled my jeans down to my ankles, kicked my legs apart, inserted her hand between my shaking thighs, and reached inside my dripping cunt with her rough finger. The finger that minutes before had been scrolling through pictures of teak Mid-Century dining room sets in such a distracting way.

"Is this what you want, my little invert?" she asked as she shoved one, then two fingers inside my cunt, curved and hard.

As I looked up from the tabletop, a beam of sunlight broke through the fog and shone through the stained glass, casting a scattering of rainbows throughout the dining room. "Oh fuck!" I exclaimed as I came with a short burst, come dripping down my legs to my knees.

Lucky draped herself over me, holding me until I caught my breath. "Welcome home," she murmured, as we kissed, folded together over the dirty canvas tarp, the cast rainbows dancing around us like a blessing.

After a few minutes, I straightened up, fastened my pants, buckled my brass belt buckle, and sucked Lucky's wet fingers clean, licking each digit sweetly, relishing the texture of her skin and my scent and kissing her after. "I like this apartment."

"I'm glad." Lucky was looking a little dreamy, and I know I was feeling tender.

"It looks like your friend, Henry, had a thing for Art Nouveau. The stained glass, the fireplace mantle, the bathrooms," I said, as I gestured at the stained glass over the bay windows.

"He did. Art Nouveau had a resurgence in the mid-1970s, and Henry decorated this apartment with a fabulous collection of Art Nouveau furniture that he bought at auctions and estate sales. Henry and I used to drive to estate sales early on Sunday morning, then come back to gloat over our loot while drinking crystal pitchers of mimosas and eating eggs benedict off his good china. His favorite dinnerware was white and cobalt blue, decorated with festoons and garlands with a gold metallic rim. He was a terrific cook. We get to reap the remnants of his enthusiasm and good taste. I know it is frivolous. Do you like it?" Lucky turned to me, looking a little concerned.

"I do like it. It isn't too fussy for you? I know you like cleaner lines," I said.

"No. It reminds me of Henry. I like the idea of him still being here, watching over his apartment and us." Lucky squeezed my hand. "You would have liked Henry. He was a huge slut and would spend days at a time at the baths. His favorite was the Barracks on Hallam near Folsom. He also liked to do cross-stitch. I still have a cross-stitch piece that he made for me based on a Mucha illustration of a swooning woman. Of course, he spiced it up by slipping her gown off her shoulder to expose her erect nipple and added a tiny pink iridescent seed bead at the very tip of her tit."

I giggled. "You'll have to hang Henry's naked lady somewhere in the apartment so she can keep an eye out for us. Hey, do you want to start measuring the rooms and windows? Although this joint is so big that we'll have a hard time filling it up with furniture!"

"I know. I'd forgotten how huge this apartment actually is. When Henry lived here, it was crammed with ornately carved Art Nouveau benches, cabinets, side tables, and chairs. He had huge elaborately framed mirrors hanging in the living and dining room, and gorgeous stained glass and metal light fixtures. At least the light fixtures and stained glass are still here." Lucky unzipped her rucksack, got out the metal tape measure, handed me the notebook, and started measuring the room and windows while I jotted down numbers.

We had done the dining room, living room, and were just finishing up on the main bedroom, when we heard the stomping of boots coming up the steps.

"It's us." John and Autumn walked up the steps and into the bedroom. "Congratulations on moving in together!"

"And congratulations on your new job," Lucky replied. "This is Behrouz."

Autumn was a tall, plump woman with long tangled copper hair, creamy freckled skin, a large gold septum piercing, and round rosy cheeks. Her husband John was short and slender with perfect mahogany-colored skin, short dreads, and a carved silver ring on each finger. They were carrying cloth bags of vegetables. I could see green beet and leek tops poking out of the top of the tote bag. We shook hands, then made idle small talk about the University of Pennsylvania, Philadelphia, the East Coast, and snow. Autumn had been hired to teach in the University of Pennsylvania's cultural anthropology department. They were both from Texas, and had never experienced a winter with snow. We teased them about snow days, blizzards, six-foot snow-drifts, and stockpiling bread, eggs, and milk.

We measured the remaining rooms, then left to eat our pecan rolls and drink tea in the park. It was just a four-block walk to the park entrance at Lincoln and 9th Street, and a half-block walk on Martin Luther King Drive to the gates of the Arboretum. Although we had walked down 9th to the park entrance many times before, both alone and together, it felt different now that we were moving into the neighborhood. I wondered if I would get to know the friendly middle-aged black man selling *Street Sheet* newspapers on the corner of 9th and Judah, the way I'd become friends with Dearie, who hung out smoking Kools and drinking cans of Old Milwaukee beer in Patricia's Green Park in Hayes Valley. The people in line at Arizmendi Bakery, where we bought the pecan rolls, were my new neighbors. Were there many queer folk living in the neighborhood? It was exciting to have so many mysteries and unanswered questions.

72

We made our way to one of the small meadows past the Mediterranean Garden and near the waterfowl pond, spread out our red-plaid blanket on the green lawn, and sat, pouring cups of hot mango black tea and unwrapping our sticky rolls, loose pecans showering onto our laps. Lucky took her boots off, stretching out on the blanket. We sat amidst clover, grass, dandelions, and violets talking about the new apartment. Geese quarreled and strutted nearby, while park-goers strolled down the winding path and over the waterfowl pond's bridge. Children watched turtles sunning on rocks, while Lucky and I lolled in the cool San Francisco afternoon sun planning our life together.

Lucky wiped her sticky fingers with a damp tea towel and brought out her phone to show me some of the furnishings she'd found. Neither of us had a dining room set, although Lucky had a 1950s kitchenette set. "I thought we could go Mid-Century for the dining room. Teak wood, modern lines. I found this set of six Danish teak Koefoeds Hornslet chairs online. They have black leather seats and tall curved sculptural backrests. I haven't been able to find a large enough teak table and was thinking of commissioning one. And a teak hutch."

"I like the warm red tones of the teak. Do you want a long skinny hutch like a sideboard, or a tall one?" I asked, scrolling through images of Mid-Century hutches on my phone. We looked together, finally finding one that we both liked, a tall one in the same finish as the chairs with two glassed-in shelves, three long drawers, and fluted grooving in the two sets of closed shelves.

We already had some curtains, but I wanted to get Arts and Crafts lace curtains for at least one room. I'd found a set of reproduction pictorial lace curtains, featuring a design by the British designer C.F.A. Voysey with stags, swans, birds, streams of water, tall thin trees, and a narrowly scalloped border. They would complement the stained-glass transom in the dining room, and act as a design foil to the Mid-Century furnishings. We planned on using my large antique Persian bird of paradise carpet in the dining room, and picking up the greens and blues of the stained glass with mid-tone peacock-blue walls.

"I'd like to get a new bed too. I like your metal bed frame and I like my 1930s wooden frame, but I'd like a bed just for us. I know it's corny, but maybe even a four-poster!" I felt vulnerably romantic admitting this craving. I poured the last of the tea into our metal camp cups.

Lucky typed *four-poster beds* into images, and we scrolled through ornate metal enameled beds, mock Far Eastern rattan beds, faux Medieval wooden beds swathed in brocade fabric, white princess beds, metal beds with posts that were shaped like trees, and stark pencil-post beds. As we scrolled through dozens of four-poster beds, we were starting to feel like Goldilocks. This one was too big, that one was too small, where was the one that was just right? Finally we came to a mahogany Venetian four-poster bed with tapered barley twist posts in a dark ebony finish. It was lower to the floor than my bed, so low that it would be impossible to use the underbed for any serious storage, but the new place had a full-length closet along one wall and closets in the other two rooms, so the lack of underbed storage would not be missed. Besides, Lucky's antique wood-and-metal steamer toy chest would look perfect at the foot of the bed. Best of all, we both loved it.

"A friend of mine posted this on Facebook while she was on a book tour and staying at Kink.com's Armory building headquarters in San Francisco. They added fancy decorative metal rings to the sides of their wooden beds in the guest room to be used as bondage tie-down points. We could do that too," Lucky exclaimed excitedly while eating the last nibble of her sticky pecan roll.

We got up, shook out the blanket, packed up, and took the long way through the Ancient Plant Garden, Australia, Chile, and New Zealand before heading toward the exit gate. We caught the #7 MUNI bus, riding down Haight Street, through the groups of grimy street kids strumming their guitars and begging on the corners, the gaggles of German and French tourists taking photos at the intersection of Haight and Ashbury, skinny bearded hipsters coming out of the Haight Street Market with bags of organic strawberries and sushi, and oblivious skaters mowing them all down as they sped along the narrow sidewalk. We got off at Market and Haight Street, then walked five blocks to my place in Hayes Valley.

It was bittersweet opening the door to my apartment, knowing that in a month we'd be opening another door. Francy was waiting for us, urging us into the kitchen to pour out her dinner into her ceramic dish, and meowing her hunger loudly. She wound her way around my ankles as I measured out half a cup of dried cat food, and she started eating greedily once it was in her dish.

"What a sweet hungry baby! Poor staving kitty!" Lucky petted Francy's ginger head. "Would you like a playmate? Another kitty?" Francy ignored her entreaties.

"I wanted to work on my memoir for a little bit," I mentioned as I rinsed out the green metal thermos.

"How about I make us a broccolini and potato frittata? I can use up the tiny waxy fingerlings that I bought last week, and I have a bunch of broccolini and plenty of Parmesan from Rainbow." Lucky nuzzled my neck. "Go write. I'll stay in the kitchen and rustle up dinner."

I meandered down the hall, opened my laptop, and started working on my memoir. I lived in digs when I was a teenager, and was researching Persian archeological excavation sites, dates, and participants, fact-checking to make sure I got my summers straight. Some summers I'd lived at more than one dig, and it was easy to mix them up. I was deep in research, starting with Hajji Firuz in 1968 and ending with Marv Dascht in 1971, when Lucky appeared with gray pottery plates, silverware, and water glasses, then reappeared carrying an iron skillet containing a hot crusty frittata.

I saved my work and shut down the laptop. "Do we need anything else?"

"Yes, why don't you bring the pitcher of water and the salad on the kitchen counter?"

I went into the kitchen and returned with a spinach and avocado salad in an olive wood bowl, and a red pottery pitcher of iced water. "Wow! This smells great! Thanks for cooking." I cut into the frittata, the Parmesan cheese crust crunching beneath my fork to reveal bright yellow-orange eggs cooked with vegetables and even more Parmesan cheese.

"I love these fancy-schmancy pasture-raised Marin eggs we've been buying from Rainbow, both the intense taste and the brilliant color."

"I know, right!" Lucky agreed. "Oh fuck. Have we become hobos? Just a couple of queer bourgeois Bohemians?"

"Probably. We buy eggs that cost ten dollars a dozen and take our Dickies overalls to the cleaners for wash-and fold-service."

"When we plug in all our electronic gadgets at the same time, they completely cover the coffee table from end to end, iPhones to iPads to Kindles to laptops."

Lucky and I collapsed in laughter at ourselves. What else was life for, but to enjoy ourselves? For pleasure and love?

I cleared the table, leaving Lucky lolled on the sofa in the parlor catching up with the news online with Al Jazeera, the *New York Times,* and BBC. As I washed the dishes, I thought about how fortunate we were. We had a refrigerator full of tasty food, all the hot water we could ever want, love for days on end, and we were moving into a gorgeous apartment. I detested smarmy gratitude lists. When folks would break out into affirmations, I cowered. They sounded false and pious to me. I was deeply grateful every day, starting with the feel of my cotton sheets and Lucky's naked body next to mine, then the luxury of a steaming hot shower with scented soap, then a pot of black tea. I had been poor. I had been homeless. I had been lonely. I had been celibate. Now I was none of those things. I dried the dishes with a striped cotton dishtowel, put them away, and returned to the living room.

Lucky had put on Leonard Cohen and "I'm Your Man" was playing. The lamp was dimmed, and Lucky was sitting in the leopard armchair while smoking her briarwood pipe. Leonard sang sexily, "I'm your man" and we were there for each other.

Lucky held her hand out to me. I dropped to my knees and crawled to her, nestling my head in her lap, her thighs strong and warm beneath my head. Lucky stroked my hair as we listened to the music together, then she tapped out her pipe, stood up, and shoved me into the bedroom gripping my belt. I could feel her warm breath on the back of my neck. My neck felt tender where minutes before she had been stroking it softly.

"I'm your man," she said as she tore my flannel shirt open, popping the buttons loose, the pearl buttons flying off and landing on the rug. She grabbed the neckline of my T-shirt and pulled me close. "Take off your clothes."

I pulled my T-shirt over my head, took off my binder, unbuttoned my 501s, took off my socks, and unlaced my boots. Finally I was naked, covered only in bruises, my tender nipples hard, and the silver hairs of my cunt in wet curls. Lucky reached out and twisted my nipples, causing them to harden into points. They were always tender and sore from her daily administrations, and the slightest touch made my cock twitch and swell.

"Oh fuck," I said, swooning.

Lucky pulled a length of rope out of the bedside table drawer, "Lift your arms." She bound my breasts in a figure-eight formation, pulling the rope tightly, tight enough to be uncomfortable, and cutting into my flesh, forcing my breasts to swell around the rope. With the chest bondage, my nipples hardened further, aching for her touch. Her face was serious and intent as she knotted rope, one corner of her tongue poking out in concentration.

The lamp cast a warm golden glow over us and we could still hear Leonard Cohen crooning from the adjacent room. Lucky smelled of today's sweat and Cedarwood Tea cologne, a spicy musty combination that I loved. She fastened leather cuffs on my wrists, pulled my hands behind my back, and linked the cuffs together. I sat on the side of the bed, smelling Lucky and feeling the rope pinch my flesh, getting lost in sensation. My breasts felt so exposed and naked, propped up by the rope tourniquet. Lucky fetched a slender cane from the pottery umbrella stand by the bookshelf, then hefted my breasts with one hand, running her palm over my nipples. She bent over, suckling them, her lips and teeth pulling the tender flesh. I didn't like having them sucked. It felt invasive and made me feel vulnerable. I tried not to squirm away, but Lucky caught me flinching.

"You're mine." She suckled my nipples more intently, watching my face, then released them, grinning at my discomfort.

I gasped as the cool air hit my wet nipples. Then she started caning my breasts lightly, not enough to leave marks, but enough to make me want more. She knocked my thighs apart to cane my inner thighs. Lucky was still dressed, and I was pink and swelling and wet and spinning with desire. Lucky glowed with intent, intent to hurt me, to own me, and to love me. She grinned devilishly. This was love, this electrical sexual connection and power exchange. I can tell you what came next, where orgasms originated, where the cane struck, how I felt when the clamps pressed my tender nipples, the noises Lucky made as she beat and fucked me, however this is merely a litany of actions, noises, and smells. What does this mean as the room fills with the funk of our passion, our moans, my bruises, our bits swelling and wettening? Is that all this is? The meeting of chemicals, pheromones, serotonin, oxytocin, dopamine, and testosterone in Lucky's and my bodies? Everything changes.

I squirmed. My nipples were still tender from crawling across the rough wool Persian carpet the night before, the chain between my nipple clamps dragging on the red-patterned carpet as I made my way from the slate-topped cabinet to the leopard arm chair where Lucky was waiting for me to give her evening head. My nipples had been tender for over five months. The residue of Lucky's touch was with me every minute of the day reminding me of us.

Lucky started caning me harder, leaving stripes and welts, my pale flesh reddening and bruising. First my thighs, then my breasts. I hated getting my breasts caned hard. It was different from other places on my body. It was this moment when I thought, "Why do I do this? This hurts and I hate it!" I wanted to stop, and in that minute of resistance and hatred for the pain, my heart spilled, breaking open to Lucky. And at that moment, a cry was forced from me; I opened my mouth to wail and tears spilled from my eyes, wetting my cheeks. Lucky didn't stop. Why stop, when this is why we started?

I sobbed as my world narrowed to only Lucky and myself in my darkened bedroom. Perhaps that is the key to this existentialist rat's nest: the answer is the creation of our mutually created cave. Each kiss, each cry, each strike of the cane, each twist of Lucky's hand inside my cunt, solidified this tiny dreamworld where we existed to pleasure our flesh and our hearts.

When I was in Alcoholics Anonymous decades ago, I was an agnostic. Although we were encouraged to use anything as our higher power, AA had cultural limitations. When I announced in the Selectively Sober meeting that sex was how I prayed, I hit that AA boundary and was subsequently scolded, patronized, and shunned. I was right though, and every twist of Lucky's hand brought me closer to the state of god.

The caning across my tender swollen breasts burned; I cried, held still, and the burning traveled from my chest to my cock, to my cunt. Swelling, hardening, dripping onto the dark-brown cotton sheets and staining them with my need. I cried, snot running from my nose and over my lips. I licked the sticky mucus indelicately. I might as well have been four and picking boogers. Shamelessly I cleaned the snot from my puffy lips with my tongue until Lucky pulled the black bandana hankie from her back left pocket, held it to my red nose, and sweetly told me to blow. I loved the combination of tenderness and pain that Lucky poured into me, and Lucky loved giving that to me.

Sniffling, I blew, grateful for the tenderness. Lucky shoved me over onto the bed, uncuffed my hands, then brought the ropes up from the four corners of the bed frame to tie me down on my back, legs spread and cunt exposed. Lucky resumed caning my breasts and thighs, switching from one to the other as I held still for her pleasure, crying quietly with every sharp, biting jolt. I could feel my cunt get wetter and wetter.

Finally I gasped, "Please fuck me!"

Lucky grabbed the rope binding my breasts, lifting me up off the bed, and twisting it savagely. "What makes you think I want to fuck you?" she hissed, then leaned over, biting my shoulder until I cried out.

Lucky fastened the clamps to my tender nipples, then held the chain that traveled between the clamps to my mouth. "Open your mouth and hold this." She shoved the stainless-steel chain between my teeth. Her mouth moved from my neck to my nipples, suckling, nipping, and licking, her warm breath and wet lips tenderly soothing then pinching each bruise and stripe. She worked her way down to my belly, following the outline of my fire-beetle tattoo with her tongue.

Lucky had never sucked my cunt, my flesh cock. She had sucked my silicone cock many times, down on her knees, looking up at me adoringly, us melting into each other. No one had sucked my flesh cock or my cunt for decades. It had never been a favorite sport for me, and with testosterone I was unsure of myself. I'd even drawn a rare boundary there, asking Lucky to refrain from sucking my flesh cock. As Lucky licked the fiery tattooed beetle on my belly, I squirmed, trying to get away.

"No!" I begged. I didn't have many boundaries, but this was one of them. Was Lucky breaking a cardinal rule of kink behavior with her insistence, or was Lucky helping me stretch my boundaries? I didn't have long to mull over this conundrum because Lucky was moving quickly.

Lucky held my thighs apart with her hands, squeezing the marks and bruises until they burned, and making my cunt swell and my cock harden even more. "You're mine. Give it up," she said as her mouth lowered onto my flesh cock.

If I had not been tied down, I would have fled. It was horrifyingly intimate. As it was, I tossed and turned as much as I was able until Lucky rose from my cunt to slap me across each cheek. "You're mine. I own you. Hold still."

Lucky held my nostrils pinched shut with the forefinger and thumb of one hand, and covered my mouth with her other hand. She held her salty, calloused palm tight over my mouth, allowing no air to reach me. As instructed, I held still until I couldn't help but stiffen with needing air. Lucky leaned over and released the hand that was over my mouth. I looked at her face. I managed a shallow breath before she quickly covered my mouth with her mouth instead of her hand. She held her breath as I tried to remain calm beneath her lips, unable to breathe. And then she breathed into my mouth, still holding my nostrils tightly shut. Lucky's breath was my breath. Her exhale became my inhale as we breathed together, our breath binding us together, and the air traveling from her body to mine, then back again. I was passive, the fleshy body that Lucky was feeding with her breath. I was passive, but my passivity was an active state of receiving Lucky's desires, giving up power, and letting the deep sexual and emotional energy travel between us. I opened my body and heart as wide as I could make myself, offering myself to Lucky.

She said more softly and tenderly, "You're mine. You can do it." She lifted her mouth from my mouth, her hand from my nostrils, and moved south with her lips, kissing and nibbling. She returned to my cunt, licking, biting, and suckling my cock and cunt lips as I whimpered. It was so difficult to hold still, to remain open. This kind of tender was a type of tender that I was not accustomed to, softer and fleshier.

I didn't think I was going to be able to come with Lucky giving me head, but Lucky had other ideas. I felt Lucky rub lube on my asshole, then she slipped a medium-sized plug in. It was just enough to fill me and cause my asshole to throb with the desire to get fucked, a visceral vibration that made it open and twitch. She continued to suckle my cock, then slowly started working her rough fingers into my cunt. It was hard to concentrate, tied down with my asshole throbbing around a butt plug, Lucky's mouth full of my cock, and her fingers circling my cunt, occasionally working their way in to remind me of how much I needed to get fucked. My cunt was heating up, the tendrils of electricity gathering there and in my belly. I was starting to forget myself as I thrust into Lucky's mouth, her teeth nipping at my cunt lips and cock. Lucky's fingers continued to promise a fucking, one, then two, then three inside me, and me dripping, clenching her fingers with my cunt muscles, willing her to force her fingers way inside of me.

"Please fuck me!" I begged, my hips rising as far as the ropes would let me, riding her mouth and hand.

Lucky continued to finger-fuck me softly and slowly, barely inside, while biting my cock and cunt lips wolfishly. My asshole and cunt were throbbing in frustration and pleasure as I ground myself into Lucky's wet mouth. Lucky started working her hand inside of me, sliding in with a twist and a pop until I was filled, stretched around Lucky's clever mitt like a glove. I was stuffed with Lucky, her spit, her fingers, her fist, her toys, her teeth. Filled with Lucky, dripping with our pleasure. Lucky growled into my cock, her fist clenching and my cunt fucking her hand, drawing it deep into my heart. I felt pleasure unfurl from my cock, through my belly.

I could see it, a fleshy pink ribbon of electrical desire undulating through my belly and chest, radiating as it traveled down my arms, up my neck, through my head, and finally shooting out of the top of my skull in a brilliant saffron-colored explosion.

My come gathered in waves as it flowed from my belly down to my cunt, and finally gushed out of me vigorously, soaking Lucky's face, chest, arm, and the sheets with my salty wetness. Lucky growled and snorted as I shouted, releasing an explosion of nonsensical babble, my body shaking, wired on ecstasy.

I started crying, overcome with the unexpected strength of my orgasm. I was leaking everywhere and had ejected the butt plug onto the sheets. Lucky lay on top of me, kissing my cheeks and petting my head. My throat was sore and gravelly from shouting and I was suddenly overcome with tears.

Lucky untied my wrists and ankles letting the ropes fall to the floor, then pulled the quilt up to cover us both. "Oh, baby, you're mine," she murmured as Leonard Cohen crooned "I'm Your Man" into the tender night.

And tender, we were so tender together.

CHAPTER FOUR

OWNED

an Francisco was becoming a dystopian wonderland, or maybe it had been one all along and the present had finally caught up with the past. From gold diggers to techbros, from North Beach to SOMA to the Castro to the Mission, from Bohemians to activists to drag queens to hippies to hipsters, the history of San Francisco enveloped me every time I left my apartment. Sometimes it was a comfort, to be surrounded by such a rich past, but sometimes it felt like quicksand, a stew of unwashed longing.

Is this how it begins? The homeless fellow outside of All-Star Donuts Cafe died. It wasn't really a cafe, it was a cheap donut place with burnt coffee and a basket of spotty bananas next to the cash register. There were always homeless folks hunched over the chipped, dirty Formica tables, the metal table legs uneven and the grimy tabletops wobbly. Each workday on my way to the MUNI bus stop on Market, the smell of crappy bacon and fried donuts would waft around the corner of the tiny triangular brick building next to a parking lot. The homeless man I'm talking about slept on the southwest corner, huddled on the sidewalk wedged up tightly next to the building. They'll be tearing down the All-Star sometime in the next few years to put up a five-story edifice to money. I thought it would be this year, but maybe not, because they're having a party in the parking lot tonight to unveil a mural painted by three street artists: CARATOES from Hong Kong, LOLO from Oakland, and TATI from Miami. All women. And the mural depicted a bouquet of wide-eyed slender waifs, its style second cousin removed from renowned San Francisco artist Margaret Keane. This is what I mean. See how easy the trip was from cheap donuts, hunger, and death to hipster street art? Oh, fuck me.

I never talked to him. He was there each morning, soaking in the greasy stink and foggy shadow. He was never really awake, and I never saw him beg. He must have eaten food, pissed, taken a shower, jerked off, shot up dope, and smoked cigarettes somewhere, but all I ever saw was him passed out. Once, I walked by hurriedly, late for work, looked down at him and realized that he'd shit himself, his ragged filthy pants pulled half off and dark brown diarrhea oozing onto the gray cracked sidewalk. His ass was pale white smeared with dirt and shit, his butt crack a crevice of unimaginable depth. I looked away, wanting to give him privacy. How could his shit and my carefully knotted silk necktie exist in the same universe, the same street corner? Sometimes I'd look at his face as I walked by, trying to see the five-year-old he'd once been, imagine that he had a cowlick, and a mother who loved him, fed him, held him, sent him to school in the morning. Then one day I read about a fatality in the *San Francisco Chronicle,* the death of a homeless person at Van Ness and Market, the brick corner of the All-Star Donuts Cafe. I read about the death wondering if it was him. I never saw him again after that. He passed like the greasy smells from the cafe, rising into the San Francisco air to disappear into the clouds. Did anyone else notice that he died? Did his mother know?

Lucky and I were moving into her apartment in the Inner Sunset in a month. I'd watch that corner as I walked past, thinking about the man who shat himself to death there. There was no marker. His ghost didn't linger. We were moving, deep in discussions over paint colors and deliriously ordering an extravagant four-poster bed and antique

84

oak barrister bookcases. But that is what San Francisco was like. It was a mixture of the most elegantly sensual and the most filthily profane. Lucky and I discussed this dichotomy over pasta alla puttanesca, over rhubarb and strawberry pie, as she washed my back, while chopping onions, when riding the trolley, and while in bed with the covers drawn up to keep away the night damp.

It was part of a larger system, something beyond our control. This beast was a racket that let people stay cold and hungry, while food was wasted and buildings were empty. I started carrying change in my pocket and would empty handfuls of coins into the hands of whoever asked me for it. I met the eyes of the people who lived on the sidewalks that I walked upon, each glance saying, "I see you." I sent out all the power, energy, and love I could as I walked past the homeless and bereft, imagining that I could heal something. Anything at all.

One night, after a dinner of a mushroom and smoked Gouda omelet and sourdough toast, Lucky and I took a moonlight stroll, looking for some fresh air and a dark alley for a little after dinner cock sucking, Lucky in her black leather jacket and I in my hoodie. We walked through Patricia's Green Park, the one-block-long and one-quarter-block-wide park at the end of Octavia. Five lanes of speeding cars turn at the park, and two small lanes flank the park. Exhaust fumes act as fertilizer for the palm trees, the ginkgo trees, and the brown-eyed Susans. The palm trees and a collection of concrete tables and benches filled the Hayes Street end, the brown-eyed Susans and a children's playground were on the Fell Street and Octavia Street end. In between were two grassy areas for dogs to shit, piss, and play and a sculpture that changed every year or so. Usually the art was made by Burners and was quasi-mythical, but the current sculpture was made of steel and involved too many sharp corners and not enough compositional forethought. It was a cool night and the fog obscured the full moon. We sat on one of the metal benches by the ginkgo trees, and discussed our day and our upcoming move. Lucky lit her pipe, the fumes and smoke rising delicately in the night air.

"Is that a new tobacco? I like it. Kind of fruity. Do we want to go with the peacock blue for the dining room and the leaf green for the library?" I asked.

"It's called McCranie's McArris; it's a Virginia blend. I like the sweetness. I'd rather we went with something softer in the library, a deeper more muted green. I bought those teak dining room chairs for the dining room and a Mariko teak and an amber-colored resin side table for the library. We need to get a fireplace screen too. Have you thought any more about the bedroom situation?"

"I don't know," I sighed. "It's more about privacy than about sleeping or not sleeping together. I need options to be alone. You have the library. You can shut the door and know that you're alone. We have the middle room, which could be a guest bedroom, but maybe it could be my bedroom or maybe it could be my studio. The apartment is huge, but I don't want us to be underfoot with each other. You know?"

"We need a place to put up friends. You need a private place to write. Why don't you make the middle room into your studio and have a sleeper sofa in there? It's big enough."

"The thing is that I also want it to be my cave. I want to be surrounded by my stuff. I don't want it to feel like a guest room or a hotel room," I whined. "How would you like to have the sleeper sofa in your library then?" I asked querulously.

"We could put the sleeper sofa in the living room."

"Oh, all right. I don't know why I'm being so crabby about sharing a room with a sofa. Let's just put it in the middle room and call it my studio. That seems eminently fair. Just no futons. I don't want to feel like I'm camping out in a dorm!"

"Why *are* you so crabby tonight?" Lucky asked me, relighting her pipe.

Just then one of the local Hayes Valley mentally ill people walked by talking to himself angrily. Jerry was in his forties, tall, good looking, with shoulder-length, tangled blond hair, chiseled cheekbones, a muscular but lanky build, and very handsome. He was a painter and wore the same torn, paint-splattered, faded blue jeans and a bleached-out blue chambray shirt every day. He was always barefoot and jacketless, no matter the weather. I once ran into Jerry in the local, now closed, bookstore, and got into an unexpected lengthy discussion with him on German artist Joseph Beuys's mediums, specifically which kind of animal fat he used in his performance pieces. I'd never talked with Jerry before. He used to yell at me in the park and call me a capitalist prisoner that was being controlled by the mafia, and tell me that I'd be shot by Satan at dawn. The art conversation was on one of Jerry's good days, but his good days were infrequent. After we talked art in the bookstore, he stopped yelling at me, but continued his rake's progress of becoming unhinged.

"It's kind of that." I gestured toward Jerry as he turned left by the palm trees onto Hayes Street. "Then there are all the HELP WANTED signs littering the windows of the coffee shops, boutiques, and chocolate stores. I live in an upscale paradise, but no one can afford to even work here anymore! I can't afford to buy shoes in my own neighborhood and recoil at paying fifteen dollars for a pita wrapped sandwich. What will happen to Jerry?"

Two young men walked by our bench in the same direction that Jerry had taken. They were in their mid twenties, not stylish, white, straight looking, clean cut, with short hair, and wearing plain jeans, T-shirts, sneakers, and dark hoodies. They were talking earnestly about buying a sofa and as they passed us one turned to the other and said, "Maybe I'll get it in leather. I just got a forty-five thousand a year raise."

"And that," I said, "is that. It just makes me want to cry. Jerry will go home and maybe paint or maybe talk to the walls, and they'll go to some hipster bar and get drunk. Then spend money and not look at any of us in the eye. It feels more and more like us versus them. There is a class war going on and the enemy is here in this city. Or is it like Pogo said, 'We have met the enemy and he is us?' What can we do to own our city again?

"And look at this shit! People leaving their crap all over the park!" I gestured at three empty Smitten ice-cream cups, a discarded Ritual coffee cup, an empty bottle of LonjeviTea's Gravenstein Apple kombucha, and a box with dried-up pizza crusts from Casey's pizza food truck. I scooped up the debris and angrily threw it into the nearby metal trash container. "I'm sorry."

Lucky turned to me, and grabbed my hand, looking at me seriously. "I have an idea. I have an idea on how we can own San Francisco again. Reclaim the city. The Lexington may close down to become a ritzy restaurant for techies, but we will own our city again!

"When I was a little girl, growing up in Ohio, my dad had a tool shed in the back yard. One of the neighborhood tomcats, an enormous battered ginger with one ear, took to entering into the shed through a busted window and spraying on my dad's drills and saws. Dad fixed the broken window, but the cat found another way inside. It stank in there and dad was pissed. One summer Saturday night, with the green smell of freshly mowed grass in the air, dad grilled steaks on the brick barbecue pit. As we ate at the redwood picnic table, dad hatched an idea to keep the pesky tomcat away from his tools. Dad downed can after can of Schmidt beer. The fireflies and mosquitoes came out and mom sprayed us down with Off bug repellent. Dad kept guzzling beer, until he was full of hops and piss. He then swaggered over to the tool shed in the dark, unzipped the fly of his khaki slacks, and methodically peed around his shed, circling three times for maximum effect. The tomcat never returned. Dad had marked his territory. We could do that."

I grinned at Lucky. "So you're talking the best ever kinky version of us shaking our canes and yelling, 'You kids get off my lawn!' We piss all over San Francisco?"

"Well" Lucky replied slyly, "I was thinking we could piss and we could come all over the city. Mark our city with our juices and reown it. Google, Twitter, Uber, and all those techbros can't take San Francisco away from us."

"I like it." I giggled. "We need to make a list of places to mark. I remember James and Laura telling me about the San Francisco Yuppie Eradication Project back in the 1990s where activists would slash the tires and otherwise deface the cars of upscale gentrifiers. He had friends that were involved. A group of women that pissed on Hummers and other ostentatious cars; they'd climb up on top of the cars, lift their skirts, and let loose!"

"Let's start tonight in Hayes Valley. Behind what used to be Marlena's." Marlena's drag bar had been a twenty-two-year institution, the oldest drag bar in the city. Now it was Brass Tacks, a cocktail bar and techbro pickup joint that was as hipster and annoying as it sounded, filled to the cheap black, gray, white, and metal brim with hipster girls looking to score with techbros.

Lucky and I rose from our park bench and scuttled across the park, down Octavia to Ivy Street, the alley behind Brass Tacks. We scoped out the dark alley. Although a row of homes abutted Marlena's with no alcoves to fool around in, the Days Inn across the alley had a line of parking spaces for their vans and there was just enough privacy and space for a quickie. We ducked behind a scraped-up silver Ford van; Lucky leaned against the hotel's beige siding, unzipped her black jeans, and pulled her cock out. I fell to my knees, opened my mouth, and greedily popped her black cock into my mouth. I starting licking and sucking the head, until Lucky became impatient and shoved her cock down my throat by pushing my head forward, spearing me, her cock touching the back of my throat. She rested, pushing deeper and deeper until I started to gag. Then she drew out slowly, dragging her cock along my tender lips and holding my head stationary. With a growl, Lucky started fucking me fast and hard.

"I'm going to fuck us into this alley. Marlena's is ours!" And with a deep yip, Lucky came deep in my mouth, her cock straight down my throat. I had drool falling from my mouth to the asphalt and my knees were sore from kneeling on stones and debris.

"We're going to mark this alley as ours with either my piss on you, or your come on me. Which is it? You choose this time," she growled.

"Piss on me! Please. Do it!" I begged.

Lucky took off her cock, pulled her jeans down, spread her hairy cunt lips, and let loose with a stream of hot piss aimed at the ground in front of me. My cunt clenched at the sight of the stream shooting from her cunt lips, her cunt swollen and red, and her piss glistening in the moonlight. When she was done pissing, she shook her hips like a dog after getting a bath, drops of piss flying. Some fell on my face and I wondered what Lucky's piss would taste like. I loved her sweat and would plead with her not to shower so that I could revel in her musky odor. Would her piss taste like sex?

Lucky helped me up. My knees creaked and I wobbled. Getting old was playing havoc on my proclivities, but Lucky understood about the fragilities of age, as they were creeping up on her too. Lucky grabbed me by the front of my black Mr. S hoodie and we kissed in the alley. Then we strolled back through the park, past the sweetly scented jasmine that tumbled over the backyard wall at the intersection of Fell and Octavia, and home to Francy and our warm bed.

The next evening, Lucky and I spread a map of San Francisco out on my tiny Victorian wooden dining table, and I took out my tablet. We decided to make a list of places in the city that we needed to own, to mark. We had a lot of ginger tea and Lucky was rubbing pot salve on her hands.

"The alley next to the Castro Theater! Twin Peaks!" I exclaimed.

"In front of the old Lexington Club. The statue of Ben Franklin at Washington Square Park and the site of the old Black Cat in North Beach. All the apartment buildings in the Mission that have been burned down to create tech condos."

"The End-Up. Dolores Park! Compton's Cafeteria at Taylor and Turk Street in the Tenderloin. Or at least somewhere on Polk Street!"

"The windmills in Golden Gate Park. The baths at Cliff House. Each apartment where our friends have been evicted and every new condo construction site. The old Barracks bathhouse."

"The purple Victorian hippie house near Rainbow at 12th and Folsom that they repainted in shades of smoke and toast. The rotunda at the Palace of Fine Arts."

"We can't bring anything back, or resurrect the dead, but we can make our mark. It's a kind of magic, carving our way into the earth, the sidewalks, and the buildings. I know this verges on woo, a kind of California quasi-spiritual ache, but I believe that by making our mark with our piss and come we'll subtly change things. Tilt the world toward us, one orgasm at a time." I turned red. "I'm sorry if this sounds wacky."

Lucky stared at me seriously. "It does sound wacky, but I get it. I get the need."

We looked at our list, then took a hot-pink highlighter and marked each location on our map of San Francisco. Then we taped the map to the wall and triumphantly pinned a red-flag-topped decorative tack to the alley behind Marlena's drag bar.

We were moving in a few weeks, but we could continue in our mission to re-own San Francisco during and after the move. For now, we needed to box up our possessions, agree on paint colors, negotiate living arrangements, and move. We would fit sex in. We always did.

The next month was two parts excited to one part frantic. We were both relieved that we were moving into a different place instead of one of us moving into the other's flat. This way the awkwardness of trying to merge books, art, dishes, and other living ephemera was diluted by the craziness of moving and the shininess of a new apartment.

We had both lived alone for several decades, so this was new territory. I would sometimes wake up at 3:30 a.m., and lie between my cotton sheets next to Lucky's lightly snoring warm body, shocked at the chances we were taking by moving in together.

Blithe and spontaneous was for nineteen-year-olds. At sixty I fretted about the potentially serious consequences of giving up my rent-controlled apartment. If this didn't work out, not only would I lose a lover, but also I'd most likely have to move out of San Francisco to an only somewhat less expensive place in the East Bay.

Besides privacy, aesthetics were another issue. Lucky was fifty and I was sixty. Both of us had definite opinions about home decorating that did not always merge. We were both stubborn, but I was hoping that love would encourage compromise.

Lucky liked clean-cut lines, Mid-Century furnishings, and cool colors. Her bathroom was a stark barrage of snowy white towels, a forest jungle of plants, and dove-gray walls. The rest of her furnishings in her large studio apartment were teak Mid-Century antiques, with floor-length, stone-colored, heavy linen curtains over natural matchstick blinds. She ate off deep blue, gray, and warm-sienna-brown Danish chunky stoneware from the mid-1960s called Granit and cooked using cast iron pans, supplemented with dented aluminum starter pots and pans. She collected tasteful German Mid-Century art pottery and owned an enormous hideous vintage shag rug in a geometric op art motif in shades of brown, cream, and ocher. Aside from the plants, a cast iron skillet or two, and the slate-blue linen curtains, I would never have given most of her home decor items a second glance, and I'm sure she would say the same for me with my red antique Persian carpets, moss-green velvet overstuffed armchairs, black-slate-topped Victorian walnut wash stand, and gray-marble-topped Eastlake dresser. I was all about the velvet, textiles, Victorian and Arts and Crafts furniture, reds, and oranges. My main concessions to the present were my gray Noritake stoneware dishes and an immense modern brushed steel and dyed wood armoire that I got during a divorce.

We started refining aesthetics before we moved, as we packed, divvying up some of the rooms according to style, and mixing most rooms like cocktails at 3:00 a.m. The main bathroom stayed as is in all its William Morris Strawberry Thief glory and the library became a mixture of Moderne and Arts and Crafts. The dining room was a paean to Mid-Century cool accented with William Morris lace curtains and a Persian tree of paradise carpet. We kept the magnificent vintage stove and used my oak dining table in the kitchen. My brushed steel and dyed wood armoire went into the parlor, along with Lucky's marvelous 1878 leather-and-oak library armchair with its open modern lines. We kept my moss-green tufted velvet sofa, but donated my ratty maroon mohair Victorian side chair to charity. We kept Lucky's collection of German art pottery for display in the dining room, however the op art shag carpet was sold to a trendy hipster boutique in the Mission. We bought a new stylishly dramatic wood four-poster bed and put Lucky's antique steamer trunk at the foot of it to store sex toys and play gear. Lucky's 1950s light oak valet was perfect next to the McCoy umbrella stand where I stored canes and riding crops. Fortunately, Lucky's prints and my artwork worked well together without too many stylistic glitches and accidents.

The library was Lucky's lair, a butch dyke man cave with overtones of extravagant *Downton Abbey* lavishness meets sleek Danish Modern. The studio was mine, more Bloomsbury meets Paris in the 1930s, meets Persia. We decided to keep all of our books in the library, but like men and women in the mosque, to keep them separated with Lucky's in two barrister bookshelves, and mine in the other two. We were leery of too much combining too quickly, besides we categorized our book collections differently, and trying to align categorization methods seemed too daunting. We combined our cookbooks in the kitchen though, Lucky's more carnivorous volumes rubbing elbows with my more vegetarian collection.

We hired painters to cover the dreaded rental-colored cream walls, spreading a montage of paint chips over my dining table during one night of exhausting chromatic decision making. By midnight we'd made our choices. The parlor walls were to be golden ocher, the library a moss green, the dining room a muted peacock blue, the bedroom a rich barn red, the foyer a honey gold, my studio a deep thistle, and the kitchen a fiery mango.

And this is how the days passed, in a flurry of intense domesticity with barely enough time to fuck or sleep. A week before we were to move into the new apartment I realized that once we moved in it would still not be over. There would be a whole other stage of unpacking, hanging pictures, unrolling carpets, unwrapping dishes, and getting acclimated to living with each other and living in a new neighborhood. I wanted to cry in frustration and anticipatory tiredness, but instead we got another cat.

My cat Francy was a Craigslist foundling, so we consulted Craigslist again, but all we found were dogs and bunnies. In frustration, we visited the SPCA on Alabama Street in the Mission one Wednesday evening. Francy was a middle-aged, one-eyed ginger tom with a poet's soul, all soft and snugly, eager to roll over with his paws in the air and used to being the king of the household. We were trolling for kittens, with the thought being that Francy would find a kitten more innocuous. It was going to be difficult enough moving to a larger apartment, without having Francy duke it out with another adult cat in the process, but we thought the distraction of a rowdy youngster might help her acclimate. The immense facility was practically deserted. In an hour, the only people we ran into were a trio of young, white-habited nuns looking for a good mouser, a Spanish-speaking extended family with twin toddlers looking excitedly for their first puppy, and an adorable bear couple wanting to adopt an older kitty. I felt like the little old man in *Millions of Cats*. Each cat was more beautiful than the next, but we were not contenders for queer cat daddies. The seal point Siamese was too noisy, the black tuxedo one too aloof, the calico too surly. After an hour, we came upon a wee Maine Coon with an enormous bushy tail, huge upright tufted ears, and a soft round belly. And with a wave of a passel of paperwork and a hundred and twenty-five dollars we were the proud daddies of a four-month-old Maine coon kitten that we named Lulu-Bear.

We were moving in a few days. We were both packed up, the new apartment had been painted, and our wooden bed had been delivered. At the last minute, we'd found a McRoskey mattress set, and we'd finally agreed just to pack all of our dinnerware and sort out what we'd use once we unpacked. We hired Delancey Street Movers, took a deep breath, and moved in together.

Unpacking was fast. I wasn't the kind of person to prolong the agony of moving in, letting taped-up boxes sit in corners for months. I couldn't understand people who exclaimed, "I haven't gotten around to unpacking that yet!" two years after moving. I liked to open boxes on Christmas, and I liked to open boxes in new homes. A childhood of moving every two years prepared me for kamikaze acclimation.

And so we unpacked. Two pressure cookers, towels, box after box of books, duplicates of Scrabble, sex toys, framed art, table lamps. The second night, Lucky unwrapped a box of balls and skeins of yarn, knitting needles, and unfinished socks.

"You knit too! That is so cool. And you can knit socks! I'm so jealous. All I can do is knit in a straight line and all I've ever made is scarves. I can't even purl."

"I haven't knitted anything for the past eight months. I've been too busy courting you." Lucky winked.

After a week, we were unpacked and firmly nested. Sofas were in the living room, bookshelves in the library, beds in bedrooms, and teapots in the kitchen. The wool Persian runner had been unfurled down the hallway and I'd already tested it for crawling comfort, having spent most of Tuesday night on my hands and knees naked, following Lucky's black Dehner boots from one end of the hall to the other and suffering rug burns on my knees in the process. The hallway was twice as long as mine and was made for begging. My nipples were sore and tender from dragging on the rough wool runner. I spent one afternoon naked, meditatively combing the runner fringe while Lucky watched from her leather chair in front of the lit fireplace in the library, briar pipe in hand and wearing a vintage maroon quilted-silk smoking jacket, leather pants, and velvet slippers, Marlene Dietrich keeping us company in the background.

Lastly, we pinned up our map of San Francisco in the library. It looked like a war battle map. We'd added two pins since fucking behind Marlena's drag bar, in front of the End-Up and another memorably in the alley beside the Castro Theater during a run of the sing-along *Sound of Music*. I will never listen to Julie Andrews singing "My Favorite Things" again without thinking of Lucky on her knees, sucking my cock with enthusiasm, while humming along.

We decided that a luxury condo construction site in the Mission would be our next foray into marking our territory, and spent an afternoon along Mission and Valencia Streets scouting out possible venues before deciding on one at 22nd and Mission. This was the site that started suspicions of mass arson in San Francisco, resulting in protests and investigations. That had not stopped developers from tearing down the destroyed three-story building and starting construction of yet another luxury building for techies, displacing more local brown families. It was the ideal place to make a statement.

By now we were old hands at public-sex activism, with our bag of lube and gloves, all black clothing so we'd blend in at night, and our stealthy superpowers. That is such a lie. Each time we did it, we were equal parts nervous and excited. This time it was a little risky. The spot we picked was policed by navy-blue-uniformed rent-a-cops and there were motion-detector lights, but it was the best spot in this construction site.

We arrived at 22nd and Mission at 11:00 p.m., keeping an eye on the building from across the street. Not many people were out, the new moon was high, and wisps of fog clouded the night sky. When the security guard passed by the corner we had staked out for fucking, we waited a minute, then scurried over to the construction site. In the spirit of derring-do, we decided to go for the full squirt. Lucky was going to fuck me until I came against the site, marking it with my come. We stumbled over piles of dirt as Lucky pushed me against a wood column in a cluttered dark corner, pulled down my jeans, and reached in to fuck me, the fingers of one hand curved around my wet cunt and the other hand holding me around my neck. I was already hot and ready for her, and all it took was a few minutes for me to start to come. My come was dripping down my leg, but we wanted to shower the new building, so Lucky turned me around facing the dirty wood framing. I rested my cheek on the scratchy wood post, smelling the sharp scent of wood and preservatives as Lucky fisted my cunt from behind, grunting quietly into the night. Finally I came with a spurt of salty liquid, sprinkling the site with my orgasm. Lucky unbuttoned her jeans, letting loose with a shower of piss through her pee-and-play packer. We collapsed giggling, then heard the shuffle of someone rounding the corner at a rapid clip. Quickly, I pulled up my pants, not caring whether they got wet, and Lucky buttoned up. We stood nonchalantly on the sidewalk by the site as the guard ran around the corner toward us.

"Get back here. Stop!" the guard shouted as he stumbled up to us carrying a small paper bag and panting. "I heard some kids fooling around. Did you see them?"

"We saw a couple of kids run off that way," I said and pointed toward 21st.

The uniformed security guard scratched his balding head, clearly bemused. He was in his thirties, portly, cheerful, and a little out of breath. He took a bite of a coconut-covered donut from a greasy brown paper bag and grumbled, "Darn kids. Now you two be careful around here. We get vandals and troublemakers. It can be dangerous this late at night and you two gentlemen don't want to get hurt."

"Yes, sir." Lucky said. "We were just walking off a little insomnia and are on our way home now."

"Have you tried chamomile tea or valerian? The wife uses those and swears by them. Better than walking around the Mission late at night!"

"Thanks for the tip. Maybe we'll give it a go. Have a good night. Hope you catch those kids."

We walked up the street a bit, hailed a cab and rode home, thankful that no one would suspect a couple of cute old geezers like ourselves of being rabble-rousers. Once home, we added a red-flag-topped pin to the construction site and pondered our next move while snuggled with Francy and Lulu-Bear in the cushy comfort of our bed.

"What about the Palace of Fine Arts? I'm imagining us in the circular rotunda, with the tall marble Greek columns casting shadows through the smoky fog and moonlight as I suck your cock. We can wear our tap-dancing shoes and glide through the columns like Gene Kelly and Fred Astaire afterward."

"Better yet, we can do it Greek style against the Greek columns, and I can be Alexander the Great and you can be Hephaestion frolicking through the columns of Persepolis before it burned," I snickered.

"Of course we'll be Djuna Barnes and Natalie Barney in front of the old Lexington, reenacting the infamous Paris Temple of Friendship on our hands and knees."

"Fleet Week is coming up! We can suck cock in Chinatown. Get dressed up in uniform and pretend we're sailors out for a good time. I'll unbutton your thirteen-button pants, each button, one at a time, ease your pants off, then get you off in the shadows of a dim doorway. Drunken sailors will pass us by, but we'll be hidden, busy sucking and fucking." Lucky flicked my nipple for emphasis.

"And against the base of the bronze Spanish-American War Memorial at Market and Dolores across the street from Whole Paycheck, the building with the private organic butterfly habitat and gardens on its roof." I was giddy with excitement.

"I love that statue with the Pegasus horse and the million pointy things, guns, hooves, swords, and wings. Fuck Whole Paycheck and fuck private rooftop butterfly gardens!" Lucky gestured wildly as Francy and Lulu-Bear scurried off the bed in alarm.

"The windmills in Golden Gate Park! Down by the Pacific Ocean and past the buffalo fields. I hear that the windmills are still used by gay men for cruising. With the salty tang of the sea air mixing with the dank fog, and seagulls serenading us as you glide into my ass, inch by inch, until we come in the park, coming together beneath the protective shadows of the windmills and the ghosts of all the men that have come there before us. I can be Sam Steward and you can be my rough trade."

"So many possibilities." Lucky turned on her side to go to sleep.

I felt Francy and Lulu-Bear jump up onto the bed again between us, solid hunks of fur and purr, curled up, snuggled around our knees. Then I heard Lucky's soft snores and I too fell asleep.

A couple of weeks after our construction site maneuver, we planned a foray to Twin Peaks. We wanted to do this one in the daytime, us overlooking San Francisco in triumph and San Francisco overlooking us in protection. We packed a Southern picnic lunch of pimento-cheese sandwiches sliced into triangles, Veronica's pickled-dill green beans, two fine slabs of three-layer coconut cake, and creamy deviled eggs wrapped in waxed paper, then packed it into a rucksack along with a quilt, a thermos of sweetened iced tea, gloves, Lucky's favorite black cock-sucking dildo, lube, and wipes. Like the Boy Scouts, our motto was "Be prepared!"

We hopped on the 33 bus and rode to the base of Twin Peaks, rising breast-like and overlooking San Francisco—Twin Peaks was originally called *Los Pechos de la Choca* or Breasts of the Maiden. We got off near the hiking trail and started walking the narrow trail through the scrubby bushes, butterflies, and wildflowers to the top. It was sunny in the city, but the closer we got to the peak, the windier and cooler it became, the sky cornflower blue overhead, and inklings of fog in the distance. The trail was dry and dusty, and the bright earthy scent of the foliage led us forward. We got to the top of the peak, leaned against a rock, and rested, taking in the city beneath our boots. There were two peaks, one named Noe and the other Eureka. Fittingly for public sex, we were on Eureka.

The city spread before us, glistening in the sun as Lucky unbuttoned my jeans. We made out, kissing against the sharp rocks, and letting the sun heat us up. I took off my hoodie, my long-sleeved striped knit shirt, and my binder, letting the breeze envelop me and the sunshine warm me. Lucky suckled my nipples into peaks, and yes, I thought of Noe and Eureka as my nipples hardened in her mouth and between her pointed teeth. Lucky took her mouth away, leaving my tits wet and cold, aching to be twisted, the electricity running from them to my cunt. I was on fire, my hips arching toward Lucky and San Francisco, begging to be filled by both. And Lucky, oh my captain.

Lucky also took off her blue-plaid flannel shirt and hoodie, her olive skin breaking out with goose bumps, and her dark brown nipples hardening in the breeze. She kneeled in the dirt, kneeled over San Francisco, kneeled to bless the city with our love and our lust. I was dripping already, dripping down my hairy thigh, my precome falling to the tawny dust as black crows circled overhead, cawing their encouragement. She caressed my cunt, jerking off my clit until I threw back my head to the sky and clouds and pleaded for her to fill me with her hand, and with a cackle she did. Lucky's gardener's fingers, those tendrils worrying their way inside of me, so knowing. And then a pop as her entire hand was inside, twisting and pressing and I let loose, my come gushing out like a spigot irrigating the trail. She kept going and I kept coming, raining my pleasure over San Francisco as she poured herself into me. I yelled into the wind until I was hoarse, my pleas traveling over San Francisco and my come watering the hills. Lucky was yelling too, the crows, Lucky, and myself a pandemonium of ecstasy.

Lucky gazed up at me and I gazed up at the sky. Suddenly I was fucked out and could not come any more, melting into the rock that we'd been fucking against. Lucky was drenched to her elbow, my throat was sore from yelling, and I was limp. Lucky rested her silvery head against my knee and I laid my hand upon her in benediction. Then Lucky stood up, the sun shining against her muscular back, unbuttoned her jeans, pulled out her pack and pee, and let loose with her piss, yelling to the open sky in triumph. Her piss baptized Eureka, showered the hills, the grasses, the winding streets below, the Google buses, the corner stores, the Sisters, the hipsters, our town.

The city gleamed beneath our boots, having been renewed by the drenching cosmic rainbow of our come and piss. The Victorian houses were washed clean, the streets freshened, the air clearer. There was something about fucking amongst the wind, the fog, the sandy dirt, and the blue butterflies that felt expansive.

Giggling and high, we cleaned up, meandered down to a field of unearthly lupines swaying in the breeze, found a place to spread out our quilt, and ate our Southern feast, nibbling sandwiches and devouring cake until there was not a crumb left. Curled up, sated, and self-satisfied, we napped on *Los Pechos de la Choca* dreaming of nothing but the present.

CHAPTER FIVE

STUFFED

T here used to be a transman in his midthirties from Noe Valley who would post in the Craigslist Man-for-Man section on a regular basis. There his photo would be, shot from the waist down, his hairy thighs spread, his bits glistening proud and hard. The title of his post demanded, *Fill my Hungry Holes*. I admired him relentlessly. I didn't have a flesh cock that I could fill him with to the top and back the way he demanded, so I wrote him a fan email instead. I wanted to be like him. I wanted to growl to my lovers to fill me until whatever they were stuffing in my cunt and my ass was squirming out of my mouth, my heart. I never heard back from him, but I thought about bumping into him at Dolores Park or Tartine, he prowling and I outwardly complacent, but inwardly from the same insatiable tribe. I would never recognize him unless he stripped, spread his legs, and demanded that I fill his hungry holes.

I like to get stuffed. I mean I love to get everything filled like a turkey on Thanksgiving. Fill my mouth, my cunt, my ass, my pisshole. I don't care what you stick in there, although I have my favorites, the ones I keep close to my bed. I love the cold, battered, 24-inch-long heavy metal chain, each oblong link sliding in one by one, the edges pinching my tender flesh, and me tasting the metal as it fucks me. I've been known to jam two eight-and-a-half-inch-long silicone Outlaw dildos into my ass, bigger than I thought possible, first one, then the other layered on top sliding in smoothly and filling me. I like to fill my pisshole with the delicate length of a long cool metal sound, opening me slowly, and reminding me of all the secret places that can be possessed, all the wet caves.

Then there is the gleaming stainless-steel ball hitch that we bought at Tractor, Farm, and Fleet last winter. It was snowing and we were desperate to find something to fill me up for the holidays. We grabbed it right before they closed at 7:00 p.m., Eartha Kitt huskily crooning "Santa Baby" over the scratchy loudspeakers and Lucky's hand clenching my overall-clad ass as we worked our way through the line of exhausted last-minute shoppers. Even now, my nipples are tender hard as I hunch over shivering, my asshole twitching, thinking about that planetary sphere sliding into my ass like the moon into orbit. We'd bought the stainless-steel hitch in Ohio during our visit to my daughter and grandchildren's home.

It was fifty-three degrees in San Francisco, with the kind of dank spitting rain we'd get sometimes that was somewhere between foggy and raining, but not quite either. I looked down through the velvet curtains in our library bay window to see whether the cars had their wipers on and what folks were wearing. Dressing for the moody San Francisco days was never easy, so we looked for clues in the street. What would I wear to the airport? Would it be my red hoodie, my wintery fleece-lined pullover, or my corduroy blazer? In the end, I settled on my olive tweed Norfolk, a seedily fashionable jacket with a plethora of sneaky hidden pockets and the ability to suavely straddle the twenty degree difference between Northern California and Ohio. Lucky wore her favorite vintage 1970s black leather jacket, with its multitude of buckles and vague safari look. We were leaving in half an hour to take BART to the airport, so we would soon be making that transition between fog and snow, San Francisco urban and Ohio Midwestern, hedonistic frolicking and parental snuggling. Lucky and I were flying to Ohio from San Francisco to spend the holidays with my daughter and my two grandchildren. It was the first time Lucky had come out with me to Ohio to meet my family, and we were nervous.

I had not introduced my daughter, Theo, to a lover since an ill-conceived marriage when I was thirty-nine to a handsome oaf who, in retrospect, we'd nicknamed Numbnuts. Numbnuts was a bumbling mechanic and had the smelliest feet of any man I'd ever met, a nasty concoction of toe-jam and old motor oil that had permeated his socks, wafting around him like a cloud. When Numbnuts and I first got together, my daughter had been pregnant. With her hormonally enhanced sense of smell, she could not bear to be in proximity to Numbnuts and his stinky feet. I'd had a propensity for handsome devils who were a little on the slow side, cheap, and often cruel. Lucky was different. Lucky was slyly handsome, yet thus far her cruelty was confined to the bedroom where it belonged, and she read Jean Genet and Djuna Barnes for Sunday morning pleasure. She was an erudite devil and I was contentedly in lust and in love. Theo was territorial and protective of me, and often claimed that I had the sense of a house cat in heat when it came to choosing lovers.

Lucky packed large and I packed small. This is not a metaphor for what was in our pants. In that respect, neither of us packed. We flew cockless. My driver's license read male and Lucky's read female, but it was a crapshoot as to how we'd be perceived at the airport by TSA. At the least, my curmudgeonly scowls got me nervous pat-downs and twirls through the X-ray machine, and Lucky's flirtatiousness, combined with her masculine demeanor and good looks, got her a collection of business cards with phone numbers handed over surreptitiously by femmes intent on discovering what Lucky might be really packing in her 501s. I was amused by the string of fluttering hopeful hearts that Lucky carried behind her like a glittery kite tail, but Lucky remained oblivious to her effect on most femmes.

Finally we made it to BART, and soon were on our way, past Daly City, past South San Francisco, past the cemeteries of Colma, past

103

the scrubby conifers, dusty hills, fog, and ticky-tacky houses beyond the city that I loved so much and called home. I hated leaving San Francisco and was mesmerized by the highway, the underpasses, the motley BART passengers, and even the wafting fog every time I traveled outward. We arrived at the airport, scuttled through security, and got on the plane safely and quickly. Lucky checked two bags, carried her laptop, and had a messenger bag slung over one black-leather-clad shoulder. One hardside aluminum suitcase was jam-packed with boots and gifts, the boots comforting and soothing her nerves, and the gifts an effort to please the family that she had spontaneously and roundaboutedly acquired through the miracle of online dating and OKCupid. The other was packed with clothing, each pair of jeans, sweater, and shirt meticulously folded with tissue paper layered between them. I carried my battered brown-leather rucksack over my shoulder and a small vintage tweed duffle bag of tightly rolled-up clothing. I'd snuck an extra pair of boots into Lucky's boot and gift suitcase and was pleased with my ability to travel light and loose. By the time we'd settled into our seats, Lucky had three scribbled femme's phone numbers stuck in her pocket, and I was digging through my rucksack for my e-reader and our flight snacks.

Somewhere over Utah, Lucky took a sip of cranberry juice and ate a handful of goldfish crackers, then turned to me. "I've been meaning to ask you, there is a queer play party on New Year's Eve? Do you want to go to it together?"

I looked at Lucky in horror. "No. I don't like play parties." My refusal to go to play parties had been a bone of contention between lovers and me in the past, but Lucky hadn't shown any interest in going to them since we'd been together. It wasn't the play part that annoyed me, but the party part. I was an introvert, far happier in small groups or alone.

"Aw, come on, they'll have a sling we can play on! It'll be fun!"

"Lucky, do I look like I enjoy having fun?" I said sharply, "No, I'm not interested."

"Will you at least think about it? Tov and Mikail will be there too," Lucky said hopefully.

I said I'd consider going to the play party with Lucky, but I lied. Although I loved the idea of play parties, the smell of pheromones and come, and the sounds of people fisting, fucking, and flogging, when it came down to it, I *disliked* rooms full of partying strangers more than I liked public sex.

I wondered if Lucky was getting sexually bored with me. I was once in a poly relationship with a lover who was a big old player. After two years, she started begging me to go with her to play parties, and then started lying to me about fucking other women. In hindsight, I can see that she got bored and was looking for something or someone different or more exciting, but she couldn't be direct about it. I ended up going to play parties with her, but I would have been happier with her going by herself. I didn't care if she got new lovers, but she needed the subterfuge of lying. Lucky's father had also been a player, always stepping out on her mother in a cloud of bad cologne. But Lucky's mother, as far as I could tell, was honest with her lovers about her flings. Obviously, a penchant for sexual adventure ran in Lucky's family, and as far as I was concerned, her curiosity about sex and willingness to be adventurous served me well, but still I had limits.

We were spat out at midnight in Columbus, Ohio. The pilot thanked us for flying with Southwest and announced the weather. He was upbeat, but it was twenty-two degrees and windy, with a bitter December chill. The thirty-one degree difference had us scurrying through our carry-ons for wool scarves and caps. Theo picked us up at the airport a little bit before midnight. All six two of her was bundled in an orange down jacket, skinny jeans, black riding boots, and a froggie green knit hat with one missing pop-eye. She wore her new violet and rhinestone cat-eye glasses, her chin-length hair was in burgundy ringlets, but she still looked wan and tired. We staggered into her battered but faithful blue Honda Civic, with Lucky crammed into the backseat cluttered with overdue library books, soccer balls, and stray hats and gloves. It was snowing lightly on the outerbelt, as Theo and I chatted about how the grandkids were doing and our plans for the holiday, until we heard Lucky snoring lightly from behind.

"So, you two moved in together." Theo managed to sound angry even though she was talking softly so as not to wake Lucky. "After only six months? What are you thinking? Wait, don't answer that. I don't want to know."

"Theo, don't be a chump. And stop talking to me as if I'm sixteen and just staggered home drunk without my panties."

"Mom! She's a player! Even I can tell that. Sorry, I mean *Dad*."

"It's okay. I've been your mom for almost forty years and I'm still your mom. Call me whatever you'd like."

What could I say? I wanted to tell Theo to fuck off about her misgivings about Lucky, but that would not earn me any points for maturity. Defending Lucky seemed irrelevant and like a losing proposition. Either Theo would grow to like Lucky or she would remain skeptical, and me griping and nagging would only make the situation worse.

"Well, when you two break up you'll finally move back to Ohio. We can buy a place with an in-law unit and live together. You're getting older, Mom. What if something happens?"

This was familiar territory. It was the "you're-getting-older-what-if-you-break-your-hip-get-mugged-dotter-about-half-crocked-with-a-faulty-memory-start-hoarding-newspapers-kittens?" lecture. I rolled my eyes. It had come to this. I remembered my mother's tone of voice as she scolded me when I was eighteen for not being serious, fucking too many girls and boys, taking too many chances, really just being uncontrollable, and knew that my daughter had turned into my mother. I remembered my scolding Theo for earning mediocre grades, getting pregnant too young, and dating men who didn't respect her enough. Life was a full cycle of parents or children reining-in one another in ferociously.

We pulled up to Theo's brick row house. Snow had started to drift down hypnotically through the dark night, lightly covering the black streets, the hedges, and Theo's windshield. The snow was soft, sticking, and would cause havoc for traffic in the morning, nature's metaphor for my daughter's annoying but loving behavior. We woke up Lucky, gathered our luggage, and made our way carefully up the icy sidewalk to Theo's home.

The house was quiet as Theo disarmed the alarm and showed us in, the children and cats sleeping. She stayed up with us sitting at her vintage red Formica kitchen table for a bit while we ate the cheddar cheese sandwiches she'd prepared, and settled in. Lucky admired Theo's windowsill herb garden, and chatted about Theo's plans for an expanded vegetable plot this spring, and offered to give her advice on heirloom varieties that would grow well in Central Ohio. I was relieved to see Theo start to thaw toward Lucky a little. It was late and Theo was used to going to bed at 10:00 p.m., while we were exhausted from the flight. Theo spread out a futon mattress on the living room floor for us, then finally toddled off to bed.

Before meeting Lucky, I had slept in my younger grandchild Alex's bedroom during visits, lying on her single bed wrapped in unfamiliar-smelling sleeping bags and quilts. I liked drifting off to sleep in my grandchild's bedroom with their ginger cat, Bacon Bits curled up next to my head, one paw patting the nape of my neck. And that was how I slept before, with a cat petting me to sleep with his delicate tufted paw pads, Alex's stuffed tiger and elephant perched on the windowsill, and the window open a crack to let in the fresh, icy night air.

Alex's thin, narrow child's bed was too small for two creaky old queers though, so we were shacking up on that futon on the living room floor. Theo, Alex, and Sam had already put up the Christmas tree. The clear lights reflected off the terra-cotta walls and the red wool stockings I'd sewn for them hung on the mantelpiece. The futon was lumpy, but we could slide the wooden pocket doors shut and have privacy. It felt a little like college, sweetly innocent and very vanilla. Sleeping on the futon mattress on the floor made me want to hump Lucky frantically, rubbing our cunts against each other's hip bones, the way I did with my next-door neighbor girlfriend when I was sixteen. We had to be quiet and keep an eye on the sliding doors for interruptions. The first night we made out with our pajamas on, Lucky with her red union suit, and I in my green tartan flannel pajamas. We pulled the unzipped sleeping bags over our heads, and lay on top of each other kissing, giggling, trying to be quiet, our hands holding each other's breasts under our pajamas, rubbing damp spots through our pajama pants with our come, and the air under the covers steaming up with our breath.

Lucky and I woke up to my grandchildren Alex and Sam and three cats eyeballing us expectantly, surrounding the futon like knights around a castle moat. Children are time intensive and demanding, something I forgot between visits, and Lucky had never been around children. Lucky was already looking a little frantic, so I sent her to shower while I scouted for tea. In the steamy kitchen, Theo was up frying bacon, while the cats wound about her ankles angling for a second breakfast. Theo had planned a full day of household shopping and bookstore browsing, culminating with a visit to the Christmas lights display at the zoo. Her childhood best friend, China, was having a baby shower on Wednesday and we needed to stop off at Target for a gift. After showering, Lucky shambled into the kitchen in a cloud of Cedarwood Tea, wearing a white cotton undershirt, a scarlet Scotch-plaid flannel shirt, blue denim 501s, black Wesco harness boots, and carrying a small shopping bag stuffed full of fancy-pants Blue Bottle coffee beans for Theo. Just like her mom, a sure fire way to Theo's heart was through her stomach. Theo ground some Bella Donovan beans, started a pot of coffee, shooed the cats, Bacon Bits and Chuck Norris, from the kitchen, and started cooking banana pancakes. By the time I'd gone into the playroom to fetch Alex and Sam for break-fast, Lucky and Theo were animatedly drinking coffee and trading pancake recipes.

Our first foray into the twenty-three-degree cold was to Target for gloves for Alex and Sam, kitchen odds and ends, and the baby shower gift. The kids stayed with their next-door neighbor, while Theo, Lucky, and I piled into Theo's car, travel mugs of coffee and tea by our sides. We slid to the mall on barely salted streets, along with a battalion of other last-minute holiday shoppers. Once at the overflowing mall, we parked as close to the store as possible, girded our loins with chocolate and dried fruit, and marched into battle. The store was overheated, and full of squalling children, crazed adults, and exhausted salesclerks. Perky Christmas carols competed with the general crankiness, but we were high on pancakes, coffee, and the pleasure of one another's company.

Theo headed with ferocious determination toward the infant section, announcing, "I want to buy China a pack and play for the party."

We followed. Lucky poked me in the side, confused. I poked her back, just as wary.

"A pack and play?" Lucky whispered to me. "Does Target in Ohio carry dildos now? Do pregnant women pack these days? What am I missing out on? Do women pack at baby showers? How do you wrap a pack and play?"

I giggled, imagining a contingent of pregnant Midwestern women, all packing silicone cocks. "I have no idea what she is talking about. Just keep quiet and eventually we'll find out."

This was one of the disadvantages and one of the delights of mixing cultures. I usually waited it out, knowing that the secret would eventually be revealed. I was reasonably certain that neither China nor her amiable husband needed a silicone cock, and that pack and play meant something entirely else in Ohio baby-land.

Lucky kept poking me in my side, eyebrows raised and wiggling. I sighed at her impatience. It was obvious that we needed to solve the mystery of the pack and play, so I asked Theo casually, "What exactly is a pack and play?"

"It's a playpen for traveling," Theo replied, oblivious to our giggles.

"Playpen? Like puppy play?" Lucky whispered. "Do the pregnant women get in the pen and feed one another biscuits through the bars? Is there barking?"

"Shut up!" I giggled.

We walked past pyramids of disposable diapers, stacks of cloyingly gendered pastel onesies, aisles of nipple brushes, bottles, and sterilizers until we came to an aisle of portable plastic baby cages, the anticipated pack and play. After much consideration, we decided upon the decidedly urban and fashionable battery-run, chirping, sage-green and chocolate-brown pack and play with an overhead play station. Lucky looked stunned at the culture clash and bewilderedly chewed a handful of bourbon truffles in quick succession. I snickered at her. I was used to it, but she had some catching up to do.

Next up was another cookie sheet, and a passel of winter gloves for Alex, who had a propensity for losing the left glove of any set. Theo made a beeline for the children's gloves, while we found a section of leather gloves. Leather gloves were on sale, and Lucky stopped in front of a display. She looked studiously through the selection, while biting her bottom lip in concentration, until she found a pair of black leather gloves with decorative stitching in a size small.

She pulled me over. "Did you see these gloves?" She drew the glove on slowly, flexing her fingers and causing the thin leather to grip her hands tightly. I felt myself getting turned on looking at Lucky's hands encased in black leather.

"You know how I like my gloves soft and tight. Touch them and tell me what you think." She looked me in the eye. "Are they tight enough for you? Are they soft enough? Touch them."

I stroked her gloved knuckle as she clenched her hand into a fist and then relaxed it, stretching her fingers out. "Can you imagine my hand inside of you?" She clenched her hand again.

She whispered, "Go on, touch the leather again. Is it soft enough? Do you like the fit? Will these last long enough?" She drew out each word seductively, each sentence loaded with meaning.

Then she lifted her hand to my face, her forefinger curled under my nostrils, and smiled slyly, her olive dimples deepening. I smelled the spicy scent of new leather, and sighed as she took her hand away. She flexed it into a fist again, turning her wrist and admiring the gleaming black leather. I started blushing. I couldn't stop thinking about her leather-clad hand on my cunt, stroking and parting my cunt lips, then gliding inside so hard and soft, her wrist twisting as she leaned into me. My cunt was getting wet and I could feel my nipples get hard inside my binder.

I tried to think of something to say. "They fit you well," I stammered.

"I like how they hug your knuckles." I stroked her leather-clad palm with my forefinger and blushed.

She said decisively, "I think these will do nicely," and leaned over to adjust my scarf, casually pinching my nipple in the process. I succeeded in not moaning, but staggered backward in surprise for a second. Lucky smiled and leaned in for a hug.

Just then, Theo rounded the corner with her shopping cart overflowing with baby furniture, children's winter gloves, ice scrapers, and cookie tins.

I tried to look dignified despite my dripping cunt and pink cheeks, as Lucky crowed about finding such spiffy black leather gloves on sale. Theo lit up and tried on a pair of gloves in brilliant orange, then glanced at the price tag and sniffed piously, saying, "They are beautiful, but new leather gloves are a want, not a need!"

As Theo herded us toward the cashier, I tossed the orange gloves and Lucky tossed a pair of emerald-green gloves into our cart. I rolled my eyes at Theo's back. I understood the necessary frugal nature of single motherhood, but found Theo's parsimonious huffiness hard to bear, and I liked to fight it by indulging her with frivolities. It was a parental duty. Usually I sent her la-di-da Blue Bottle coffee beans, cotton sheets, and European shoes, so I was happy now to be able to fuel an immediate desire. Besides, if you asked me, leather often fell under a need rather than a want.

By that evening, the snow sprinkles had deepened to thick flurries. We'd picked up the kids from a neighbor's house, grabbed some dirty rice and red beans at the creole joint DaLevee in the Short North, and made it to the zoo light display at 7:00 p.m. On the way back home, Alex and Sam fell asleep in the backseat, sticky candy canes in hand, with me between them, Candye Kane crooning the blues, and Theo and Lucky up front fondly discussing my bossiness. The moon was a horned sliver in the blue night, the snow magical, and I felt exhausted yet satisfied.

Once home, we put the kids to bed, then changed into our jammies. We met at the table in Theo's orange kitchen, and I looked up Marion

111

Cunningham's overnight yeasted waffle recipe on Lucky's laptop as Theo put on a kettle of water for ginger tea. We could see the snow falling slowly outside the kitchen window, framed by the spidery bare branches of the pear and cherry trees in the small backyard. Lucky mixed the powdery yeast and warm water, added sugar and salt, then the flour, and covered the turquoise pottery bowl of batter with plastic wrap to rise on the counter overnight.

The next day was Christmas Eve. We planned to spend the day prepping food for Christmas dinner and trying to keep the kids occupied. Between the excitement of Grandpa visiting, meeting Lucky, the impending unwrapping of gifts, and school being out for winter break, they were wound up to hell and back. I'd been tense with worry about whether Theo and Lucky would get along, and how Lucky would handle the onslaught of rambunctious kids, but everyone seemed to be doing fine. I'd even caught Sam and Lucky whispering in the zoo gift shop, then later looking nonchalantly at each other with much eyebrow wiggling and smirking at the checkout counter as they bought something.

We finally settled into our sleeping bags on the futon at 11:00 p.m. I was exhausted, but I was used to fucking every night and Lucky's teasing in the leather glove department had me hot for a quickie. I reached for Lucky, but she shoved me over, lying on top of me with her full weight.

"Please fuck me," I begged.

She laughed at me quietly. "Do you really think it is proper to fuck in your grandchildren's living room? I don't think so! One, the mess. You know how you are. Two, the noise. Again, you know how you are. Three, propriety! Didn't you learn anything in that fancy South Carolina finishing school your daddy sent you to?"

"Please. I'll be quiet. I'll stuff your underwear in my mouth. Please, I need your hand inside of me," I whined. I pleaded. I pouted.

All Lucky did was laugh at my discomfort, twist my nipples until I almost came, then tell me to lie still with my hands behind my back, and unbuttoned the fly of her union suit, wiggled her hand through the fly, and proceeded to quickly jack off while watching me squirm. She came with a short grunt, kissed me sweetly, shoved her come-covered fingers into my mouth to be licked clean, turned over, and prepared to fall asleep.

"You're mean!" I exclaimed, my cock still throbbing with unfulfilled need.

"That's my job, sweet cheeks," Lucky retorted.

I spooned Lucky, my cunt throbbing and my nipples burning, and then fell asleep too.

Christmas Eve morning started at 7:00 a.m., with waffles at eight. I staggered into the kitchen to find Theo on her second pot of coffee while putting away clean dishes, a foot of snow covering the backyard, and cardinals at the bird feeder. The rich smell of Blue Bottle coffee filled the steamy kitchen.

"So, what do you think of Lucky?"

"Well, she seems okay," Theo admitted as she stirred sugar into her coffee. "Better than the last one at least! No. More. Players. That's the rule!"

"Oh Theo, knock it off. I can take care of myself and I'm your mother, not your teenaged daughter. Or son. I'm glad you approve though. Are you dating anyone right now?" I added half-and-half to my black tea and looked at Theo's coffee longingly.

"I'm not interested in having a boyfriend. They're too much work. I'm busy with my job and my kids, but maybe that will change once the kids are in high school." Theo peered at the bowl of fermenting waffle batter on the counter, removed the plastic wrap and poked at the batter with a wooden spoon. "Is it supposed to look all bubbly and gross like this? I am seeing someone once a month, but it's just for sex."

Theo usually had a trick or two on the side, and they almost always started wanting more from her within a few months. "Is he starting to squirm yet?"

Theo grimaced. "I know. It sucks. I told him I wanted to keep it

113

casual, but now he wants to meet the kids and go out to the movies. I'm going to have to break up with him soon."

I commiserated with Theo, but I also felt sorry for the guys she was dating. Theo had the habit of swooping in, fucking them witless for three months, then dumping them swiftly. If anyone was a player around here, it was my feckless daughter.

I could hear the sounds of Lucky singing "I Enjoy Being a Girl" as she showered upstairs, then her boots on the wooden steps coming downstairs. Lucky swaggered into the kitchen, exuding good cheer and sandalwood.

"Good morning. Let me get the waffles made." Lucky kissed me, added the eggs and baking soda to the bubbling waffle batter, then poured herself a cup of coffee, drinking it black. "Whoa! There is snow out there!"

I boiled water for another cup of morning tea. At the last minute, I decided to live dangerously, popped an antacid pill, and instead drank my first cup of coffee since my birthday, stirring in copious amounts of sugar and half-and-half until it was like drinking a hot, liquid, coffee-flavored candy bar. Fuck consequences! I fried the in-house smoked bacon we'd bought from the Clintonville Community Market, while Lucky made waffles at the table. Alex, Sam, and Theo shoved it in as fast as we cooked. I felt like I was running a diner. Maybe a hipster Oakland diner, but a diner nonetheless. Finally, Lucky and I ate. And ate. The waffles were tender, the outsides crisp from the butter that Lucky had been basting the waffle iron with and the insides light from the yeast. The kitchen was steamy and smelled of coffee, bacon, and maple syrup. Outside it was white and dreamlike, while inside I was coddled by my lover and my family.

We spent most of the day indoors, except for a morning sledding excursion to Schiller Park followed by a lunch of buttery grilled-cheese sandwiches and canned tomato soup. After lunch, Lucky and Sam played a fierce game of Battleship beneath the Christmas tree, the tiny Christmas lights twinkling as Lucky and Sam annihilated each other gleefully. Theo took two of the cats upstairs for an afternoon nap.

Alex curled under my arm on the sofa as I read her *Millions of Cats* by Wanda Gág. The little old man had found the scraggly kitten in the high grass, taken it home to his wife, she'd bathed it, and they'd plumped the kitten up with bowls of cream. I'd reached the end.

"'It's the most beautiful cat in the whole world,' said the very old man, 'I ought to know, for I've seen—hundreds of cats, thousands of cats, millions and billions and trillions of cats—and not one was as pretty as this one.'" I closed the book.

Alex looked at me dreamily and whispered, "I want a blue button-down shirt just like Daddy's! I don't like dresses and I want a super-short haircut for my birthday," then closed her eyes and fell asleep.

I covered her with the quilt, and wondered. She'd always been a rough-and-tumble girl, dragging fire trucks bigger than her around at age three, and now crazy about softball. I believed that queerness was at least part genetics and our very small family was packed with bisexuals, lesbian separatists, closeted elderly single gentlemen, woman-loving sherry-tippling single gentlewomen in Boston marriages, and queers of all ilks. Maybe Alex would grow up to be a butch lesbian. I smiled, remembering Sam's stage of wearing pink glittering gowns and tiaras when he was three. Now he wore skater clothing, and was into *Doctor. Who*, chess, baking, and sharks. Things change. I made a note on my phone to buy Alex a blue button-down shirt when I got back to San Francisco, and went into the kitchen for a glass of water. My tummy wasn't happy with the coffee I'd had at breakfast so I popped another antacid before dinner.

I was sipping a cup of ginger tea and browsing through cookbooks when Theo came into the kitchen, laptop in hand. "Feel better now? Did you manage to get some sleep?"

"Yep. I'll heat up some beef stew for dinner, then I want to start making pies for tomorrow. Are you okay with leftovers?" She retrieved a plastic container of stew from the freezer, removed the lid, popped it in the microwave, and opened her laptop.

Lucky wandered into the kitchen yawning. "Sam and I fell asleep under the tree for a little bit."

The microwave dinged. Theo got out the stew and ladled it into shallow red-yellow-and-white-striped bowls.

Theo called the kids and we sat down to a Christmas Eve dinner of beef stew and buttered rolls. The kids were cranky and sullen with pre-Christmas excitement.

"I made grandmother's recipe for the stew," Theo said as she started in on her second bowlful of stew.

"I still have her typed and grease-stained recipe card for the stew. The recipe is from *McCall's* magazine in the nineteen sixties. I wish I had her recipe for beef stroganoff. It was her special company dinner and had a tin of beef consommé in it. So sixties!"

Sam and Alex were kicking each other under the table and squabbling about who got the last dinner roll. Finally I cut it in half, gave each a half, and told them to chill. We finished our stew to Theo fretting over recipes and the kids fretting over tomorrow.

After dinner Lucky and I were sent out into the wilderness of Columbus, Ohio by my daughter to buy a turkey baster, a string of small clear lights, garbage bags, tape, lard, and half-and-half. Ohio liked to snow for my visits, and a wet snow had been falling softly since midmorning. Ice trucks and plows were already out, preparing the streets for a Christmas day of squiring squalling excited kids and sleepy caffeinated parents to relatives' homes, and other folks to packed movie theaters and Chinese restaurants. We were grateful for some time alone. Alex and Sam had reached their optimal level of preholiday anticipation and were whining, too wound up and reluctant to go to bed. Theo had resorted to assigning them household chores on different floors just to keep them busy and separated until bedtime. They were plotting insurrection, but not until after they'd absconded with their gifts on Christmas Day. We'd left Theo frantically scrolling through pie crust recipes, muttering about flakiness, ice water, butter vs. shortening vs. lard, and swilling black coffee laced with whiskey, tempered by listening to the Indigo Girls.

Most stores were already closed for the holiday, but Theo had directed us toward a decrepit mall on the South Side that was usually open on holidays. She Google mapped it on Lucky's phone and sent us off. It was off a desolate side road filled with construction, but after getting lost in the snow twice we finally found the mall. There was a grocery store, a Tractor, Farm, and Fleet, a cheap haircutting salon, the ubiquitous Starbucks, and a bank. It was everything one could possibly want on Christmas Eve. The parking lot was full in front and empty in the rear, kind of like a reverse mullet. We parked next to the grocery store, went in, and managed to get everything except for the turkey baster. Tractor, Farm, and Fleet was our only hope. The store was almost deserted, the only shoppers looked desperate and bewildered, with shopping carts filled with wrapping paper and last-minute gifts of toys and tools. To two urbane queers from San Francisco, Tractor, Farm, and Fleet was an exotic wonderland of Middle America sprinkled with kinky sex toy possibilities. We decided to start at the right and work left, the bright overhead lights illuminating us as we fondled and giggled over butchly overalls and hoodies, J-Lube, riding crops, bales of barbed wire, sundry dangerous-looking metal tools, and shoulder-length latex gloves. I found a blue button-down shirt for Alex and we grabbed the last turkey baster in stock for tomorrow's dinner, with a rubber bulb in the shape of a plump brown turkey. We almost made it out without any sex toys until Lucky's eyes lit on a shiny chrome hitch ball that bore a remarkable resemblance to a pricey butt plug we'd seen at Mr. S a month ago. She pounced on it, I raised my eyebrows in mock indignation, and we added it to our basket. We checked out, the chirpy, mustached, flannel shirt—wearing bear of a clerk wishing us happy holidays, as Etta James huskily made promises that she was not going to keep over the loudspeakers, and then we started back home.

We were on the highway and nearly home, when Lucky pulled over to a rest stop. It was deserted and I wondered why we were parking there. Lucky turned off the car lights, unbuttoned her black jeans, took off her packy, fished into her man-bag, put on her biggest cocksucking cock, and stroked it, tilting her hips up. "I want you to suck my cock. Now. Get me off. I've been waiting too long."

She grabbed my head and shoved my head roughly onto her cock. I love sucking cock. I love getting stuffed, that feeling of opening and the lack of control. I love the messiness of cocksucking, the spit, drool, and tears as I gagged, choking on her cock. The smell of Lucky's cunt, out of reach yet less than an inch from my mouth, and my lips chaffing as she fills me. I wanted to be Lucky's boy, Lucky's girl, Lucky's man, and Lucky's woman. I wanted to be Lucky's everything.

I opened up my mouth, feeling Lucky's cock hit the back of my throat. Lucky thrust into my mouth as she held on to my neck and head, tightening her grip on my neck. It was hard to breathe and I could feel drool gathering in the corners of my mouth and cooling as it trickled down my chin. She bucked beneath me as I made gulping noises, gagging as her cock buried itself in my mouth, stuffing me full of Lucky. My cunt was on fire and my nipples were painfully hard. All I wanted was Lucky speared down my throat as deep and hard as possible, and coming in my mouth and out my cunt. The windows were fogging up and all I could hear was the quiet sound of falling night snow, her grunts and growls, the wet slobber of her cock pushing into my mouth, and my gulps and moans. With a final shout of, "Fuck me!" Lucky came in my mouth, her cock slamming into the back of my throat one last time. She leaned back and relaxed as I put her cock away in her bag, buttoned up her 501s, and wiped the spit and tears from my face. My lips were puffy and sore from cocksucking. I wanted her hand inside of me desperately. It had been three days of no fucking, my cunt and ass unstuffed. I was becoming carnivorous and feral, desperate to be filled, but I knew that I wasn't getting any until we were back in San Francisco. My cunt, my ass, my pisshole, and now my mouth were empty.

"Baby, that was good. You're a good little fag cocksucker." Lucky turned the key in the ignition, set the heat on high, and whistling "The Lady Is a Tramp," drove us the rest of the way home.

Lucky did not relent at any point on Christmas Eve, but kissed me chastely before dropping off into a deep sleep. I stuck my hands under my armpits to keep them away from my cunt and thought of England, but it didn't help. I tossed and turned until Bacon Bits came into the living room and curled up in the crook of my neck, purring me to sleep noisily, orange tail swishing under my nose.

When Theo was little I used to make her eat a bowl of oatmeal sweetened with dried fruit before she was allowed to open presents on Christmas morning. Being a hippie, I also banned sugar from our diet, saying that it was a mood-altering addictive substance. I saw the error of my ways once Theo grew up and left the house, but she had never forgiven me for a childhood bereft of chocolate Easter bunnies and Halloween candy corn. I was dutifully remorseful, so I made a point of sending her California chocolate and home-baked cakes and cookies regularly. In rebellion against her austere upbringing, Theo had not maintained what she felt was the unreasonable family holiday ritual of oatmeal on Christmas morning. She prided herself on her holiday morning breakfast of sugar-bomb baked iced cinnamon buns and whipped-cream-topped hot chocolate on a tray in the living room so that the kids could mainline sugar while opening their presents. I found the combined sugar rush, excitement over new toys, and early morning hours too rowdy for my taste, but it was only once a year so I sucked it up for the sake of ultimate peace.

Alex and Sam woke up at 5:00 a.m., and parked themselves behind the closed pocket doors between the dining room and the living room where we slept near the Christmas tree. I could hear them whispering and shuffling, hoping to wake us so we'd let them into the room with all the gifts and their stockings.

"Shhhh. Mom said we aren't allowed to wake up Grandpa and Lucky," whispered Alex.

"You're making all the noise," replied Sam.

"Shut up. We're gonna get in trouble!"

"I'm gonna tell on you!"

"Santa won't bring you anything!"

"I know there isn't a Santa."

Lucky was still sleeping the sleep of the well sucked. At five thirty I gave up. I stealthily got up without waking her, gathered the wayward grandkids, and went into the kitchen where Theo was putting an enormous pan of cinnamon rolls into the oven and drinking coffee.

Theo divvied up cooking tasks. "Alex, help me whip the cream for the hot chocolate. Sam, do you want to grate the bittersweet chocolate that we sprinkle on top? You can wake up Lucky in thirty minutes when the cinnamon rolls are done."

I grabbed an extra-large mug of coffee for Lucky and went into the living room, sliding the door closed behind me. "Hey you, Christmas will officially begin in about fifteen minutes. You might want to guzzle this for a head start."

Lucky poked her head out from under her pillow. "What the fuck time is it?"

"Five forty-five, kiddo. Rise and shine. Theo, Sam, and Alex will be coming in here with a platter of cinnamon rolls and too much anticipation, so you'd best get up and chug this coffee."

I hefted Lucky up out of bed, settled her with the mug of coffee in hand, and put away the futon mattress and bedding just as Theo arrived, triumphantly bearing an enormous tin tea tray decorated with bluebirds perched on a cherry tree, and loaded with a red Fiestaware platter of hot iced cinnamon rolls and red mugs of fragrant hot chocolate.

"It's that French blogger, David what's-his-name's recipe this time. It is all about the hot milk and chopped bittersweet chocolate. I used the Scharffen Berger that you sent me last month, and yes, of course I tarted it up with whipped cream! Are you sure you don't want any?"

Lucky shook her head blearily while clutching her coffee firmly, and I declined the hot chocolate due to heartburn. Theo sat cross-legged beneath the Christmas tree and handed out presents, rotating between Alex and Sam with an occasional gift tossed our way. I'd gone overboard on board games, pogo sticks, and stilts for both grandkids. Theo loved birds and collected bird salt-and-pepper shakers, so I bought her a set of vintage ones in the shape of a girl bird in a bonnet and a boy bird in a top hat, both with demonically sparkling rhinestones for eyes. My Great Uncle Garland, one of the elderly single gentlemen in my Southern family, painted rustic outhouses, and I'd given Lucky one of his earlier outhouse paintings framed in a walnut spool-style Eastlake frame from the mid-1870s. Lucky and I traded gifts of cuff links. I gave her a pair of vintage Tiffany gold cuff links in the shape of stag heads with sapphire eyes and she gave me a pair that had a tiny handcuff key concealed as part of the design. Bacon Bits and Chuck Norris got a handful of frisky felt catnip mice from Rainbow Co-op, but ended up ensconced in empty boxes and torn-up wrapping paper. The grandkids' and Lucky's zoo gift shop plotting had resulted in a red-butted furry baboon hand puppet that I named Queen Victoria.

Alex was enthralled with the puppet's red butt and spent the rest of the morning holding the puppet, snorting, and chortling, "Queen Victoria has a big red butt!" Then she would make the puppet shake its ass and she'd collapse in giggles.

Lucky leaned over and whispered, "That inflamed red monkey butt looks like your ass after I'm done caning it. That's why it is the perfect gift for you, my little monkey butt."

By noon Alex, Sam, and Theo were crashing from the sugar. Lucky and I volunteered to start the roast turkey and sent everyone off for naps. I removed the twenty-five-pound hunk of bird from the brining bucket on the back porch and patted it dry while Lucky chopped sweet onions and tart apples for our traditional cornbread and apple stuffing. I fried the sage sausage, and when I was done Lucky mixed everything in a large metal mixing bowl.

"Baby, I'm going to show you how to stuff a turkey. Watch closely." Lucky whipped out a pair of black nitrile gloves from the back pocket of her jeans. She put them on, snapping the cuffs, then flexed her hands. I jumped at the snapping sound, my cunt getting wet in Pavlovian response.

"I gotta warm this sweet little bird up," she said, and reached into the turkey's cavity slowly until she was in halfway up her forearm. "Come closer so you can watch my hand. Stand next to me. There you go. Closer. Right next to me. Just rest your hip against my ass the way I like it."

I was mesmerized, turned on, and horrified all at once. I was in my daughter's kitchen in Ohio while my lover did dirty things to and fisted a clammy cold dead turkey carcass. Lucky removed her hand from inside of the turkey, poured a dollop of olive oil onto her gloved palm and rubbed her hands together, getting them slick and shiny.

"I need to make sure the flesh is tender, so I'm going to smooth this olive oil into the inside and then the outside of our bird," she said, like a perverted Martha Stewart. She reached in again, meeting my eyes. "See how I'm making sure our bird is all slick and slippery inside. I'm turning my hand around and pressing into its tender flesh with my knuckles. I've got to make sure that I grease up every spot. Put your hand inside too and grab my fist. Go on. Don't be shy." I reached in the opening, felt Lucky's greased up fist, and gasped. I imagined her sliding into me the way she'd slid into that turkey and my hips moved forward against her ass. I couldn't help it.

Lucky grabbed a garlic clove, then separated the cold, feather-pluck-marked skin from the turkey breast. She took the clove and slowly inserted it with her index and middle fingers under the loosened skin. "See how I gently loosened the skin? Now I'm sliding the garlic in between the skin and the flesh." She moved her hand around, the two fingers straightened out and sliding carefully, reaching the entire breast and pressing in with her fingertips. "I'm softening up the breast flesh and making it flavorful. You know how important it is to soften things up before you cook them, right?"

"Oh baby," I moaned. "You are so fucking unfair. So fucking mean. We haven't fucked in days!"

"That's why I'm the sadist, monkey butt."

"Hey you two," Theo stood in the doorway rubbing her eyes. "Tell me what you want me to do next."

Theo came into the steamy kitchen and I backed away from Lucky's ass. I did all but throw myself onto the snow in the backyard to cool off. I washed dishes. I folded laundry. I peeled potatoes. I took out the trash. I fed the cats. Anything to stop thinking about Lucky's right hand in my cunt and her left hand at my throat.

Dinner was terrific and the table was packed with Christmas orphans. Theo's heavily sun-tanned gay couple next-door neighbors, her filmmaker, gluten-intolerant, vegan landlady, two hopeful exes, and a freshly single teary-eyed girlfriend, along with three pals from my activist days twenty years ago all came. The freshly fisted turkey was juicy and tender, the mashed potatoes a glory of Yukon gold, cream and butter, and the roasted Brussels sprouts with bacon, pecans and maple-balsamic vinaigrette vanished quicker that you could say "Queen Victoria has a red monkey butt." We had Theo's pumpkin pie, my sour cream raisin pie, a pomegranate cheesecake, and Lucky's pear pie for dessert. We were truly stuffed. After dinner, we sipped tea and played a rowdy game of Cards Against Humanity until the tryptophan, carbs, and sugar started kicking in. Folks started leaving at nine, and by 10:00 p.m. Lucky and I were flat on our backs on the futon mattress with Theo, Alex, and Sam upstairs asleep.

"That was so good," I said. "I'm really glad you came with me to meet my family. Do you like them?"

"I'm stuffed. I like your kid. Sam is a firecracker and Alex is a sweetie."

"Theo likes you. At first she thought you were a player though."

She kissed my cheek. "Could you go get me a plate with a few of those ginger cookies? And while you're at it bring back a dollop of lard."

I padded into the kitchen, arranged some cookies on a plate, then scooped out a couple of tablespoons of lard and put them on the side of the dessert plate. I came back into the living room, shutting the doors behind me, and sat on the futon mattress next to Lucky. We shared the ginger cookies, then Lucky smiled at me slyly.

"Lie on your stomach," she said, and rolled me over. She pulled my pajama pants down and sat on my thighs with her palms resting on my ass. "Poor monkey butt. All stuffed full of food and nothing else. You need to be stuffed don't you?" I heard the snap of a glove and watched as she scooped up the lard with her right hand. "You're my petit porc, aren't you? Gotta have things stuffed into your ass and cunt until they are coming out of your mouth."

She caressed my asshole with two lard-smeared fingers, then told me to spread my legs. She reached over to her bag that was above my pillow and pulled out the chrome hitch ball, then rubbed lard all over the mirrored surface. The metal was icy cold and felt wonderful against my hot asshole. I inhaled and my breathing became fast as Lucky pushed the ball inside me. I opened up, feeling my cunt juice drip down my legs and my cock get hard and swollen. I shook and groaned, my belly tensing. My nipples ached.

"No coming. No fucking. You're mine, my petit porc. Lie still. Put your hands up over your head away from your tits. Close your legs."

Then Lucky took off her pajama pants and lay on me full length, her raspy cunt hair brushing against my ass and her soft belly warm against my back. She spread her cunt lips, smearing my ass with her juice, and started humping my ass. I could feel her cunt get wetter and her cock get harder against my ass. I had to resist moving to meet her.

"Hold still. Fucking stay still." She opened her lips up farther, her cunt splayed over me, grinding into my ass. "Don't you wish I was fucking you right now, my cock sliding in and reaching deep inside your ass? Oh yeah, coming out until the tip is barely in, then slamming in so fast and deep that you feel it in your gut, and fucking you so hard and fast that you're grunting with each stroke?"

I could feel the hitch ball inside of me, but it wasn't enough. I needed to be filled. My eyes teared up in frustration. I was never going to be able to come again.

I lay on my belly, my ass filled with lard and metal as Lucky got herself off, humping me like a dog on a stranger's leg. Her cunt left a trail of come as she rubbed faster and faster. She grunted as she pushed me into the futon, my cock flattened and exposed against the sheets, my juice pooling between my closed legs, and my ass throbbing around the chrome ball. With a deep almost silent moan, Lucky came. She rolled over and we both started giggling.

"Go clean up kiddo. You have lard and come dripping all over your monkey butt," she chortled.

When I came back to bed, freshly cleaned chrome ball hitch in hand, Lucky was curled up and snoring lightly. I crawled into bed and fell asleep empty.

We were flying home at noon the next day. We had a big breakfast, then Sam and Alex insisted on packing our lunches for the flight. They had flown before and remembered starving over Kansas, looking down at farms, fields, and roads and wasting away to nothing in the air. Or so they exclaimed dramatically. We left with two enormous bags of holiday dinner leftovers, assured that we would last the eight-hour trip intact, and with Queen Victoria the monkey puppet tied to the outside of my rucksack with a red bungee cord. Alex and Sam felt strongly that the Queen should be out and about for her first flight, rather than packed away like so much dirty laundry and we concurred.

The flight home was uneventful. We ate three kinds of pie during our layover in Chicago, and both of us napped during the leg from Chicago to San Francisco, our heads on each other's shoulders and Queen Victoria nestled between us as a chaperon. The Midwest, children, and grandchildren were a different type of exhaustion from work and our urban existence in San Francisco, and we were tuckered out. We gratefully staggered into San Francisco International Airport at 5:00 p.m., splurged on taking a Super Saver van home, and were deposited on our apartment doorstep by six thirty.

I loved arriving in San Francisco after leaving Ohio. Ohio was so quiet, bland, and low-key, but San Francisco was an assault on my senses. The elaborate Victorian houses mixed with the tacky new tech-driven glass monoliths, the combined smells of fresh coffee, exotic jasmine, and sharp piss, the multilingual murmur of people, and the incredible volume of movement, people, and noise renewed my happiness at returning home.

We wearily climbed the carpeted steps to the second floor, unlocked our front door, and dragged our luggage into our bedroom. Our returning home ritual involved much petting of Francy, hot showers to clean travel from our skin, and a pot of heavily sweetened Scottish breakfast tea. There was a note from Tov reading, *The cats claimed a dire*

125

need for caviar and salmon. I did not fall for it. Lucky had first dibs on the shower while I put the kettle on for tea. Francy was a forgiving feline. After eating and belly rubs, she settled down in Lucky's open boot suitcase for a nap, her head resting on a Wesco harness boot and her body stretched out on a Dehner patrol boot. Lulu-Bear was more temperamental, ignoring us both for having the gall to leave her for Ohio. The apartment filled with the smells of sandalwood soap and the sounds of Lucky belting "I Enjoy Being a Girl," then she came out of the bathroom wrapped in her Pendleton green-plaid robe, and I made my way into the bathroom. I adore showers. I love the hot water pouring over my skin, the spicy smell of soap, and rubbing slick soap bubbles over my hips and breasts. I came out of the bathroom looking forward to finishing my tea and eating out for dinner, but Lucky had other plans.

Lucky was lounging on the bed with her hands behind her head, wearing a smile, her biggest blackest cock, and a tight black tank top. My lips parted; she stood up, grabbed me by the back of my head and shoved me to my knees. I opened my mouth with a moan, but Lucky just teased me by circling my lips with the head of her cock. It had been days. I was dizzy with need, but stayed still.

"Do you need it?"

"Yes!"

"I didn't hear you."

"Please, may I have your big black cock?"

"What do you say?" Lucky demanded, slapping my ass. "Did I hear you say *Sir*?"

"Please, Sir! Please, Sir, fuck my mouth with your big black cock!"

Lucky thrust her cock all the way inside of my mouth. I could feel her cock hit the back of my throat as she started fucking my mouth, taking quick deep stabs the way she does when she is already close to coming. It had been too long. I needed Lucky inside me and I knew she felt the same. Lucky needed to be inside, surrounded by my ass, my mouth, my cunt. I gagged as she held the back of my head, fucking my throat and grunting with her first come of the night. Lucky fell to the carpet and pushed me down. I was lying on my belly, ass up.

"Open your ass. Now."

"Yes, Sir!"

"Again!"

"Yes, Sir!"

"What do you say?" Lucky slapped my ass again. "What about my cock?"

"Please, Sir! Yes, Sir! Please, Sir, fuck my ass with your big black cock!"

She squirted a dollop of lube into her hand, lubed up my asshole and sunk her cock into my ass in one quick move.

With each stroke, Lucky grunted, "Again!" and I replied, "Yes, Sir!" as we fell into a rhythm, Lucky pulling out until I wailed, "Please, Sir! Yes, Sir! Please, Sir, fuck my ass with your big black cock, Sir!"

I was so ready for her to stuff me. It had been days of Lucky teasing me, and me with a hard-on, desperate to have her cock, her hand inside of me, my cock and nipples painfully hard and my cunt rubbing together slickly as I walked around, never getting any relief. I snuck my hand down between my legs and started jerking off as Lucky fucked my ass furiously. This was not a slow subtle fuck, but brutal and fast. My other hand twisted my nipples, my nipples that had been ignored by Lucky *and* me for four too-long days. I came, my hips rising to meet Lucky's, and she came again, this time shouting with relief before collapsing on top of me.

"Thank you, thank you, thank you!" I managed as Lucky turned me over roughly, then slapped my face until it stung.

Lucky pulled on a black nitrile glove, then with a twist of her wrist slid into my cunt. I was babbling by then, with her kneeling between my legs, her fist inside of my cunt, and me pulling my nipples, which were like mountains, pointed and rock hard. Lucky put her forefinger and middle finger inside my open mouth and I started sucking her fingers, fucking one hand with my cunt and the other with my mouth. I wanted everything filled by Lucky, her reaching inside and grabbing my heart. She removed her fingers from my mouth to slap me hard again across my face. I felt a wave start in my chest and ripple down my belly and my cunt, then a powerful burst of come shot out of me, soaking Lucky from her hand to her armpit and even to her chin.

Lucky collapsed on top of me, our sweaty bodies limp and sated, both of us breathing heavily.

"Oh, baby. I'm so glad we're back home. I love you," I murmured.

"Me too, my little tacchino. Me too," Lucky replied drowsily.

CHAPTER SIX

HITCHED

W hat is home? Is home the feel of your soft, rounded belly pressing against my lower back as we fall to sleep? Is home the clink of house keys tossed upon the side table when we come home, one set of keys following the other, nestled side by side? Or is home the fact that I'm never home? I'm always longing to breathe in the feeling of home, letting it become part of me, then exhale as my heart travels into the world and I become part of it.

I trace my dissatisfaction and restlessness to being an exile from the home of my childhood, the home that I do not deserve by dint of my nationality. I am an American who was raised in Iran during the reign of the Shahanshah Reza Shah Pahlavi. I have not returned home to Iran since I turned seventeen in 1972, yet was it ever my home? I am of Scottish and German heritage, not Persian. Can I call Iran home? Do I belong anywhere? I know that I belong in San Francisco. I know that I belong in our apartment. I know that I belong next to Lucky.

I woke up at 5:00 a.m on a Sunday morning in June in a melancholy mood. I slid out from under our covers, careful not to disturb Lucky, who was still snoring softly, olive limbs curled up. She was recuperating from a short summer cold and needed her rest. I made my way into the bathroom to piss. I looked at myself in the bathroom mirror critically. My hair had thinned out when I was diagnosed with low thyroid in my forties, and when I started transitioning in my fifties, my hairline had gradually receded as I molted limp straight brown hairs down the shower drain every morning. My decades-long short on the sides and back, part on the left, and a thick bad-boy lock of hair flopping over my forehead wasn't working anymore. My lank forelock had bit the dust and now looked more like fluff. My pal Nona had even spoken the dreaded word "comb-over" at me. It was time to throw myself at the mercy of my barber again. Apparently there was no age limit on vanity.

I limped to the kitchen to start some tea water. I remembered when I went to bed at 5:00 a.m., instead of waking up at 5:00 a.m. Then I remembered that I used to spend hours sitting cross-legged on the floor painting, and now I was a gimpy old fuck with an inflamed left knee limping my way down a dark hallway grumpily at dawn. Things change. I turned on the gas burner on our 1940s Wedgewood stove, filled the red enameled kettle, then made a large pot of smoky Taylors of Harrogate Scottish breakfast tea and sweetened the pot with several heaping spoons of brown turbinado sugar, fed Francy and Lulu-Bear who were meowing frantically at my feet, and limped into the parlor to brood, drink tea, and wake up.

I curled up on the window seat in the bay window overlooking the park and wrapped my brown corduroy robe close, nestled the silk quilted collar around my neck, and tucked my cold toes under a Kurdish kilim-covered throw pillow. I'd pulled the bittersweet-dark-brown velveteen drapes open. It was a drizzly foggy morning, with the fog winding its way through the treetops. I liked cooler weather and hoped it would stay misty and chilly throughout the day. We had plans to go to the Civic Center farmers market for leeks and clementines, Blick Art Supply for more gouache paint and brushes, and to Arizmendi Bakery to pick up some sticky buns, shortbread, and croissants.

I poured another cup of tea and sighed. I worked part-time at the main branch of the San Francisco Public Library, but hoped to retire within a year. There had been budget cuts at work, so some much-needed positions were going to stay unfilled. The gentrification of San Francisco was affecting middle-income and poor folks strongly. The main library was blocks from Twitter headquarters, so we felt the reverberations more strongly than some branches. The increased evictions, heightened enforcement of the sit-lie ordinance, and brutal harassment of the poor meant that we were dealing with more mentally ill, more homeless, and a greater number of stressed-out patrons. It was painful and heart wrenching to watch, and I often was grateful that I'd worked in crisis management and social services before becoming a librarian. The experience came in handy. This wasn't how I wanted to start my Sunday, but I worried. It was too easy to suck up their pain. I wanted to heal each of them, remove their suffering with a calming touch. I would feel my heart softening with empathy when they came to me for help. Often, the only assistance I could offer was to acknowledge their humanity, their pain, and the hopelessness of their situation. I rarely felt I did enough. I hated taking the F-Market streetcar to work. Invariably, the police would board to check fares at the MUNI stop in front of the Twitter building at Market and 10th. People in rags living out of shopping carts made their way down the sidewalk in front of Twitter's magnificent 1937 Art Deco building, while booted officers yanked folks off the trolley and wrote them $274 tickets. A new law was going into effect in March that would let seniors and disabled people whose annual income was under the Bay Area median income level of $67,950 ride MUNI for free. I was hoping it would cut down on the massive ticketing on MUNI. I'd been telling my patrons about it and helping them sign up for the program.

I drew the line at feeling guilty for our elegant Victorian apartment and somewhat decadent lifestyle. We both earned below the relatively exorbitant Bay Area median, shared our income, and our only dependents were two roly-poly cats. Lucky also received dividends from investments made when she was a high-rolling techie, so we lived very comfortably. I'd been briefly homeless in my twenties and I considered us extremely fortunate. Lucky volunteered with Francisco League of Urban Gardeners, I answered the hotline at San Francisco Suicide Prevention, and we donated money to a few favorite nonprofits annually.

I poured the last dribbles of tea from my Brown Betty pot into my bear orgy tea mug and looked out at the fog as it started to dissipate. Francy and Lulu-Bear were curled up together on the Empire récamier, their fur mottling beautifully with the amber upholstery. I heard the pad-pad of Lucky's bare feet on the carpeted floor as she woke and came into the parlor. She stood over me looking disheveled and sleepy, then tousled my mussed-up morning hair.

"Hey you. Have you been up long?"

"Just a little. Do you feel any better?" Lucky rubbed her eyes, yawned, and sneezed a tiny high-pitched achoo.

"Some. I took some Emergen-C last night." Lucky smiled, then reached inside my robe and tank top and squeezed my right breast, working my nipple until it started getting hard and I groaned softly, shifting my legs. She parted my robe and reached for my cunt, slowly running her fingers from my cunt opening up to my clit, then stopping to pull on my clit, jerking it off. She smiled as I leaned back against the cold window glass and opened my thighs farther, my cunt wet and my clit hard.

"I'm feeling a little better, but I like how you're feeling even more," she said as she leaned in with three fingers and slid them inside of my dripping cunt, her thumb rubbing my cock and her other hand pinching my nipple. Unlike with other lovers, it never took much to get me going with Lucky.

"Yes, yes," I panted, as I started fucking her fingers back.

She slipped her fourth finger in, folded her hand, and twisted inside of me filling me up with her fist. I loved Lucky's hand inside of me first thing in the morning. Her skin pressing on my flesh, her hand moving inside of my hungry cunt, and her moist breath on my neck brought me home. I came quickly, contracting around Lucky's wrist as she twisted her fist inside of me. It was one of those fast first-thing-in-the-morning

132

comes. Just enough to let you know that you're awake and in love. She slipped her hand out of my cunt as we lay together on the window seat, soft belly to belly and chest to chest. I stroked and squeezed her ass, that meaty rounded shelf of a butt, so difficult to fit into jeans and so luscious when naked and under my palm. Lucky started humping my thigh, her cunt open and damp, leaving a snail trail of precome down my leg. She smelled of yesterday's sweat and morning sex, a deliciously pungent smell that filled my throat. I burrowed my nose closer to her armpit for more and worked my fingers between her asscheeks seeking her asshole, circling it teasingly and then wetting my fingers with her cunt juice and fingering her soft musky asshole with one and then two fingers, fucking her. Lucky groaned and sped up, her hips and cunt pressing hard against my leg, sliding faster as her asshole opened up under my fingers to second knuckles deep, and she started to come. She grunted twice in snorts of pleasure, then came.

"Foggy outside," Lucky murmured lazily, her legs entwined with mine.

"It'll burn off. Waffles?" I asked as I sniffed her pits happily. I loved the smell of ripe pits and especially Lucky's.

"Yum, waffles and bacon and coffee. And you," she said as she pinched a faded bruise on my right breast from Friday night's romp, the sharp jolt causing my hips to twitch and me to giggle.

I got up and made my way through the glass-paned French doors, the soft peacock-blue dining room, and into our kitchen where Uncle Garland's painting of a barn-red, rundown rustic outhouse hung over the oak table. Lucky had made a bowl of yeasted waffle batter last night, which was rising on the gray-veined soapstone kitchen counter. I added egg and baking soda to the red pottery bowl, then stirred. I heated water for another pot of tea for myself and a French press of coffee for Lucky, plugged in the Art Deco stainless-steel waffle iron and started baking waffles at the table, then removed some smoked bacon from the freezer and put the frozen bacon into a covered frying pan to defrost and fry. The kitchen was starting to smell cozy like Sunday. I turned on Nico crooning praises of the dawn with "Sunday

Morning," singing along with the tiniest baby piano notes and Nico's lonely voice.

I could hear Lucky in the shower, the water running and the heart-stopping domestic sound of her lustily belting out "I Enjoy Being a Girl." I never tired of hearing her sing that song in the shower. It meant all was right with our world. I set the oak kitchen table, laying out green-and-natural-striped linen napkins and pottery plates. I trimmed the bouquet of periwinkle thistles, fragrant rosemary, and surreal-looking rosy protea in an aqua McCoy pottery vase that I had on the table. The flowers were from the gals at Church Street Flowers in the Castro, where we had a standing weekly order. The scent of waffles, frying bacon, sandalwood soap, and coffee along with the joy of a beautiful world to look at and the buzz that comes from being well fucked, well beaten, and well loved had me feeling smug and lazy in all the best ways.

We ate breakfast eagerly, then retired to the parlor to read the Sunday paper. I used to get the paper edition of the Sunday *New York Times,* but had stopped before I met Lucky. I could never keep up, so stacks of unread newspaper would pile up, taunting me with my carelessness and inability to slog through current events without either wanting to throw myself out a window or nap. I downgraded my paper subscription from daily to weekend, then to Sundays only, finally canceling it in favor of the less accusatory digital subscription. When Lucky and I moved in together, I discovered that I had a lover who plowed through the Sunday *New York Times* like a schoolboy through smut and we renewed the paper subscription. I enjoyed having the hard copy *New York Times Book Review* section once more, and on Sundays Lucky wallowed happily in beheadings, natural disasters, coups, and financial escapades.

I returned to the window seat with my laptop while Lucky fetched the newspaper from the doorstep, then spread out on the green velvet sofa, coffee in hand. I went to the *New York Times* website and as usual, the headlines were gloomy, sure to have me in a funk within minutes.

Stream of Foreign Wealth Flows to Elite New York Real Estate, ISIS Declares Jordanian Airstrike Killed a U.S. Hostage, and *Unequal Education: How Elementary School Teachers' Biases Can Discourage Girls From Math and Science* started wiping out my joy, smoothing it over with despair and pain until I came to a headline that made my stomach drop and my heart pound. As I read, the world slowed down, just like in a movie. *Iran: Travel Restrictions for U.S. Citizens Lifted* the headline read. It couldn't be! For years, the Persian government had required that all U.S. visitors travel with a Persian government authorized private guide or group tour. I read through the article. Three times. For loopholes. There did not seem to be any. For the first time since the revolution that overthrew Shahanshah Pahlavi in 1979, Americans would be allowed to freely visit Iran without a Persian sponsor. Additionally, all banking and shipping sanctions had been lifted. One of the many positive repercussions of the banking sanctions being lifted was that tourists could use their credit cards while in the country. As it sank in I started to cry, tears rolling down my cheeks. I could return home. I'd been waiting for over forty years to go back to Iran, my other home. By the time my daughter was an adult, Iran was nearly impossible for me to get into and I was unwilling to pay guide fees and be monitored while visiting my old haunts. And then I shrieked.

"We're out of here. They've opened up Iran again. I can go back!" Just as suddenly as I was planning my trip, I remembered that I was a man on my passport yet I had breasts and a cunt. And that Lucky was a woman on her passport, yet looks pretty fucking manly at first glance, and second and third. I started pacing quickly across the Tabrizi carpets. Back and forth. "Fuck! Can we get in? Suppose they want to look at my cock? I don't have one. You're a woman. Will you need to wear a headscarf? Will they think I'm a woman because I have a cunt? Will I have to wear a headscarf? I have facial hair. But what about the breasts? I don't even have the same name I had when I lived there before! And the secret police! What about the secret police? What if they arrest and torture us for being the sons of the Great Satan?" I could not stop thinking about gender, danger, and Iran. I mean, not

135

real danger, but maybe *complications* might be a better word. Complications and lots of them.

Lucky laid the *New York Times* science section down on the coffee table. She looked both amused and concerned. "Take a deep breath, sit down like a good boy, and tell me what the hell you're going on about!"

I sat on the sofa next to Lucky and reached over for her paw, holding it and twisting the gold-and-diamond-horseshoe art-deco ring around her forefinger distractedly.

"The rules have changed. I mean, for traveling to Iran. And we can go now, that is if you want to come with me. But I might be a girl and you might be a girl. Do you want to? Go there, I mean?"

"Let me get this straight. The laws have changed for visiting Iran and you want to go there. You want me to come with you and you are worried about gender. Did I hit it all there?"

I felt enthused by the thought of traveling to Iran, bemused by the thought of any girlishness between us, afraid that they would not let me into the country, and embarrassed at my inarticulateness in explaining my worries. "Yes. I want to go back. I never thought this would happen. Will you come with me? Oh fuck." I started crying again, overcome with equal parts trepidation and relief.

"Of course I'll come with you, monkey butt. Stop crying and babbling. Let's buy our tickets today. But first."

Lucky hauled me up by my overall straps, goose-stepped me over to the slate-topped mahogany Victorian washstand that we used for a liquor cabinet, yanked my denim overalls down, planted me on the gold-and-blue Isfahani antique carpet, and bent me over the cold stone table top. I squirmed as she pushed me over, feeling the hard slate edge against my chest.

"I know how you get when you're scared, afraid something will happen and they won't give you a visa. Afraid they'll arrest you and throw you in prison because of some long-forgotten teenaged transition. Afraid they'll hang you for being queer," Lucky said as she held me down, her forearm wrapped around my chest tightly. "You're all wound up, aren't you?" Lucky twisted my right nipple, the more sensitive one. I could smell her, a sexy and familiar combination of sandalwood soap, coffee, come, and sweat.

Lucky ran her hand over my striped knit Jockey shorts and cupped my cunt, feeling my dampness spread. She pulled my shorts down roughly and with a quick twist, shoved her fingers, then her hand inside my cunt, crouching over me with her full weight and leaving me breathless. I immediately groaned with relief, my orgasm sending a stupendous amount of come gushing down my leg, soaking my overall pants legs and puddling onto the rug. I collapsed with a moan, my cheek resting on the icy slate washstand, my fear drained from me by Lucky's hand. Lucky's hand inside of me was both my ballast and my way into the present when I became overwhelmed. Some folks de-escalate and unwind with drugs or a martini. I'd take a quickie with Lucky any day.

Lucky lay on top of me, holding me. "Better?"

I smiled, licking the salty, calloused palm of her hand, which was curled up next to my head. "Better. Let's go buy airline tickets now." I kissed the faint bruise on her wrist, the bruise that marked my orgasms on Lucky's body.

We snuggled up on the window seat with my laptop, cruising travel sites for tickets. Lucky was self-employed and since I worked part-time, we both had flexible schedules. I pined to fly with Lufthansa, my favorite airline as a child. I had fond memories of warmed hand wipes, fuzzy slippers, friendly women in tight uniforms, and metal wing pins. Fortunately, Lufthansa made regular flights from San Francisco International Airport to Imam Khomeini International Airport, so for a little more than a thousand dollars each we were able to book two round-trip flights to Tehran for my sixty-second birthday in October.

That evening while Lucky was out singing karaoke with gardening pals at the Mint in the Castro, I spent hours sitting in my leopard armchair in front of the fireplace in our library brooding about the nature of home while staring at copies of our confirmation email from Lufthansa and compulsively clicking through Persian websites on my laptop. *Tehran 24/7* was one of my favorite sites, updated regularly. Would I even recognize Tehran? They had just opened a highway from Tehran to Tabriz right before my family had returned to the States, the first modern highway in Iran. Now Tehran was surrounded by freeways and highways, and even had a subway system. Transportation wasn't the only thing that had changed. Drinking alcohol had become illegal after the revolution. No more wild discotheques, John Glenn vodka, and gin and tonics at the Iran American Cultural Center. Women had to wear head coverings and dress modestly, and men were not allowed to wear neckties, that Western tool of the devil. One of the results of the revolution and overthrow of the shah in 1979 was that streets, monuments, and parks were renamed, making me worry that I would not be able to find my way around. My onetime home's address at Ghaani Street was obliterated. Where did it go? If not Ghaani, then what? The almost decade-long Iran-Iraq War from 1980 to 1988 had changed the landscape even more dramatically, leaving bombed and burnt-out buildings.

I woke up on Monday morning from my recurring nightmare of the past twenty-five years that I was lost in the postwar, bombed out city of Tehran. I could smell dust, destruction, and death in the air. As I stumbled around the crumbling vacant buildings, I ran into others and asked for directions to my old home on Ghaani Street. They told me not to worry, but no one knew where it was. I ran from empty street to empty street, homes falling down and compound walls leaving dying gardens exposed, rosebushes brown, and goldfish ponds dry.

I spent the following week frantically researching Iran's current policies on homosexuality, gender, and dress codes. Homosexuality had always been stigmatized. Sometimes gay men and lesbians were whipped or hung by the state. There was an activist organization called Iranian Railroad for Queer Refugees that smuggled endangered Persian queers out of the country. Gender dysphoria was recognized, and transgender folks were officially considered legal and treatable in 1987. Once they were approved for sex reassignment, they were expected to undergo hormone treatment and surgery immediately.

Blatant human rights violations in Iran had gradually lessened in the last year or so, and homosexuality was starting to become officially recognized by clerics. Once that happened, we hoped it would become decriminalized. The new rules changed things. In an effort to placate potential tourists, the headscarf for women was no longer mandatory and men were allowed to wear neckties. Iran was a long way from celebrating Pride the way they did in Istanbul, but change was happening.

The next few months were a flurry of hepatitis A and typhoid inoculations, Persian language lessons, and research. We threw a Persian potluck to get into the mood and so that we could answer all of our friends' questions at once. Ian brought a magnificent platter of sticky homemade baklava, all the time fussing over it and confessing that he'd made three batches before he felt that he'd gotten it right. Tov and Mikail brought fudgie dark chocolate brownies, the tops sprinkled with fleur de sel. Nona, Laura, and James brought an enormous glass bowl of distinctly non-Persian banana pudding complete with vanilla wafers that James had made. Laura was allergic to gluten and dairy and Nona existed on air, so James was elated to get the chance to feed everyone the dessert of his poor-folk Central Valley childhood. We were just as delighted to eat it. Ebony and Faye brought a heavenly dill-infused Persian kuku sabzi, plus an armful of brilliant blue irises. Our sideboard groaned under the weight of food and flowers. Our friends were evenly divided between thinking we were foolhardy twits who would end up either thrown out of the country or imprisoned, or brave adventurers that were going to spend three weeks touring ancient monuments. We were in good company in our travels to Persia, but were we modern Gertrude Bells, or were we feckless inverts like the Swiss writer and morphine addict Annemarie Schwarzenbach? We were none of these. We were two older American queers, one seeking their past and the other along for the ride.

We watched *Journey to Kafiristan* about Annemarie's journey to Persia in 1939, reread *Garden of the Brave in War: Recollections of Iran* by my old family friend Terry O'Donnell and *Persian Pictures* by Gertrude Bell, made flash cards of common Persian words and numbers from one to twenty, and cooked too many khoresh stews. I fretted over chadors and headscarves, while Lucky dreamed of endless mounds of black Caspian Sea caviar. Then Lucky fretted over villainous turbaned clerics, while I sighed over the rose gardens at Hafiz's tomb in Shiraz. Taking turns was our style.

We were careful to pack no shorts, short-sleeved shirts, fitted long-sleeved shirts, or T-shirts. Although Lucky was officially a woman, we were counting on her ability to pass as male, together with the relaxed rules for *farangi*, or foreigners, to free her from the female dress code. Even though it was no longer mandatory to cover the hair and many women wore jeans, we did not anticipate meeting any Persian butches. Maybe the actress, activist, and filmmaker Kiana Firouz was the only Persian butch out there. I knew that was unlikely, but I wondered how signifiers such as butch and femme would translate culturally. Would we even recognize a Persian butch if we stumbled over her in a teahouse? We took turns worrying while accumulating a stack of books on Iran, along with a passel of fears and expectations.

We developed the habit of spending Sunday afternoons learning Persian in the park. We would walk through the weekend crowds of bicyclists and coffee drinkers to Arizmendi Bakery, buy a large bag of baked goods, and walk another three blocks to Golden Gate Park's Arboretum. Once through the park gates, we'd meander to the Fragrance Garden, to sit on our favorite green wooden bench with a butter-stained brown paper bag of pecan buns and ginger shortbread and a file of flashcards, surrounded by butterflies and the scents of rosemary, lemon verbena, and lavender, our fingers sticky and sweet. My Persian came back, and my vocabulary progressed from a three-year-old's to a five-year-old's, with a sailor's ability to cuss thrown in for good measure. Lucky learned the numbers to ten, some basic sentences, intonation and sentence structure rules, and started calling me her *kucheeki gul* or little flower.

As it got closer to our departure date, I became more and more nervous. My biggest fears circled wolfishly around home and gender. Could I go home again? To paraphrase Gertrude Stein, what if there was no home there? Would we be picked up by Basij, the uniformed morality police, for deviance? Would chadored women surround Lucky in the streets, spitting their disapproval?

One sunny Saturday afternoon in July we went on a North Beach excursion for deli sandwiches and books, taking the N-Judah underground to downtown, then the #45 MUNI bus through the tiny grocery stores and bustle in Chinatown to Columbus Street in North Beach. There was a translucent layer of fog over everything and it was only sixty degrees, a little chilly for August in San Francisco but perfect as far as I was concerned. The 45 was crammed with Chinese grannies clenching bags of vegetables and chickens, wiggling children sucking on candy, and serious bearded hipsters. I felt a swarm of affection for San Francisco, the wispy fog, the chattering crowds, and the surly MUNI bus driver, and squeezed Lucky's paw in mine as we sat together in the back of the bus.

We got off the bus at Columbus Street and strolled a block to the revered Molinari's Deli for sandwiches. The tiny joint was packed with tourists and Italian families, Midwestern and Italian accents mingling over the smells of cured meats and olive oil. We took a number, then grabbed a hard roll from the bread bin, and good-naturedly bickered over which sandwich to share. Molinari's sandwiches were husky and came cut into halves. If we bought two sandwiches, we'd have soggy, garlicky leftovers in the bottom of our knapsacks. One sandwich was just right for the two of us, but which one to choose always required negotiation.

Lucky's eyes got big at the Molinari's Special, piled high with seven different Italian cold cuts and mozzarella. Lucky tended toward the meaty side of the menu, whereas I was borderline vegetarian. I wanted a less carnivorous sandwich and put in a plug for the Luciano Special with prosciutto and fresh mozzarella, but we compromised and bought the Renzo Special with spicy copa, prosciutto, and mozzarella. Lucky chose a lime Pellegrino and I got an Orangina.

Finally our turn came, our sandwich was made and bought, and we scooted out to buy a box of cannoli from Stella's Pastry across the

141

street. We pushed our way through the tourists, outdoor cafes, and restaurant barkers toward Washington Square Park.

Before lunch, we stopped off so that I could take a leak at the round metal pissoir next to the park. I pushed the wide button for the door to open, and when it slid open, Lucky grabbed my hand, pulling me into the forest green pissoir and letting the sliding metal door roll shut with a metallic clang. Her eyes gleamed with glee as she leaned against the sides of the toilet, unbuckled her brown leather belt, unbuttoned her jeans, each button making a pop as her fly opened, revealing a bulge in her red knit shorts. She fondled her cock casually, drawing it out for me as I fell to my knees on the filthy concrete floor. The pissoir reeked of stale piss, picnic trash, and pine cleaner, but all I could smell was Lucky as my mouth closed over her cock, my hands flat against the gritty floor to balance myself.

Lucky clenched my head tenderly as I gave her head, her dimples deep, murmuring French indecencies into the air. "Mon chouchou, ma puce, suce ma quéquette!"

She didn't come, but she buttoned up her jeans and motioned for me to piss. I sat on the rickety white toilet seat, suddenly pee shy, until Lucky knelt before me commanding, "Piss. Now. Do it," and I forced out a trickle.

Her hand darted out to intercept the stream of piss and with that, the trickle became a flood, drenching Lucky's hand in urine. I moaned as Lucky started jacking off my cock, her wet fingers sliding on either side of my tiny erection. Then she slid home, her fingers reaching inside of my cunt, curling up to yank my come from me. My cunt was slimy and hot, my thighs helplessly opening under her rough hand. The chipped toilet seat creaked as I leaned back against the green metal walls of the pissoir so that she could stuff more of her hand inside of me. I came within minutes, washing my piss off her hand in a salty gush of come. We got up, kissing, cleaned our hands on the wipes that we'd packed in my rucksack, and left the toilet, weaving our way through picnickers, Frisbee players, musicians, and playing children to our favorite bench.

It was after lunch and while sitting at our favorite forest-green wooden bench, the one dedicated IN MEMORY OF "THE KING" MARK THOMAS JAMES 1953–1997: A GREAT GUY, RICH WITH THE SPIRIT OF NORTH BEACH, that I breached something I'd been brooding over for the past few weeks. We toasted to good food and park benches, and then I brought it up.

"Have a cannoli," I began nervously, hoping to soften my proposition with pastry. "Let's get hitched."

It's true that we'd been shacking up for almost two years and I was in love with Lucky. Lucky was in love with me too, but I did not consider either of us the marrying kind. Marriage both terrified and fascinated me. I'd been married three times. None of the marriages had been successful, and on some level I worried that formalizing love and lust was a relationship jinx. It was the Persia trip that got me thinking of making us legal. If we were married, we'd be a straight couple on paper and documentation is what counts with the Persian authorities. Marriage would validate my maleness for Iran despite my C-cup hairy breasts and my cunt. On paper I was a man and Lucky was a woman. Marriage would cinch our heterosexuality despite our blaring queerness. At least that is what I told myself. Was I rationalizing my romantic nature with politics?

Lucky spit out her soda and stared at me in disbelief, "What did you just suggest? Marriage!" She crossed her denim-clad legs firmly and glared at me. The gry-and-brown pigeons that had been lurking near Lucky's Wescos hoping for crumbs flew off at her outburst. "I don't do marriage. Never have, never will. Marriage reinforces heteronormative power relations and is counterproductive to queer equality." Lucky tossed the last bite of her sandwich into her mouth, glared, and crossed her arms over her blue plaid ombre Pendleton-clad chest.

I flinched at her anger, giggled in nervousness, and stared into the distance at the statue of Ben Franklin. "Look, it might make it safer for us in Iran. And wouldn't we be toying with and mocking heteronormative power relations by passing as straight?"

143

"I am not an assimilationist!" Lucky sputtered, her hazel eyes deepening to green in anger.

"I never said that you were an assimilationist and getting married would not make you one either. For real. What it might make you is safe though," I continued. "Besides, think of all the wedding drag. Monogramed cuff links, ruffle-front shirts, tuxedos, silk socks, and cummerbunds." I wiggled my eyebrows, but Lucky was not buying it.

We got up from the park bench and walked down Columbus toward City Lights Bookstore. Lucky took my arm and sighed, "We have a good thing going and marriage could fuck it up. We're fucking queer. That is *q-u-e-e-r* with a capital Q." She sighed. "I also know that you're right about marriage smoothing things over in Iran." She licked cannoli filling out of the flaky shell distractedly, then nibbled the edges of the pastry.

"I'm sorry for bringing it up, but I mean it. We're leaving soon so we would need to do the deed sooner rather than later. Let me know what you think within a few days. We can have a shotgun marriage at city hall. We don't even have to tell our friends. It can be our dirty little secret." I nudged Lucky.

We continued softly bickering about marriage as we wound our way down the street, through the late afternoon crowds of tourists, and into the doorway and stacks at the tiny bookstore. Once there, we made a beeline for the Middle East section.

Lucky leafed through a copy of Cyrus Copeland's memoir, *Off the Radar* and sighed, "I love you, but this is a little weird. I'd be a grandmother."

"I have that book at home. Cyrus and I went to school together in Shiraz," I sighed. "Betty would become my mother-in-law."

"I wish there were more queer erotica out there! Betty liked you. She said you were a regular whippersnapper," Lucky said as she opened a copy of *The Marketplace* by Laura Antoniou.

"So write some erotica then," I replied as I browsed Persian phrase books.

"Then there are Social Security and tax benefits. Medical rights.

Oh fuck," Lucky thought out loud. "This isn't a bad idea, but it wasn't what I expected."

I'm a romantic, but I'm also a skeptic. Lucky and I were living together nicely, thanks to terrific chemistry, love, and a mutual fetish for domesticity. Give me a half-naked butch dyke in jockey shorts hovering over an ironing board, wielding a bottle of spray starch, and a heavy metal iron and I'm yours. That is what I had with Lucky and I didn't want to fuck it up. Would a slip of paper from city hall fuck that bliss up?

Eight weeks before we were set to leave for the Middle East, I came home from dinner with my friend Birdie. I'd known Birdie ever since she and I had briefly dated fifteen years before. We quickly figured out that although both of us were bottoms with no sexual chemistry between us, we made fine friends. Birdie was a fey silver fox butch from the deep inbred South with a wicked self-deprecating sense of humor and a sexy swagger. We'd had dinner together monthly for years, trading off on picking the restaurant. Tonight it was a full moon and we'd ended up at A La Turca in the Tenderloin. They had a butch Turkish cook there whom I never tired of flirting with as she slapped meat around skewers with her muscular hairy arms glistening with sweat. I'd imagine that the cook was Cherifa and I was Jane Bowles. We'd loll in the desert, smoking opium and fucking all night under the Moroccan sky. I rolled home, all jolly and filled with dolma, feta, and lamb.

The house was quiet when I unlocked the door, and it smelled damp and spicy. Lucky must have just taken a bath. She was in the library. She was awake in the semi-dark, sitting in her Mid-Century butterscotch-colored leather chair in front of the fireplace, with a faceted tumbler of Blanton's Original Single Barrel bourbon on the teak-and-resin side table next to her chair. The only light was the low flickering flames from the fireplace, and she looked thoughtful. Her normally impeccable pompadour was mussed, she was wearing her favorite charcoal-gray plaid pajamas, and Patsy Cline was crooning

"Walkin' After Midnight." Lucky's bare feet were propped up on our needlework naked-lady footstool. She was smoking her rust-colored cherrywood pipe, the aromatic fumes from the Manor Heights tobacco forming a fragrant cocoon around her.

Lucky smiled. "Sit down. If I married anyone it would be you. I still think marriage is a tool of the patriarchy, but I don't want to put us in any danger while we're traveling in Iran. I've thought about our getting married, but I never thought it would really happen. Marriage just seems like something that happens to other people, but not to me. I never thought I'd be a groom, and I'm certainly no bride. I love you though and I want us to turn into old geezers together. Will you marry me?"

I sat down on the carpet at Lucky's feet, massaging each clean brown toe. "What happened?"

"We took a chance moving in together and the sky didn't fall. I love you more than before and I love our life together. It's hard being two prickly people together like us. Here we are trying not to leave and wanting to stay. We can do this together."

"And hating to process." I added. "Please don't forget hating to process."

"You hate to process more than I do, kid." Lucky took a sip of bourbon and grimaced. "There was an article on BBC today about another lesbian refugee from Iran. They tried to force her to transition, but she fled instead. Her parents said that they would kill her if she disgraced the family with homosexuality. Besides, there are tax, medical, and federal benefits here at home too. Maybe it's time for us both to stop being afraid of permanency." Lucky tousled my hair and her face started to relax. "What the fuck monkey butt, let's do it!"

And as if all the goddesses and satyrs were smiling down on two jaded old queers, Ella Fitzgerald's voice broke into "Let's Fall in Love" and the fireplace sent out hot red and orange sparks. I leaned over to suck on Lucky's toes, licking the damp little cave between each toe, nibbling her arch, then the sensitive spot near her ankle. I adored being on my knees and looking up at Lucky's face, her eyes dropping closed and her cheeks flushing with desire, listening to her breath deepen. Lucky reached down and grabbed her cock. I could see its eight-inch length under her pajamas. She was packing the longer one, the one made for mouth-fucking. My nipples ached and my mouth watered with anticipation. I reached under her flannel pants legs and stroked her strong shins, rubbing the long hard muscles, then tenderly licked behind her dimpled knees. I reached up to unbutton the fly of her worn flannel pajama pants. The fire cast a warm apricot light on us, the rest of the room in purple shadows. Lucky's sandalwood soap, the fireplace smoke, the bourbon, and the burning tobacco from Lucky's pipe surrounded us as I freed Lucky's cock, leaned in, and swallowed it gratefully. This is what I lived for, sitting on the floor with the wool rug scratchy and rough beneath me, bent over with Lucky's hard cock between my soft lips sliding down my wet throat, and the smell of her cunt rising, pulling me closer. I was turned inside out with pleasure. Lucky's cock pushing inside of me, filling me, the sensitive lining of my mouth being stroked, my lips engorged around her cock. I started drooling, spit dripping down my chin and down her cock, wanting to fuck her deeper until I was filled with her so hard that the space between her cock and my skin disappeared. No distance between us; our skin, our membranes merging into something electrical. A chemical change and we become a different animal snorting and sloppy, hoofs clanking, all synapses afire. I pulled out, stroking my overstimulated lips with the head of her cock, feeling my eyes roll back with pleasure. Lucky shifted, jamming her flannel-clad leg between my legs so that I could ride her as I sucked her cock, my cunt pressing onto her leg. My cunt sliding like the rider of a hobbyhorse, with her leg bobbing up and down, up and down. My throat was my cunt and I came, her cock rubbing inside my mouth so hot and wet. Then my mouth was moving faster, spit puddling onto Lucky's fly, the salty sweet smell of sex wafting around us both, her hands tight on the back of my head shoving me down harder as her hips arched upward, soft flannel and hot flesh, and she was coming inside my mouth as I came again, this time on her leg, the most perverse hobbyhorse imaginable.

★ ★ ★

We bought our marriage license online, made an appointment at city hall for the day before our flight, October 10, rustled up Birdie and Tov as witnesses, and asked Ian if he would become an honorary Deputy Marriage Commissioner so that he could marry us.

Getting married felt incredibly transgressive, as well as a little awkward and frightening. Of my previous three marriages, one had ended in widowhood and two in *d-i-v-o-r-c-e*. Lucky had never been married in any shape or form, but she was the kind of person who was blithe once she had made up her mind. She spent the next weeks whistling show tunes and cruising vintage ruffled tuxedo shirts online. I gnawed my cuticles raw, popped antacids, and baked cake. We were also getting ready for our Iran trip, so things were hectic.

We told our friends that we'd concluded that marriage might keep us from undergoing a stint of nonconsensual torture in a dank room at Tehran's Evin Prison, and joked that it was like a shotgun wedding, except that the President of Iran was the one holding the firearm to our stately heads. This wasn't entirely true though, we loved each other and had a need for the kind of intimate family that only a romantic partner could fulfill. It was something different, not more and not less, but different from close friends, blood family, or chosen family.

Fortunately, checking Bride or Groom was optional on the marriage application form so we checked neither and left it blank. Gender wasn't on the form at all. Lucky identified as female and butch, whereas I identified as genderqueer. Would we be pronounced man and wife like in the movies? Who was the wife and who was the husband? Were we both husbands? Both wives?

I had more of a propensity for privacy than Lucky, and was prepared, willing, and eager to keep it small. An elopement in name, almost in deed. Lucky felt differently. As Lucky eloquently put it one night five weeks before our wedding, while standing in our bedroom wearing nothing but red boxers, striped sock garters with black socks, I Hate Perfume Cedarwood Tea, and a white muscle tank top, "If I'm getting married, we're having a party!"

148

I was flabbergasted and flummoxed. "Have you ever even seen a bridal magazine? Talk about heteronormativity! Weddings are a deluge of rose petals, matching outfits, tulle, champagne toasts, bad catered food, and drunken uncles. Can you imagine Betty giving you away?"

"Here, take my daughter, she never would wear a dress," Lucky said, in a spot-on imitation of her mother, Betty.

"Okay, we can do a for-real wedding, but please let's keep it small. And no tulle. I hate fluffy bridal puke!"

Lucky immediately texted Betty to buy an airline ticket: *Buy tix for October. Getting married on the 10th. You'll be giving your little girl away.*

Betty responded within minutes, setting off a flurry of texts about wedding dates, clothing, open relationships, and heteronormative privilege, mostly from Betty. Betty was concerned that marriage would mean that Lucky would lose her carefree ways, become Republican or Libertarian, and that our sex life would suffer. It was obvious that the apple did not fall far from the tree.

Lucky had changed from a reluctant fiancé to an enthusiastic groom within a week of saying yes. I was blindsided by her unexpected eagerness, but it felt like an adventure into a possibly delectable unknown. Why not, indeed! I tried not to roll my eyes over the deluge of sentimentality.

There was a lot to fret over. The drag seemed like the easiest. I got our tuxes dry-cleaned, polished our boots, and shined our cuff links. There were rings, cakes, invites to send, vows to write, and flowers. Maybe there were even punch bowls and ice sculptures. It was a bit of a bamboozle. I'd forgotten about Lucky's love of a good party.

Lucky had her heart set on a ruffled dress shirt, and it had been surprisingly difficult to find modern ruffled dress shirts. Most that I'd found were either vintage or costume shirts, and neither Lucky nor I were vintage shapes. We were too husky to fit into the shirts I'd found on Etsy and eBay. I finally bought a handful of costume shirts and hoped that the fabric wasn't too cheap.

The shirts were delivered by UPS on a Thursday. It was late in the evening by the time we got around to opening the package. I'd picked up our laundry from the cleaners that morning and was untying the twine from the stacks of clean clothing wrapped neatly in crisp sky-blue paper, then putting the laundered clothing away. Francy and Lulu-Bear had fled from their nest on the bed, the noise from the crackling wrapping paper having driven them away. Lucky ripped open the UPS package of new dress shirts.

Lucky removed pin after pin from the pink ruffled front shirt until she shook it loose. She pursed her lips as if she'd swallowed a noxious still squirming bug and examined the shirt's tag critically. "This is cotton poly! It has sixty percent polyester. Feel it! It's slimy. This feels like something Humbert Humbert would wear to spy on ten-year-old girls through the bushes."

I'd raised a monster. Lucky had been content with common vintage cotton poly blends before we'd met, but I'd been sewing her shirts for the past year. I'd taught her about pima cotton, linen, shirtings, and oxford cloth. Shell, horn, and corozo buttons. Spread collars, button-down collars, club collars, and cutaway shirt collars. I'd lectured her on the indignities of polyester, exclaiming that polyester should please archeologists, as it would live long after human flesh had rotted off its bones. Polyester and McDonald's hamburgers had a lot in common in tenacity, and both were no longer part of our lives.

"This will never do!" Lucky said indignantly. "Can you sew us two ruffled shirts by October?"

I was brushing up on my Farsi, had a bad case of the pre-trip jitters, and was planning a wedding. The idea of sewing two ruffled tuxedo shirts put me over the edge. All those ruffles, the pressure of getting the fit right, buying fabric. It was too, too much.

"There's no way! I don't have the time. Why don't we find a tailor to make them?"

Lucky looked miffed and disappointed, and I felt guilty, but I couldn't push myself to crank out two ruffled shirts in the next eight weeks. "I'm sorry. Sewing ruffles is a bitch, and I haven't sewn one since Theo was a little girl. Let's go to Britex Fabrics on Saturday and pick out fabric. How about I sew our bow ties instead?"

Saturday was sunny but cool, with puffy white clouds filling the deep-blue sky, almost a parody of Saturday mornings. At 10:00 a.m., fortified with Blue Bottle coffee, Irish breakfast tea, maple bacon, and yeasted pecan and banana waffles, we walked the three blocks from Market and Third to Union Square.

Lucky was suave in an olive-green chambray shirt, black 501s, a brown leather bomber jacket, a black bandana in her left back pocket, and Pikolino brown wingtip ankle boots. I wore a striped long-sleeved T-shirt in shades of rust and pink, a black wool vest, blue jeans, a worn black leather jacket, and black Frye lace-up ankle boots with bright red laces. We had gotten up early to dedicate the morning to solving the wedding shirt problem.

We grabbed more coffee and tea for fortification at Emporio Rulli in Union Square, and were sitting among the flocks of camera-toting tourists, tall palm trees, and greedy pigeons. We walked past La Perla, Chanel, Jimmy Choo, and John Varvatos to Britex Fabrics. Britex was an anomaly, a four-story upscale fabric store packed with reams of couture fabric, a massive selection of buttons, and a passel of surly Russian clerks. The Russians were separated, one to a floor, as if containing all that aggression on one floor might lead to textile-fueled uprisings and insurrection.

We headed for the cottons on the second floor. Faced with the floor-to-ceiling-shelved wall of imported cotton fabric, Lucky browsed the traditional shirtings on the left, while I went directly to the more flowery Liberty of London cotton lawns on the right. I found a rose-strewn print in slate blue, shades of red, and ocher and brought it over to Lucky.

"Have you found anything you like yet?"

Lucky was fondling an Italian pima cotton in sea-glass green with a rapturous gleam in her eye. "Feel the soft hand of this shirting. It's imported from Italy."

Just then the second-floor Russian sales clerk darted over to us like a heat-seeking missile riding in an ocean of pungent 1980s Giorgio perfume. "The fabric must speak to you!" she hissed. "Vat are you making?" She sparkled, wearing a rhinestone-encrusted, stretch purple denim jumpsuit that clung to her hefty voluptuous figure, her hair a mountain of dyed red ringlets festooned with lighter purple silk artificial flowers.

"We're getting married and need to get shirts made," Lucky ventured nervously. The clerk had a strong air of intimidation and authority.

"Ah! A vedding! You need vite cotton for tuxedo shirts then." She started yanking bolts of white shirtings from the wall of fabrics vigorously, thrusting them into Lucky's hands.

"No. We want colors." I took the bolts from Lucky and put the white fabric back on the shelves hastily.

The salesclerk looked insulted, her haughty drawn eyebrows arching and narrow pearly pink lipsticked lips pursed in shock. "All grooms vear vite," she pronounced firmly, grabbing the white fabric from the shirting shelves and unfurling it for our approval, her gold costume jewelry rings flashing.

"No. We want colors. I'll come get you when we're ready to buy fabric." I put the white fabric bolts back again and shooed her away.

"I'm all about the love that dare not speak its name, but talking fabric? Wow, she is hardcore."

"Well, Lord Alfred Douglas, I like this Liberty print," I said, and unfurled my floral Liberty with a flourish.

Lucky laughed. "I'm not wearing flowers, but I like the way this cotton feels." She held out the pima cotton she was caressing. "Maybe I can find it in a slate blue to match the background in your flowered fabric. What do you think?" She pinched my ass surreptitiously, winking at me as I jumped in surprise.

We found a slate-blue pima cotton imported from England and entreated the huffy Russian salesclerk to cut our unorthodox fashion choices. "This fabric vill never vork!" she muttered as she cut the Liberty floral and the dark slate-blue fabrics, her r's rolling harder than her hips, then thrust the fabric into our arms and flounced away in a tizzy of indignation.

We paid downstairs, searched Britex's book of recommended tailors, scribbled down the name of a tailor a few blocks away, and left, happy to have solved at least one wedding drag issue.

I was eating dinner that night with Birdie. We went to Zen Yai Thai in the Tenderloin, Birdie's favorite cheap Thai joint in the city. The place was unassuming, but attractive, brightly lit, with paper napkins stacked neatly on stainless-steel trays, matching wooden chairs, red walls, white china dinnerware, and black-topped tables, crowded with Thai families. In addition to the menu, there was a blackboard with daily specials written in Thai near the register. It smelled spicy and fabulous.

Over an appetizer of tod mun racha fish cakes, a shared green papaya salad, mus sa mun curry chicken, and pad woon sen, I entertained Birdie with the tale of the cheap tuxedo shirts and the overbearing Russian salesclerk at Britex.

During our dessert of fried banana and ice cream I complained, "I don't understand Lucky. First she complained about heteronormative privilege and didn't want to do it, but now she's getting fussy about shirts! She's more excited about the wedding than I am."

Birdie set her spoon down and eyeballed me seriously. "Marriage is a special ritual. Lucky has never been married and has spent decades believing that she would never get married. Only in the past few years have gay people been allowed to get married. People need ritual in their lives. It adds meaning, and establishes formality and grace to decisions. Think about graduation ceremonies and anniversary parties."

"I've never had a graduation ceremony. And I don't do anniversaries. Not in my genes," I grumbled.

"Just because you've avoided ritual all your life, does not mean that you can expect Lucky to do the same. Lucky loves you and you love Lucky. This is about love and promises and dedication." Birdie laid her delicate freckled hand over mine, her age spots buried in the shallow wrinkles. "What can I do to help?"

"I know you're right, but this is hard. When do we ever grow up?" I groused.

"Ask Lucky what she wants. Just do it. I can help out. Let me know what you need," Birdie said gently. She picked up her spoon and resumed eating her dessert.

That night I came home to Lucky sitting in her leather armchair in front of a flickering fire in the library, surrounded by cats, tweed, and holding a pipe tobacco, with her laptop on her lap. I spied the glossy cover of a bridal magazine peeking out from under the chair. It appeared that asking Lucky what she wanted would be easy.

"I'm sorry if I've been cranky about the wedding. I'm not very good at this kind of thing. You know, celebrations and parties," I stammered, feeling awkward.

"Oh, baby." Lucky put down her pipe. "I know that you're uncomfortable with this part. I've already ordered engraved wedding invitations, and I was thinking of both of us getting white brogues dyed to match our shirts." Lucky showed me the web page with the wedding invites. "I picked Barcelona for our font. Kind of swirly, but I like it! And this deckled paper in smoke gray. What do you think?"

I cracked up. "Deckled paper? Brogues to match our shirts? You in slate blue and me in rose madder? Do we have matching shoelaces too? Are you going to become a groomzilla?"

"It doesn't have to be an agonizing submersion into either rainbow gay wedding gewgaws or pink and silver straight gewgaws. We. Can. Be. Ourselves." Lucky pulled me over to her lap. "Sit right here and tell me all about it. It'll all be okay."

Now seemed to be a good time to revisit the play party conundrum. There was another queer play party scheduled at the Citadel before the wedding and our Iran trip, and Lucky had been dropping plaintive hints about going together. I'd been thinking about it. It was obvious that Lucky was not bored with me, and I was confident of her love, lust, and dedication for me. My problems with polyamory had been with lovers who were liars, and Lucky was truthful.

"Hey, you. I've been thinking about that play party that you've been moping about. The quarterly one put on by the Bay Area Queer Mashup and held at the Citadel."

"I haven't been moping, I've been wistful! There is a big differ-ence," Lucky chided me good-naturedly.

"I know. I was teasing you a little. I'm sorry. I don't want to go to it. For real. Why don't you go by yourself though? You'll have a good time and you already know a bunch of people who go to that one."

"I'd rather go with you," Lucky said, but I thought there was more to it.

"Tell me what's going on with you. Do you miss play parties now?"

Lucky looked thoughtful and replied slowly, "I do. I miss being around the energy."

"Why don't you go without me? Didn't you say that Tov and Mikail have been going to them? I don't mind at all. Maybe it's time we open up our relationship."

"Maybe," Lucky said with hesitation.

"Go frolic baby, but come home to me." I kissed the palm of Lucky's hand and snuggled her close.

"You're not jealous?"

"No. Lying makes me crazy, but you're not a liar."

And so it went. Lucky went with Tov and Mikail to the quarterly Bay Area Queer Mashup play party at the Citadel. Adrian was there, wearing a metallic rainbow tail and silver hooves, and, as I found out later, Lucky found a curvaceous black-haired femme to fist in the sling.

Lucky came home at midnight reeking of pussy and Chanel No. 5. She came home to me in my pink paisley Liberty of London pajamas sprawled out on our bed happily drinking sweetened hot black tea, eating toasted pound cake, and teaching myself to read tarot cards. The deck was spread out haphazardly over the quilt, with Francy and Lulu-Bear helping by patting cards playfully, and I was listening to Mark Eitzel croon "Snowbird" from *Music for Courage & Confidence*. It had been blissful to spend the evening in solitude, in pleasurable abandon-ment with Francy and Lulu-Bear.

"Baby! Did you have a good time?" I asked, gathering up the cards.

Lucky started disrobing, throwing her sweaty clothing into the hamper. "Let me take a quick shower, then I'll tell you all about it..."

★ ★ ★

Lucky's happy-go-lucky equilibrium was finally thrown by wedding rings. We wanted to appear genuinely married in Iran, so we needed some form of traditional wedding bands. We Googled "gay wedding rings San Francisco," but the options were either a minefield of rainbows and pink triangles, or they were blandly boring. We checked Etsy and after getting lost in a black hole of knitted Viking hats for cats and silkscreened steampunk-gear neckties, we found a Canadian jeweler who'd created a darkened hammered silver band flanked by gold rails that we both loved. We ordered two rings.

I had gotten out my sewing machine the week before, and made us both matching bow ties in a slate-blue, fuchsia, and silvery-gray paisley Italian silk brocade. We'd trolled Amazon for white brogues and bought two pairs, and I'd taken them to the cobbler to be dyed slate blue and rose madder.

The weekend before our wedding, I was a nervous wreck. Invitations had been sent out. RSVPs had been received. Ian was baking our wedding cake and Tov was nervously in charge of flowers. Our shirts had been sewn, cleaned and starched. There was champagne and nonalcoholic Golden Star Tea in the pantry, and Betty, Theo, Alex, and Sam were flying in two days before the ceremony.

On Sunday, I bounced around the apartment alternating between packing for the trip to Iran and checking that we had everything prepared for the wedding, with Lucky in the kitchen frying Marcella Hazan's eggplant patties while listening to the Pretenders. The smell of garlic and Chrissie Hynde's voice singing "Brass in Pocket" wafted through the apartment, while Lulu-Bear and Francy slept curled up in the kilim-covered bay window seat in the parlor.

After dinner, I washed the dishes. Secretly, I loved washing dishes. I loved immersing my hands in hot soapy water, drifting white soap bubbles, the act of scrubbing, the smell of lavender dish soap, and the satisfaction of cleanliness. No one ever believes you when you tell them that you love washing dishes. It was a sensual meditative experience for me. That night, as I zoned out over the sink of dinner dishes, letting the magic of dishwashing calm me down, Lucky had other plans. I had just finished cleaning the greasy remnants of eggplant patty off the last plate, when I felt Lucky's arm across my neck.

"The bedroom. Now." She marched me through the kitchen doorway, down the darkened hall, and into our bedroom. The sheets were turned back and I was already wet and hard. I was always wet and hard for Lucky. Wasn't that why we were getting married? I know that I'm juvenile. I'm a thirteen-year-old boy with only one thing on my mind, and Lucky had my number.

"Take off your clothes."

My hands shook as I disrobed. How quickly I went from frantic worries about weddings, to the Zen act of dishwashing, to this state of fleshy preparedness for Lucky, my body and heart open to her. My world was this room and Lucky's hands, her breath, her skin, her sweaty scent. I started melting, my insides dissolving, precome dripping down my thighs, my nipples hard and tender.

Lucky arranged me spread-eagled on the bed.

"Don't move." She undressed and put on her cock.

She eyed me critically, deciding her course of action. I knew that look but was barely coherent enough to appreciate it. She attached leather cuffs to my wrists and ankles, then ropes to the cuffs, and tied me securely to the bedposts. Simple, yet effective. I could feel the night air cool my open wet cunt and squirmed. She fiddled in the toy box at the foot of the bed, digging about with great clangs, humming, "It's Now or Never" under her breath. I never understood her idle savoir-faire attitude when we started. What was Lucky thinking?

Lucky fastened clamps to my nipples, suddenly and tightly enough that I yelped in surprise. I could feel my cunt swell, but there was no friction. Nothing down there to rub against. I whimpered in frustration.

"We can't have you unmarked for your wedding, can we? And Betty, Theo, Sam, and Alex will be here tomorrow, so it's now or never." Lucky grinned carnivorously, her canine teeth poking out with promise, and attached six clamps to my labia, three on each side. The clamps felt like teeth and Lucky was my wolf. I whimpered more, my hips rising from the bed.

"Please, please," I begged.

"Please, what, my little invert?" Lucky took her cane from the umbrella stand and tapped my decorated tits. "Please what? Please hit me harder? Please stop?" Lucky caressed my cunt with her hand, spreading precome and tweaking the clamps, then fucking my mouth with her wet fingers. In and out, one hand on my throat, the other jamming her fingers down my throat until my eyes started to tear up. I started to come and Lucky stopped abruptly, pulling her spit-covered fingers from my mouth.

I was babbling by the time Lucky started caning my chest, and begging her to stop when she stuffed her day-old briefs into my mouth. I tried to stay still, but it was impossible. I mean, maybe it was possible for someone else, or maybe it was possible if the clamps were not fastened to my tender flesh, or maybe it was possible if it wasn't a few days before we were getting married and I wasn't jacked up on antici- pation. Lucky removed the nipple clamps, only to give me three hard strikes across each breast.

"There, now maybe you'll remember me on Wednesday. Do you think we should leave 'obey' in our vows?" Lucky asked teasingly while drawing the cane downward, over my belly and to my thighs.

"Yes!" I mumbled through the stinky cotton briefs, my eyes watering.

"Good answer! Now, let's give you something to remember for your plane ride on Thursday." Lucky laughed as she struck me five times on the inside of each tender white thigh.

"You're mean," I giggled as I managed to spit out a bit of under- wear, spit dripping from the corner of my mouth.

"I'll give you mean." Lucky jabbed her hand into my cunt, wrist deep with one quick motion, twisting her fist inside of me and wrenching my come out of me. I didn't expect that. Not at that partic- ular moment, but once started, I was like a wind-up doll and couldn't stop coming.

I sprayed her with my come up to the brown tufts of hair in her armpit and screamed. I screamed over and over, Lucky grabbing fistfuls of come from me like a miner seeking ore. "Fuck, fuck, fuck!"

Lucky clenched her cock, reattached the nipple clamps, hovered over me, and dove into me balls deep. Her cock, hips, and harness pushed the clamps on my labia, twisting them sideways.

"I can't come any more!" I moaned. Lucky stopped for a few seconds and I relaxed, thinking we were done. Then she quickly started fucking me again. With a long "Noooooo," I started coming again, over and over.

"You're mine and you'll come when I want you to come!" Lucky growled as she slammed unto me, fucking me, drawing out and letting the thick tip of her cock tease me, rubbing my cock and the clamps, before punching in deep and hard. Lucky was dripping sweat onto my chest. I couldn't stop coming. Fucking Lucky was all I was good for in that moment, our bodies slamming against each other's.

We were both yelling and coming hard. Her in me, and me in her. Where did we stop and end? We were feral creatures, sniffing out pleasure in each other's arms. Shivering and spent, wet and smelly, we finally slept.

The next morning, I rose tender, bruised, and whistling, with fresh cane stripes across my chest and thighs. Lucky had a bruise circling her wrist like the moon around the sun. Betty would be here in a few hours, and from that moment onward we would be switched on. We would be entertaining or being entertained. I stumbled into the shower, lathered up with sea-salt soap, dried off, put on my brown corduroy robe that made me feel like Gertrude Stein on a particularly erudite day, went into the kitchen, and made strong coffee for Lucky and black tea for myself. I brought our morning beverages into the bedroom on a tea tray.

"Good morning!" I handed Lucky a cup of steaming black coffee as she sat up in bed. "In two days we'll be hitched. In two hours Betty and Theo will be swooping through our apartment scattering advice like breadcrumbs."

"Are you ready for mom? Think she'll give us a tantric how-to sex book for a wedding gift?"

"Ha! Your mom is a card. She's great. I wonder how she'll get along with Theo?"

"I'm sure they'll find things to talk about."

The morning went swiftly. We picked up the gang from the airport. We'd rented a van for the day so we could retrieve them all at once. Theo, Alex, and Sam arrived at noon and Betty at twelve thirty. From noon onward, the day was a cacophony of children, cats, parents, and grandchildren. By dinnertime, we'd given in to chaos, ordered pizza from Marcello's, bathed Alex and Sam, then settled them in the library in front of a stack of movies.

"Do you think they're old enough for *The Rocky Horror Picture Show?* Lucky asked, aghast as a corseted Dr. Frank N. Furter arrived in his elevator cage singing "Sweet Transvestite," crimsoned lips articulating the words "faithful handyman" lasciviously.

Betty answered, "Darling, it's San Francisco! They need to remember something exciting and forbidden about this trip!" She ruffled Alex's and Sam's damp hair.

"It's okay, Lucky. They're nine and twelve years old. Hell, their dad let them see *The Hunger Games,* which was totally inappropriate. I think they can deal with a musical," Theo added.

We retired to the parlor, leaving Sam, Alex, Lulu-Bear, and Francy curled up in sleeping bags on the carpeted library floor and in the capable hands of Dr. Frank N. Furter and company, a huge metal mixing bowl of buttered popcorn between them.

We settled in the parlor with the brown velvet curtains open to the night. I brought out a tray with a pot of ginger tea and a plate of shortbread.

"Now kids, I wanted to get you a little something but couldn't bring it on the plane so here you go. Go on. Open it!" Betty brought out a large envelope.

"Mom! You don't have money to be spending on us."

As Lucky opened the card with a picture of two grooms on the front, a spoonful of purple glitter spilled out. I snickered at the glitter, knowing that glitter was only second to hairballs for Things We Do Not Want To Find On The Carpet. Betty had given us a gift certificate to Cole Hardware. It read, *For the power tool of your choice. Congratulations on your powerful love and your powerful marriage! Love you both—Mom.*

"I figured now that you're finally living in this big apartment, you might want to do some renovating. Keep going! There's more in the envelope." Betty beamed.

Lucky shook out the envelope and an elaborate, purple-marbled gift certificate tumbled out. "Wow! You bought us tickets to Body Trust's Peaceful Mountain Portals of Pleasure Retreat Center in Seattle." Lucky blushed.

"Betty, that is awesome and so sweet of you!" I gave Betty a hug. "We need a miter saw and I've heard nothing but excellent things about the folks at Body Trust."

"It was so hard to find a workshop for genderqueer folks. I found tons of tantric workshops for lesbians, gay men, and straight couples, but I was pretty sure you two needed something special."

Theo handed us a square box wrapped in garish iridescent rainbow-striped paper with an immense glittering rainbow bow. "The kids picked the wrapping paper. They said that rainbows are special for gay people. And they made the gift. Well, at least one of them." She grinned.

I unwrapped the box. In it was a Christmas ornament shaped like a unicorn with a frame in its tummy. Alex and Sam had decoupaged a photo of Lucky and me into the frame. There we were, in our black leather jackets, grinning from the tummy of a rainbow glitter unicorn Christmas ornament. We were speechless. The unicorn was nestled in top of a folded-up Christmas stocking. Theo had made Lucky a red wool Christmas stocking with her name cross-stitched in blue on the cuff. I'd made Theo's stocking when she was younger, and Theo had made matching ones for Alex and Sam. Now we all had matching stockings. It looked as if Lucky was officially part of the family.

I poured us all another cup of ginger tea and passed around the plate of cookies. We chatted for a while, talking about our plans for tomorrow. I wanted to spend the morning running last-minute wedding errands, and the afternoon relaxing. Betty and Theo both wanted to go to Golden Gate Park, and Theo wanted to take the kids to the Ice Cream Bar a few blocks away in Cole Valley. We had gone there the last time they had visited San Francisco and Sam was still raving about the L-O-L-A Cola Float. He had chatted up the charming soda jerk when we were there and she had graciously shown him their directions for making their house-made cola. He'd since become obsessed with making cola, so I'd bought him a collection of obscure cola ingredients for his birthday: orange oil, nutmeg oil, coriander oil, and neroli oil.

The next day was the day before our wedding. I was starting to realize the seriousness of the occasion and I was getting nervous. Even Lucky had a case of the pre-wedding jitters, with Betty and Theo clucking around us like a pair of mother and daughter hens. We ran errands, shared a Keller's Farm sundae at The Ice Cream Bar with cornmeal shortbread, crème fraîche and Morello cherry ice creams, cherry sauce and rosemary syrup, fed the squirrels and let the kids run wild in Golden Gate Park, bussed it to the beach to watch the ocean and collected sand dollars while drinking coffee, hot chocolate, and tea, came home, then went to bed early.

When I was only ten, I performed my first crime. One summer I walked to the tiny mall at the foot of State Street, opened the glass door to the air-conditioned drugstore, and surreptitiously stole a bag of rubber bands. Why did I shoplift rubber bands? I don't know. It might have been for a rousing summer game of Chinese jump rope, for by then I was too old for braids. My mother busted me and sent me hangdog and sweaty back to the drugstore to return the filched goods. Ever since then I'd had a phobia of rubber bands. The medical term is *lastihophobia,* but no matter.

When I was forty-five I used to walk a route to the MUNI bus stop that, apropos of nothing, became strewn with rubber bands. Day after day, I walked through a sea of rubber bands. At first I recoiled, but after a couple of weeks of avoiding the worm-like rubbery coils, I started thinking about the nature of fear. I'd look down the rubber bands and my stomach would clench. I was also afraid of love, and somewhere in those walks my fear of love and my fear of rubber bands converged, until one day I started collecting rubber bands and stuffing them into my pockets. Every time I bent over to rescue a rubber band from the gravelly sidewalk, I said to myself, *I'm not afraid of love, I'm not afraid of love*. I collected rubber bands, filling an empty thirty-two-ounce Miracle Whip jar full of them. Stuffed to the brim. I spent months performing this strange prayer, blindly groping my way into a state of fearlessness.

When I wished for a Lucky, was I endowed with Lucky because I'd cast a wobbly spell at forty-five? A couple of nights before our marriage, I told Lucky the story of my stint with juvenile delinquency and my redemption. I confessed my fear of love and even brought out the Miracle Whip jar filled with dried-up rubber bands. They looked like desiccated worms, curled up non-arthropod invertebrates waiting to burst free. I'd made a label for my jar of fear that asked, WHAT ARE YOU AFRAID OF? I'M NOT AFRAID OF LOVE. Lucky listened to me, patting my face the way you'd pet a baby or a cat to calm it. When I was done, would I be absolved by the universe? Was the ritual of love and fear that started at ten finally ending at sixty-one?

I lay in bed on the night of October 9 thinking that by this time tomorrow night, Lucky and I would be married. And by this time the following day we'd be on our way to Tehran! I could hear Lucky whistling "Get Me to the Church on Time" as she packed bars of Spanish Santa Maria Novella sandalwood soap, Uppercut Deluxe pomade, manicure supplies, coconut oil, and other grooming necessities into her buckled brown leather toiletries kit in the bathroom. It was a comfort to hear butch birdsong drifting through the apartment, a lullaby and a love song both.

It is true, behind my gruffness and moodiness I'm a sentimental and romantic kind of fellow. It wasn't just the amazing sex, but also

163

the amazing domesticity. I wanted to show Lucky how much I appreciated her, but I was usually silent and undemonstrative. Did she see through my stoicism, or did she wonder if I was emotionally stunted? Was I enough for Lucky? How could I show her how much I cherished our time together? I touched the metal wedding rings in their boxes on the nightstand. Did we know what we were doing? What kind of emotional cliff were we jumping off of? I fell asleep to the sounds of Lucky packing for Iran, with Francy and Lulu-Bear settled behind my bent knees, our cotton quilt drawn up to my chin, and clutching my childhood threadbare stuffed horsie to my chest.

I woke up at 5:00 a.m. on the morning of our marriage, and silently crept from our bed, leaving Lucky to sleep in. I was too nervous to sleep or fuck, so I fled to the kitchen for hot tea and crumpets. Actually, there weren't any crumpets and if I were still a drinker I would have been guzzling mimosas, but I'm not and I wasn't. Our ceremony was scheduled for 11:00 a.m. I drank tea, showered, shaved, got dressed, and started breakfast for the gang. Lucky was blissfully calm. Lucky and the cats were amused by my fluttering about, but with a talent for self-preservation, stayed out of my way, scattering into the library where Sam and Alex had fallen asleep.

Betty, Theo, Sam, Alex, and Lucky staggered into the kitchen in twos still wearing pajamas and robes as I fried bacon and stirred buckwheat pancake batter. I tossed a handful of chopped pecans and diced bananas into the pancake batter. We ate breakfast, then took turns showering. By ten thirty everyone was dressed in their finery and waiting impatiently to leave for city hall.

At 10:00 a.m. our doorbell chimed; it was Ian, Tov, Mikail, and Birdie. Tov had brought an enormous armful of peach and pink peonies, primrose and tea-green hydrangeas, cream and buttery-yellow wild roses, cream and blush tuberoses, green bells of Ireland, and leaf-green hypericum berries from Church Street Flowers, along with two green and violet boutonnieres made of tiny succulents, berries, and jasmine. Jasmine had scented our first night together, walking to my place from Café Flore, and its strong cloyingly sweet scent brought back memories.

Ian had volunteered to bake us a simple three-tiered wedding cake, but went into grand master kitchen top mode and created a masterpiece. The first tier was a spicy ginger cake, the second a buttery pound cake, and the top tier was a pistachio chocolate cake. The amazing delicacy was covered in black fondant with a cream-colored iced doily draped gracefully on the top layer, a cream-colored damask pattern on the bottom layer, and lustrous black silk ribbon between each layer. It was very fey and exceedingly fetching.

"How are you all holding up?" asked Tov as Ian put the cake on the dining room sideboard.

Lucky kissed my cheek and chuckled, saying, "I figured it was about time to make an honest woman of the little lady," while I sputtered unintelligibly.

"It might be a little too late for that," Theo chimed in.

"That's Grandpa Behrouz! He isn't a lady!" yelled Alex and Sam.

"Did you two ever think about having a leather ceremony?" Ian wondered as he arranged the cake on a green glass cake stand.

"Please, don't encourage them. They don't need any help misbehaving!" Theo sniffed in mock haughtiness.

"Not really. I mean that's not my style. I've never even worn a collar. What about you?" I turned to Lucky. "Is that something you wanted to do?" I'd never asked Lucky about collaring, and she'd never brought it up. I was generally oblivious to leather community culture, so I didn't miss it. Was I depriving Lucky of something she craved?

"I've thought about it"—Lucky squeezed one of my bruises and kissed my cheek—"but I'm not deeply drawn to the idea. I'm too private for that kind of shindig."

"Mikail and I are having a collaring ceremony this fall," Tov announced, his arm around Mikail's shoulders as Mikail blushed. "We need to talk later. I want you to help me with planning the ceremony."

"Congratulations, you two! Of course I'll help out." I looked at my watch and gasped at the time. "I love you all and I'm terrified. Let's do it." I grabbed Lucky's hand as we left for city hall.

It was romantic. It was scary. It was touching. Looking into Lucky's hazel eyes while taking our vows wasn't what I'd expected. I may have been married three times before, but never during the passionate flush of love and lust. Lucky and I were still in throes of adoration, which changed everything. As we exchanged our vows and slid the rings on each other's fingers I felt myself falling differently in love, a metamorphosis into a couple, but not in that creepy way where you cling to someone desperately. Not in that way where you somehow become each other sliding into each other like aquatic protozoa, but in that way where you know and love each other on a heartfelt level. KNOW with capital letters and heart opening like a flower in slow motion. I leapt off the cliff, finally relaxed, with my fear and trepidation leaving me in a gust of relief. Maybe it was possible that marriage would not kill our love.

Betty and Theo had collaborated with Ian to arrange for a traditional sendoff. After the wedding, we exited the grand marble steps of city hall while our friends and family tossed red and pink rose petals at us. Lucky and I were both flushed and giggly, brushing fragrant flower petals off our black tuxedo jackets. The wedding ring on my finger felt strange but marvelous. And I mean marvelous in the most deconstructed way: to be filled with wonder or astonishment. Getting married to Lucky was a marvel.

"Can we call you Grandpa Lucky now?" asked Alex and Sam as they threw flower petals at us and tried unsuccessfully to look solemn.

"Yep. I guess you can do that." Lucky's dimples deepened with happiness.

After our wedding ceremony, we went home, ate cake, and caroused with our family and pals. Poppy and Tiny made it. Poppy had come around and now grudgingly admitted that we were a fine couple. It was also the first time Theo and Betty had met many of our friends. By the end of the afternoon when we'd seen the guests off, we were all exhausted, wrung out with excitement and happiness.

No one wanted to cook, so we walked a few blocks to Park Chow for dinner. It was kid friendly, quiet, and comforting, the perfect antidote to rich wedding cake, champagne toasts, rose petals, and clamorous conversations. Over spaghetti with meatballs, hamburgers, pot roast with mashed potatoes, and gingerbread with pumpkin ice cream and caramel sauce we tried to reassure Betty and Theo about our trip to Iran. They were afraid we'd be beaten up and imprisoned for being trans, butch, queer, and big-mouthed and all of my assurances that Persians were the friendliest folks in the world could not assuage their fears. As we walked home from Chow, I was filled with appreciation for the smell of jasmine, the shining moon, the night breeze, the babbling of children, the feel of the metal wedding band encircling my finger, Lucky's hand holding mine, and the company of Betty, Theo, and the grandchildren.

The rest of the night was a blur of cleaning, until Lucky realized that she had last-minute packing to do, and struggled to fit too many pairs of boots into a suitcase that was already filled with tissue-paper-coddled dress shirts and jeans. We managed a silent quickie at midnight, then snuggled Francy and Lulu-Bear relentlessly, slept, woke up, had another silent tussle, showered, ate wedding cake for breakfast, and left the city for Tehran, still damp behind our ears and between our legs.

CHAPTER SEVEN

TORTURED

heo, Betty, Alex, and Sam had packed us into a SuperShuttle and we had zoomed precariously to the airport. Everyone else had stayed back at our apartment. Betty was touring Napa with a gentleman friend that weekend, and Theo, Alex, and Sam would be vacationing in San Francisco for a week.

It took twenty-four hours to reach Iran, with me crossing off every minute in my mind. I had not flown overseas since I was a teenager flying from Tehran to New York, and the last time I'd crossed over into Iran was through the Turkish border town of Gürbulak in 1965. Lucky had traveled to France and Canada as an adult, but had never been to the Middle East. For twenty-four hours my heart raced miles ahead of my body, flying home. I popped antacids and swigged sweetened ginger tea, excitement and worry filling my body in equal measure. On the third leg of the trip from Frankfurt to Tehran, I gave in to exhaustion and collapsed against Lucky's shoulder. Lucky had been calm throughout the flight, flirting with stewardesses, soothing babies, knitting, snoozing, snacking on salted nuts, drinking beer, and watching action movies. Tasteless food, crowds of frantic travelers, cranky children, stuffy airplane cabin air, and nervous traveling companions left her with an ever-expanding Buddha-like smile. I was grateful that we traded places so well: her calm with my disarray, then later on we would switch to my soothing with her irritation.

We arrived in Tehran's new Imam Khomeini International Airport. My parents and I had left Iran when I was a teen via the old Mehrabad International Airport, leaving my second home for what would turn out to be decades. Imam Khomeini International Airport had not been conceived of yet. I came back home to Iran at 2:00 p.m. the day after my sixty-second birthday. The airport was like any large modern airport, cavernous, with noise echoing off the high ceilings, travelers hurrying with their wheelies and knapsacks, polished gray marble floors, golf carts full of elderly and disabled folks, lines and more lines to wait in, no-smoking symbols, and bilingual signage in both Farsi and English.

As a child, I'd lived in Iran twice: for two years in the early 1960s, and for four years in the late 1960s and early 1970s. I'd flown in and out of the country several times, and once had arrived by VW camper van rather than airplane.

When I'd crossed the Turkish border into Iran in a van in 1965, I'd thrown myself dramatically to the dusty earth, pressing my tender preadolescent lips into the Persian dirt with joy. There was no ground to throw myself onto at Tehran's Imam Khomeini International Airport, and I missed that moment. Persians are sentimental about the earth of their county, and I was the same. All I could think was, *Iran is my home.* The words buzzed through me like an electrical current. This was a homecoming.

The line to go through customs was long and crowded, but moved quickly. There were more than a smattering of Americans in line, eager to explore Iran now that the travel and economic sanctions had been lifted.

Lucky looked around at the crowds of Persians and tourists at the airport. "Is this how you remember it?"

169

"No. Back then women wore Western clothing, even miniskirts. There were fewer chadors and I don't remember any manteau at all. Men wore bell-bottoms and fitted flashy disco shirts unbuttoned to expose hairy chests with gold chains. Of course, this was the early 1970s, so some of that was just the era. This airport is different too. Lots fancier."

"It looks as modern as the San Francisco airport." Lucky took in the high ceilings held up by steel columns, and the bilingual signage in the airport.

"The airport we used to arrive at in the '60s and '70s was much smaller and kind of dingy. People told me I wouldn't recognize Tehran, so I'm expecting to be surprised and maybe disappointed. I know my main hangout, the Iran-American Cultural Center, was bombed, and they were building the freeway when I left. I've seen pictures of the newly built subway. We just had buses and taxis before. I want to show you around town, but I'm afraid I won't recognize anything. Even the streets were renamed after the revolution. I hope you love it too."

"I'm sure there will be a lot you'll recognize. You've shown me pictures on *Tehran 24/7* and you recognized things there," Lucky said soothingly.

"But those were generalities, like *kuches, jubes,* and *zoor-khaneh.* Or people picnicking in the park, the bazaar, and Mount Damavand. Nothing is the same. I'm sorry." I was worried that I'd let Lucky down. I wanted to show her the country I loved, but it had changed immensely in forty years.

"Then I guess we'll discover Tehran together, won't we? Me for the first time, and you as my temperamental and forgetful guide." Lucky kissed my cheek.

We made it through customs easily. The middle-aged uniformed customs official merely glanced at our passports that proclaimed us a man and a woman before welcoming us with an enthusiastic and hearty, "Velcome to Iran, meester and missus! You need taxi?" He pointed us to the taxi boarding area as he waved us onward. I cried with happiness as Lucky steered me forward through the crowds of Iranians and newly hatched tourists.

"I thought we were going to pass as men here," Lucky said with curiosity.

"He saw our passports. Anyone who sees our IDs will think we're a man and a woman. Everyone else will think we're two guys."

We staggered through the automatic doors outside to hail a run-down yellow Paykan taxi to take us the fifty-plus miles to the Hotel-i Golestan on the poetic Hafiz Street. It was fifty-nine degrees, sunny, with brilliant blue skies. I clenched Lucky's hand as we rode in the backseat of the cab. The cabbie was a middle-aged man, with a splendid gray bristling mustache and eyebrows, a powerful chest, a well-fed belly, deep laugh lines, and a sparkling gold front incisor.

I was nervous about speaking Persian in Iran after so many years, afraid that my accent would be undecipherable and my vocabulary incorrect. I took a deep breath, hoped for the best, and said to the driver, "*Salam alaykum. Hale shoma chetor-i?*" ("Hello, how are you?")

The cabbie looked surprised, "*Salam. Hale shoma chetor-i agha? Shoma Americai ast?*" ("Hello. How are you, sir? Are you American?")

"*Bali. Man America-i hastam. Esme man Behrouz va doost-i man Lucky hastam. Man chahal sal peesh dar Iran zandagi mekardand.*" I said. ("Yes, I'm American. My name is Behrouz and my friend's name is Lucky. It has been forty years since I've lived in Iran.")

"*Salam aghay-i Behrouz va aghay-i Lucky. Esme man Nadar.*" ("Hello Mr. Behrouz and Mr. Lucky. My name is Nadar.")

"*Bebakhshid. Man kheli kami Farsi baladam. Ingilis-i baladid?*" ("I'm sorry, but I only know a little Farsi. Do you know any English?")

Lucky looked confused and a little annoyed. We were talking too quickly and it was the first time she had ever heard native Persian speakers. "What did you two just say? All I could figure out was *salam* and *shoma*!"

"We were just saying hello and our names. I asked him if he spoke English. I bet he does. Most Persians learn English in middle school," I told Lucky.

171

"Yes! I e-speak English. You in Iran long time?" Like cabbies worldwide, our cabbie was chatty. His name was Nader. He was an engineer who loved David Bowie. He had a wife who worked as a nurse and two teen daughters. We listened to "Rebel, Rebel" while driving on the freeway into the city as Nader chain-smoked Winston cigarettes, flicking the ashes out the open window and swerving through traffic vigorously.

"You good friends or you brothers?" Nader asked us, looking back at us sitting in the backseat of the cab.

Lucky looked to me to see what I'd tell Nader. We'd decided ahead of time to tell strangers we were close friends but tell officials that we were married, however making this decision while in San Francisco was one thing and testing our shiny new Persian identities with Nader the cabbie was another. "We're good friends."

Lucky ventured a nervous "*Salam.*" We'd been practicing Farsi, but this was the first time she'd spoken it to a real Persian.

Nader looked startled at Lucky's voice. It identified her as either female or a man with a very high-pitched voice, but he recovered. "*Salam* Meester Lucky!"

The drive from the international airport into the city took a little over an hour, most of it on the new freeway. Well, new to me. When I'd left Iran they had just opened the first leg of the freeway system, and it had seemed impossibly modern back then. I missed the camels and donkeys by the side of the road. I glimpsed Mount Damavand, its familiar snow-capped peaks overlooking Tehran, and I teared up again with love.

"Baby, look. It's Mount Damavand. Isn't it gorgeous?" I pointed out the mountain in the distance.

Lucky squeezed my hand. "Yes, it is."

We approached the busy center of the city, crowded, noisy, and alive. Lucky looked a little pale as we narrowly missed plowing down a gaggle of giggling uniformed schoolgirls crossing in the middle of a busy six-lane boulevard, only to nearly sideswipe a scooter being driven by a manic, elderly, gray-bearded cleric and piled high with neon plastic crates crammed full of squawking chickens.

"Aren't there any traffic rules here? Oh fuck, watch out for that little dude on the bicycle!"

"I told you driving here was a little lawless. Tehran-i are known for their wonderfully erratic driving skills." I grinned, stuck my elbow out the window and sniffed the diesel fumes. It felt and smelled like home. The street was lined with tiny crowded shops and trees. Music spilled from shop loudspeakers and men gathered on the sidewalks to smoke cigarettes, argue, and gossip. It reminded me a little of the Mission in San Francisco.

Suddenly, Nader squealed left across four lanes onto a narrow, one-way, one-lane cobblestoned *kuche* and careened several blocks. The *kuche* was lined with *jubes,* poplar trees, and beautiful, elaborate, painted-metal compound gates in front of homes. Women in black chadors strolled down the alley carrying string bags of groceries and alley cats walked majestically on top of brick compound walls. We were in mid-Tehran, and despite my fears, much looked familiar.

"See the *jubes!*" I pointed out the shallow waterways flanking the street excitedly to Lucky. Trees grew beside the two-foot-wide water channels, and there were narrow arched bridges over them every block or so.

"Hotel-i Golestan is near by. We may have passed. I look," Nader informed us. With a curse and a fresh Winston, Nader stopped and put the taxi in reverse, driving quickly backward down the narrow one-way street flanked by *jubes,* barely missing trees, a vendor selling greens from a red wheelbarrow, and several hapless pedestrians until he reached an intersection with a statue in the center that he'd passed on his way down, then made a sharp turn to the right.

"Oh my god. He is crazy!" whispered Lucky, clenching my hand tightly.

"No, no, no. That is how you drive here. We all drive backward on one-way streets when we need to. It's easier and faster that way," I explained patiently. I knew as soon as I said this that I'd crossed over into another culture. I could feel America slipping away and Iran taking its place.

Lucky blinked incredulously. "I suggest that you don't try this in San Francisco," she said drily.

The taxi screeched to a halt. *"Agha joon, een ja Hotel-i Golestan hast!"* ("My dear sirs, here is Hotel Golestan.") Nader tossed his smoldering cigarette to the pavement and hopped out, opening the car doors for us.

It felt disorienting to be called *agha,* not *khanom.* When I left I was a sixteen-year-old girl called *khanom-i* Jenny. Returning to Iran, due to the transformative magic of testosterone and men's drag, I'd become a middle-aged man called *agha-i* Behrouz. It was more jarring and difficult to make this gendered change in Farsi than in English.

I knew that Tehran would be different from when I left in the early 1970s. I'd talked to folks who had returned after decades and they'd mentioned in part horror and part amusement Tehran's pollution, growth, and the religious influence, but even with the new freeways, modern skyscrapers, and surplus of clerics, Tehran still felt like home.

Lucky got out of the taxi, her legs shaking. Hotel-i Golestan was in a four-story beige stone 1970s building located on a cobblestoned street, between a teahouse with dark windows and a small packed chair store, chairs of all colors and varieties spilling willy-nilly from the front door. I took a deep breath of the familiar smells of Tehran, exhaust fumes, grilled kebabs, cigarettes, roasted corn, and ripe fruits and vegetables. The hotel's entrance was flanked by two four-foot potted trees, there was a stained bright red carpet in front of the doorway, and three Iranian flags fluttered over the hotel. It was off Hassan Abad Square in Southern Tehran, near the historic Grand Bazaar, the Royal Jewelry Museum, and Park-i Shahr. Some might have called the hotel shabby, but I thought it was homey and I loved the centralized location. We got our suitcases from the trunk, bargained with the beaming Nader for the fare, and staggered into the lobby of the Hotel-i Golestan, "Suffragette City" blaring from Nadar's car as he careened away.

The lobby was small and badly lit. It had an ornate walnut front desk with a vase of a dozen red roses on the countertop, manned by a young, wiry, bored-looking clerk in a yellow polo shirt, with thick black wavy hair, muttonchop sideburns, a luscious unibrow, and a verse of poetry tattooed upon his forearm, the elaborate Persian calligraphy wrapping its way around his muscular hairy limb. He was preoccupied with texting someone and took a minute before he looked up at us.

"*Salam! Man ghablan otagh reserv kardam. Esme man Behrouz Bedford hast,*" I said as confidently as I could manage. ("Hello! I reserved a room. My name is Behrouz Bedford.")

"I e-speak Engleesh." The clerk opened his reservation book and found our reservation. "Meester Bedford and Meester Bronson? You have one room?"

"Yes. We have one room. *Yek otagh.*" ("One room.")

"You have one room and you have one bed?" The clerk pursed his narrow lips, looked at our reservation, then looked skeptically at Lucky and me for a long minute and shook his head sadly at the crazy ferangi men. He rang his bell for assistance. "One bed not good for you."

The manager hustled over, smiling officiously. "'Ello! This room has one bed. It for married meester and missus. You two meester. You want room with two bed. We have." He raised his bushy white eyebrows, looking at Lucky and me hopefully.

"We are a missus and mister. We are a man and a woman. We are married." I reached into my rucksack for our passports and our marriage license, displaying my wedding band ostentatiously as I laid our documentation on the counter. I said dramatically, "Lucky is my wife."

Lucky blanched at the word wife, but stood fast. The manager and the clerk conferred excitedly in fast Farsi before they handed us back our marriage license and passports, "*Agha-i Bedford va Khanom-i Bronson,* velcome to Hotel-i Golestan!"

With that solemn pronouncement we became a straight married couple, worthy of sharing a bed in Tehran. The clerk scurried from behind the counter, picked up our suitcases, and led us to our room. I suddenly felt straight as fuck as my wife and I walked up the carpeted stairs and down the narrow carpeted hallway toward our room.

Our room was midsized, with a queen-sized bed covered in a gold satin matelassé coverlet, a large window overlooking Khaiboon-i Hafiz with white lace sheers and gold brocade drapes, two maroon overstuffed modern armchairs, three cheap blue and gold Persian carpets, a modern brass and frosted glass chandelier, a massive oak armoire, a white mini-fridge, and a small table with two straight chairs. The walls were painted robin's egg blue and there was a still life of pomegranates over the headboard. The room smelled like lemon cleaner and faded cologne.

Lucky was looking cranky. Between jet lag, feeling left out when Nader and I were talking Farsi, and heteronormative privilege, she was heading for a meltdown.

"I'm sorry," I started saying.

"It's okay this time, but next time you're the wife," Lucky barked.

I didn't think this was the proper time for a conversation on why the word *wife* was so jarring and the possible misogyny behind this reaction. I also wanted to live to be sixty-three, so this seemed the ideal time for some decompression and alone time; I started unpacking and headed for the bathroom to take a shower, leaving Lucky staring in tired fascination out of the bedroom window at the busy street below. We could hear street vendors barking their wares to passersby and dusk was falling.

Fortunately, the water pressure in the hotel was good and the shower was hot. The hotel had been remodeled recently: the shower stall was tiled in hexagonal tiles in shades of pink and turquoise and the floor was tiled in pink marble with gold metallic veining. There were pink towels on the gold metal towel bar, matching bright gold fixtures, and a pink marble sink and sit-down toilet. The whole thing was very femme spa meets faux Versailles.

I unwrapped a new bar of amber-scented soap, reveling in the hot water, sudsing my chest, and tweaking my nipples until they were hard. I washed myself, cleaning off the dry airline air and sweat of too many hours in flight and airports. Then I soaped my asshole, fingering myself lightly. Just enough to feel more human, my cunt swelling up, getting wet and hard. We hadn't fucked since that quickie the morning we left, and I missed Lucky's hand inside of me already.

I wrapped myself in my robe and stepped out into our bedroom.

Lucky was sprawled on the bed, naked except for her rubber harness and her eight inch black cock, her brown nipples hard and pointed, her cock pointing toward the ceiling and waiting. She had lubed it up and was stroking it, smiling sexily. When I came into the room she arched her hips, pointing her cock at me. "Get over here."

I could feel my cunt getting wetter as I walked over, my breath becoming jagged. Lucky reached over to the bedside table, picked up a pair of tit clamps, and gestured for me to come closer. I came over, breathing heavily, and she twisted my nipples, then fastened the clamps onto each tip. I gasped at the sharp pain.

"Get up here, now." She smiled lazily, jacking off slowly.

I climbed over Lucky, her cock beneath me, waiting to fill me. She stroked the thick length of it, and said, "Sit on my cock."

I didn't need to be told twice. I grabbed Lucky's cock, aiming it at my asshole that only minutes before had been filled with my fingers. As Lucky pulled on the chain between the tit clamps, I teased myself with her cock, pulling the head in gradually, fucking her slowly, inch by inch. I wanted to tantalize us until we were desperate to fuck. I filled myself with two inches of hefty cock, then withdrew until just the head rested on my asshole. My asshole twitched needily, but I waited until I groaned and my whole body twitched. I then sank halfway onto Lucky's cock slowly, letting each inch of it slide into my grateful asshole. Lucky was gasping, her hips arching, and she pulled on my tit-clamp chain with excitement. My nipples burned, the pain from the clamps swelling my cunt, everything hard and dripping. I couldn't hold off another minute, and with a groan, I sank onto the full length of Lucky's cock and started fucking her in earnest. I jacked myself off as I fucked Lucky, pulling on my slippery engorged clit and stroking my labia, all hard and swollen with desire. I wanted Lucky inside of me, beside me, filled with me and me with her. It was always like this with us, this hotness. I sped my rhythm up, slamming into Lucky's groin and filling myself over and over, feeling her cock reach into my belly. Lucky grunted and came, yanking my tit-clamp chain with her neck thrown back and sweat pooling between her olive breasts.

177

"I can't get off!" I panted. I was too tired from the trip and too excited by being in Iran to come. Lucky smiled, her hand fondling my hairy breast and then wandering to my throat for a playful squeeze.

"Oh, baby. Let me help you," Lucky threw me off of her, got up, bent me face down over the side of the bed, grabbed the back of my neck, then thrust her cock into me, sinking it full length in the first stroke.

"Oh, fuck," I moaned as Lucky pulled out nearly all the way, paused with the tip of her cock inside of me teasingly, then sunk in again until her hips rested on my ass. She tantalized me slowly, until I started to beg, "Please fuck me, please. Deeper. Please." I was desperate. Lucky drew back, waiting a second, then slammed in fast and started fucking me quickly. She went all the way in with each brutal stroke, growling as she forced my hips into the side of the bed. I grunted with each stroke, as her cock filled me, stretching my asshole. "More!" I gasped. I reached down to my drenched cunt and rubbed my clit between my forefinger and middle finger. Lucky grabbed a faded bruise on my hip, twisting the tender flesh. The unexpected jolt of pain pushed me over the edge and with a yell, I finally came.

We lay there panting for a minute, the smell of our sweat filling the air.

"It's a good thing I remembered how to cure jet lag with the five *s*'s. Sex, shower, sleep, stroll, and supper. Now all we need is sleep, stroll, and supper." With that, Lucky set her phone to ring in an hour, put her arm around me, and we snuggled under the covers for a postcoital afternoon nap.

We woke up to darkness and the alarm clucking like a chicken. Lucky rolled out of bed to take a quick shower as I tossed on my denim overalls, a long-sleeved orange-plaid flannel shirt, harness boots, and a brown corduroy jacket. She came out of the bathroom, letting a burst of sandalwood-scented steam out with her, and got dressed in jeans, an olive-green-and-red-striped crewneck wool sweater, her worn brown leather jacket, and a pair of Wesco engineer boots. It was time to hit the streets for the last two *s*'s, supper and a stroll.

We went downstairs and asked the desk clerk where the closest kebab-i was located. He recommended Kebab-i Grand, just five blocks away. It had cooled off and was a little chillier than San Francisco at night. There were wispy clouds flitting across a three quarters moon and the streets were still noisy, bustling with people and street-food vendors.

We found Kebab-i Grand easily. It was small, crowded, lit by strings of clear party lights, and filled with spicy smells of chelow kebab. We were ravenous, finishing our plastic plates of a giant mound of basmati rice, grilled charred tomatoes and onion slices, lemony juju kebab, juicy kofte kebab, lavash, and buttery tadig without exchanging a single word. We topped off dinner with small glasses of black tea, almost falling asleep over our table in exhaustion, and staggered back to the hotel sleepily.

We woke up the next morning in Tehran. It seemed like magic that we were here and not in San Francisco. I could hear the ice-cream cart vender screeching *"bastan-i"* in his shrill high-pitched voice, children laughing, and cars honking their horns. I opened the wine-colored brocade drapes and poked my head out of our bedroom window. It was breezy and mild, perfect for a day of carousing in the ancient Grand Bazaar and Park-i Shahr. We dressed quickly, giggling in anticipation of an adventure, and made our way to the tiny hotel restaurant for a traditional Persian breakfast of flat, still warm barbari and sangak breads, quince jam, sour-cherry jam, salty goat milk feta, mint leaves, sliced tomatoes and cucumbers, dates, and small glasses of hot sweet black tea.

We spent the morning walking through the bazaar, soaking up the sounds and sights. It was familiar yet foreign to hear Farsi spoken in the streets. It was like being in a dream about flying, where you do something that you know is impossible, yet concurrently it is natural. Persian words filled my head, occasionally a familiar word penetrating my consciousness. The tone and rhythm, as soothing as a song, could have lulled me to sleep.

The historical Grand Bazaar was divided into corridors or neighborhoods, each lanky road covered by high, arched, ornate brickwork ceilings. The stores were mostly tiny and cramped, piled high with goods. We easily found my childhood favorite, the metal section, through the clanging of metalworkers banging out and engraving trays, jugs, and bowls. I loved the sharp scorched smell of metalworking chemicals. Lucky was fascinated by the *ghashang* magpie sparkle of all the gleaming gold, silver, bronze, brass, and copper, and honed in on a particularly charming antique copper and silver squat-lidded tobacco urn engraved with ornate filigree arch motifs, bargaining the shop-owner down in her halting Persian. We sat on a Persian carpeted bench as the shop-owner pressed glasses of tea and sugared almonds on us, alternatively flattering and insulting us with his entreatments to buy his goods.

We made our way through the rug section, the carpets vibrant and glowing and presided over by black-haired, tea-quaffing men entreating us into their carpeted caves. Nearby was the spice and nuts section, with burlap bags of fragrant cinnamon, cumin, dried *limoo* and other delicacies. We lingered to ogle the overflowing bins, and bought several bags of pistachios and cashews for later. We were finally stopped dead by the jewelry and gold corridor. The covered hallway glittered and gleamed like Oz, with tray after tray of gold filigree work, carved carnelian seals, faceted jewels, delicate chains, and more. We meandered slowly down the jewelry aisle, feeling glazed and overstimulated. I'd wanted a gold puzzle ring for years to replace the one I'd gotten as a teenager, which had been stolen. We stopped at one of the sparkling shops. I tried on several rings and bought one. Worn out from the Bazaar, I was too tired to bargain. Insulted and chagrined, the shopkeeper added a pair of cheap silver and enameled Isfahan-i cuff links to our purchase to make up for the lack of haggling. We gathered our purchases and hurriedly found our way out of the bazaar, desperate to be away from the hordes of shoppers, visual stimulation, and narrow aisles.

To our relief, it was a little less crowded in the streets. We knew that the gigantic Park-i Shahr was close by. It was sixty-four acres large, just a wee bit smaller than New York's Central Park. We meandered through the streets until we found the park.

There was an elderly bearded man running a roasted-corn cart in front of one of the park's rose gardens, so we bought some hot corn and headed for a wood-and-metal bench to eat and decompress. A rectangular pool with several fountains was behind the bench. The soothing sound of falling water, the sweet scent of roses, and steaming charred corn quickly revitalized us. We watched two teenagers playing badminton on the brick sidewalk, a group of middle-aged people sitting on a blanket in the grass and reciting poetry to one another out loud, a gaggle of blue-jeaned teen girls giggling and roller-skating, a cleric reading a book, and a couple kissing behind a tree. Men walked hand-in-hand with one another and women strolled arm-in-arm, all conversing animatedly. It wasn't like the States, this gentle physical affection between men and men, women and women.

"I told you!" I nudged Lucky. "It's different here. Those are all straight men and women holding hands and with their arms around one another's shoulders. We can hold hands here and no one will suspect a thing."

"I have friends in Israel and Turkey that tell me it's the same there. I like it." Lucky cautiously rested her hand on my knee.

I brought my new puzzle ring out to fiddle with it. I wanted to see if I could remember how to put it together. My friends and I had spent many hours daydreaming in high school classes while playing with our rings, and I was confident I'd remember how it worked. I was wrong. Lucky cracked and ate pistachio nuts, watching my futile efforts to reassemble my ring. Finally, she took out her phone and found a YouTube video that showed the solution. We watched the video together while sitting on a park bench in Tehran, then walked back to Hotel-i Golestan holding hands, like all the other straight men we'd seen in the street and the park. We'd gone from a queer unmarried couple, to a queer married couple, to a straight married couple, to straight male best friends within days. Our gender and sexual orientation jet lag was as overwhelming as our physical jet lag, but right now I was just happy to be holding Lucky's little hand.

Once back at Hotel-i Golestan, we decided to take a little nap as we were still feeling the effects of the long flight from California to Iran. Tuckered out, we crawled under the gold quilted covers, set our alarm for one hour and quickly fell asleep, waking up just after sundown. We had a bottle of *doogh* in the mini-fridge, along with some apples and bread, but we needed a hot dinner. We were still tired, so I offered to go out and bring back something to eat. I remembered that there was a tiny falafel store a block away, and I figured that some steaming falafel patties and bread would be perfect. I threw on my clothing, a quilted jacket, and a striped wool scarf leaving Lucky smoking her pipe and reading the news on her phone in a maroon faux-suede overstuffed armchair by the window.

Out on the crowded streets, I quickly bought a greasy bag of falafel along with another bag of sweets. I was humming "Strangers in the Night" as I walked up the carpeted hotel stairs and down the dimly lit hallway to our room. Slipping my key into the door, I opened it to an ominously silent dark room that smelled like stale unfiltered cigarettes. The window was opened a crack, with the sheers blowing eerily in the breeze. The little wooden desk chair was overturned on the floor by the bed, and the rumpled satin coverlet trailed off the bed onto the rug. My heart stopped. Where was Lucky? Baffled by the unfamiliar tobacco odor, Lucky's absence, and the room's disorder, I reached over to turn on the light switch, only to have someone tackle me from behind in a choke hold. The intruder wore black leather gloves and a soiled mustard-colored polyester sports coat, and smelled of cheap citrus cologne and cheaper tobacco. I dropped the bags of food as he tightened his grip on my throat with his forearm, shoved me forward onto our bed, then cuffed my wrists behind my back. Adrenalin rushed through me. Was this the Persian secret police? Had they already gotten Lucky while I'd been picking up the falafel and were now coming back for me, the homosexual son of the Great Satan? I struggled, but my assailant was firm, slipping a mask over my eyes so that I couldn't see and an oily rag into my mouth so my calls for help would be muffled. I could hear the traffic outside, and wondered frantically how I could get over to the window to get a passerby's attention. We'd only been in Tehran for one day! The secret police couldn't be onto us this quickly.

I tried to kick the stranger, but my bad knee locked up and I was useless. He hauled me up, sitting me in a high-backed metal chair and tying my ankles to the chair legs and my waist to the chair back, then he slapped me across my face. Back and forth, until I could feel my cheeks sting and was dizzy. Silently, he started punching my arms and chest with his fists until I was breathless. All I could think about was getting away so that I could help Lucky. His weight settled on my lap with a waft of cloying cologne and arid tobacco. I could feel his hard cock through his trousers pressing against my thigh as he settled down, nudging me with it as if to remind me that he was in control and that he liked it all too much. I then felt the prick of a knifepoint along my jugular and quickly stopped squirming. He unfastened my overalls, exposing my knit top. What if this person was a criminal, not the secret police? What if Lucky was already dead and bloody in the shower? I was shaking with fear as I felt the sharp knife tip run slowly from my tender neck down my chest and rip my shirt. I sobbed through the gag as he grasped my shirt and violently tore it open with one abrupt motion, then pulled my binder up exposing my breasts to the cool stuffy air in the hotel bedroom.

As he pressed the knife blade against my nipple, I flinched in anticipation. Then he leaned in and whispered into my ear, "Well, well, well, you aren't a *kucheek-i pesar* now, are you? You're just a *kucheek-i dokhtar! Bah-bah*, my *kucheek-i gul.*"

I gasped with relief, as my cunt flooded and my cock hardened. It was Lucky all along! Lucky beating me up and frightening me. We'd talked about doing this while we were in San Francisco, but that had been months ago and I'd forgotten the vague plans. Apparently, Lucky had not forgotten and I was reaping the rewards.

Lucky scrolled down my chest with her knife, lifting my shorts with the knife tip and nestling the blade between my labia. I groaned as she traced my sensitive labia with the sharp knife tip, spreading my legs further. She brought the knife up again, nipping at my tits with the pointed end of the cold blade until I flinched.

She stood up, removed the filthy rag that she'd stuffed in my mouth, kicked my thighs apart even more, then yanked my overalls and shorts down to my knees, "What a handsome *pesar* you are! Look at that little wet cock sticking out." She flicked my clit with her blade, making me shake, and rubbed the cold metal blade up and down my cunt until my hips twitched toward her, the animal scent of my arousal mixing with her cheap cologne and the tobacco smoke. I groaned. I didn't know what was coming, but I wanted whatever Lucky gave me. I wanted everything.

I felt a soft tapping on my sensitive inner thigh, a gentle nudge. Just a little reminder of what I liked. Lucky was still for a second, letting the atmosphere build. Her desire to hurt me and my desire to have her take me filled the hotel room, driving out all the stale smells that came before it. We both took a breath, then she came down with her cane on my inner left thigh. I groaned with relief. Over and over she struck me until I forgot that I liked this.

Why did I want this? This was all about giving up. Stopping was not a choice for me, for either of us. All I wanted to do was hand myself over to Lucky like a layer cake in a pink box tied up with twine. This was all about giving up and giving myself over. I hated this. Then suddenly I relaxed completely and I was Lucky's.

I'd given up, and started sobbing. Lucky continued hitting me, nailing me into the present. I thrashed about in the chair trying to get away, knowing that I couldn't get away and loving that I couldn't get away, while Lucky beat my thighs. First the left thigh, then switching sides to the right thigh, taking time to run the cane gently between my legs along my burning soaking cunt before attacking the sensitive hollow between my labia and my leg. She reached down, fucked me for a second with three fingers curved inside of me, and I shook wanting to come but I couldn't. She took her fingers out, then drew her cane over my breasts, pinching my sensitive nipples until they crinkled up into tender nibs begging, just begging.

"Please, please. Do it," I begged, not knowing what I wanted except that I wanted more. More Lucky, more touch, more pain, more fucking.

Lucky beat my breasts. I hated getting my breasts beaten, the bitter pain as the cane struck my soft flesh. Again, I wondered why I did this, as my cunt muscles swelled all hard and erect waiting for Lucky's hand. I was still crying, my snot running into a slimy puddle under my nose and over my lips. My cunt inviting Lucky's hand. If my cunt could write, it would have written an invitation in purple on linen paper with a fountain pen in the most ornate calligraphy possible, *Please fuck Behrouz now.* My nipples were hard like agate and I was so turned on that I started coming with each stroke of Lucky's cane, come spurting out of me like the Manneken Pis statue in Brussels, a boy pissing into space.

Lucky stopped caning me and caressed my aching breasts, tweaking each tip until I moaned, my hips tilting upward. I felt a soft piece of cloth under my snotty nose. It smelled of sandalwood, like Lucky. It was one of Lucky's bandanas.

"Blow," Lucky said softly, then wiped my nose tenderly.

There was a moment of silence, then I heard a click as Lucky lit another cigarette with her lighter. I could smell the raw tobacco as the smoke drifted across my face. Lucky took a drag, blew the smoke into my face, and I coughed, trying to turn my head to avoid it. She grabbed me by my jaw, forcing me to face her and continued to blow smoke into my face. I thought I was going to start crying again, and then she stopped. It was quiet. Too quiet. I heard Lucky rustling around behind the chair as she unfastened the cuffs on my wrists, brought my arms around, laid my hands together in my lap, then refastened the cuffs. She shifted on my lap, undid my blindfold, then flicked soft gray cigarette ash onto my arm, rubbing the still warm ash into my skin.

"Tell me you want it. Now," Lucky demanded, her eyes glowing

185

green as she held her red-hot cigarette a half inch over my pale forearm, singeing the blond hairs. "Tell me what you need."

"Please, please, please. Yes. Do it. Do it now!" I begged.

Lucky brought her cigarette down on my tender inner forearm, leaving it there for what felt like minutes as the cigarette tip burned into my flesh. I gasped and growled as my skin burned, the pain spreading out, opening me up even more. She withdrew her cigarette, settling it down again a quarter of an inch from the first burnt circle of flesh, then a third time, forming a perfect triangle of circular burns. It was so beautiful. My breath came out in short puffs. My burnt flesh throbbed painfully but my cunt throbbed even more so, desperate for release. Lucky leaned down and kissed me sweetly, my arms relaxed in my lap.

Raising up with a growl, Lucky untied me and threw me onto the nearby bed, facedown.

"Please, please, please..." I pleaded with Lucky as I pushed my cunt against the bed, clenching the coverlet above my head.

I heard the snap of a nitrile glove being pulled on, the soft squirt of lube, and Lucky parted my bruised and sore thighs with her hand. Three fingers, four fingers as her hand folded and my cunt drew her inside. I shuddered in expectation as Lucky started fucking me, hunched over with her beloved hand inside of me, fucking me open and willing. And I sang, moaning, unintelligible words pouring from me while Lucky growled, our desire rising together and her grunts urging me further. Her fist harder and deeper while I met it, my cunt contracting and clenching Lucky's hand and wrist. My sore breasts and nipples rubbing the sheets as we fucked, with the pain traveling into my greedy cunt urging me higher. A wave of come started in my chest, undulating through my belly and shooting from me, and I held Lucky fast with my cunt as my come squirted out, drenching her chest and upper arms. Lucky, yelling in triumph as she came too, us coming together and coming together, a million times together.

Lucky collapsed on top of me, holding my arms. Both of us drifting, awash in come and tenderness for each other.

"Baby," I murmured before I felt myself fading into sleep.

We woke up at 3:30 a.m., the way older folks sometimes do. We woke up, retrieved the bag of cold falafel and the bag of sweets, and ate them ravenously while sitting up in bed, scattering greasy fried chickpea crumbs onto the sheets in our eagerness. I woke up, in Iran. With Lucky.

1 0 0

CLASSIC

COCKTAILS

The Ultimate Guide
to Crafting Your
Favorite Cocktails

Sean Moore

Skyhorse Publishing

Skyhorse Publishing books may be purchased in bulk at special
discounts for sales promotion, corporate gifts, fund-raising, or
educational purposes. Special editions can also be created to
specifications. For details, contact the Special Sales Department,
Skyhorse Publishing, 307 West 36th Street, 11th Floor, New York,
NY 10018 or info@skyhorsepublishing.com.

Skyhorse® and Skyhorse Publishing® are registered trademarks
of Skyhorse Publishing, Inc.®, a Delaware corporation.

Visit our website at www.skyhorsepublishing.com.

10 9 8 7 6 5 4 3 2 1

Library of Congress Cataloging-in-Publication Data is available
on file.

Print ISBN: 978-1-62914-703-1
Ebook ISBN: 978-1-62914-839-7

Printed in China

CONTENTS

INTRODUCTION

White Wine Glass

Red Wine Glass

Margarita Glass

Martini or Cocktail Glass

Cooler Glass

Pilsner Glass (footed)

Iced Tea Tumbler

Pilsner Glass (standard)

This book is a collection of 100 classic cocktails, some are relatively recent—the Cosmopolitan, for example, dates only to the late 'eighties, whereas several date back to the 19th-century—The Tom Collins, for example, was first memorialized in writing in 1876, by "the father of mixology" Jerry Thomas in his *Bon-Vivant's Companion*.

The important thing to remember about all of the recipes in this book, is that they are basically guidelines—the most important thing is that you enjoy the taste, and you should therefore feel free to adjust the balance of ingredients to suit your personal taste, or even add ingredients if you wish: you want your barman to be a perfectionist, but you don't need to be!

BAR-KEEP BASICS

The most important ingredient in most of the drinks featured here is the base alcohol, and the quality of the drink will improve exponentially with the quality of the drinks you buy—cheap spirits are cheap for good reasons, so use the best ingredients you can reasonably afford.

| Seidel | Brandy Glass | Hurricane Glass | Rocks Glass |

| Cooler Glass (faceted) | Old Fashioned Glass | Highball Glass | Pint Glass |

The same logic applies to any fruit juices that are called for: wherever you can you should use freshly squeezed juice, it makes a huge difference using freshly squeezed oranges, for example, rather than juice from a carton.

In many cocktails, ice is one of the most important ingredients—many cocktails are simply shaken with ice and then strained into a glass. Ice does far more than simply chill your drink: it dilutes the alcohol, making the cocktail less potent, and improving the flavor at the same time. Your ice should be fresh, and if you want the best possible results, freeze filtered water for use in your mixological masterpieces.

Finally, don't worry too much about the glasses—don't be intimidated by the suggestion that you need a highball or a martini glass: feel free to improvise. If you get bitten by the cocktail bug, and want to serve "authentic" cocktails in the "correct" glasses, then a collection of the glasses shown above will cover most of your needs.

Cheers!

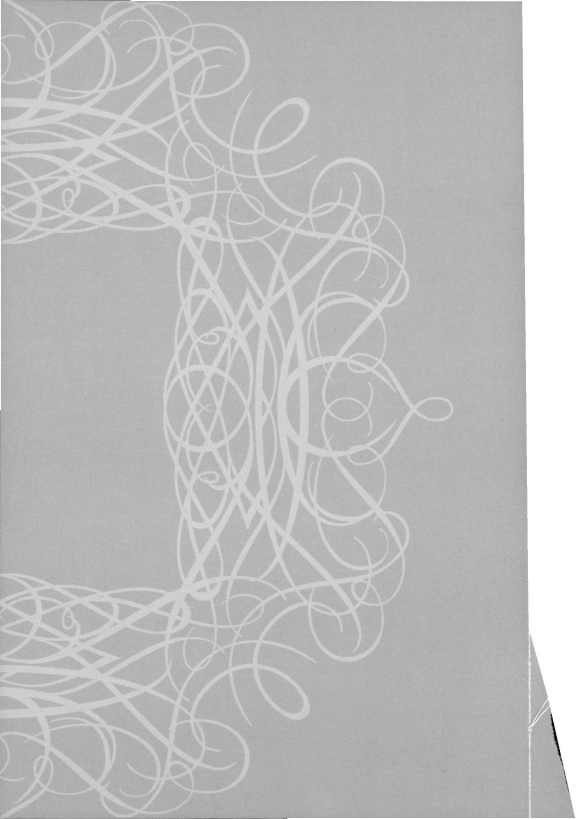

BRANDY

Between the Sheets

1 oz brandy
$^1/_2$ oz light rum
$^1/_2$ oz triple sec
Sweet and sour mix

Pour cognac, rum and
triple sec into an ice-
filled rocks glass. Fill
with sweet and sour
mix, and serve.

Bombay Punch

16 oz sweet sherry

16 oz brandy

3 oz triple sec

3 oz maraschino liqueur

2 750 ml bottles
champagne

1 liter club soda

6 oz simple syrup

Combine ingredients in
punch bowl over a block
or ring of ice and stir.
Garnish with fruits.

Brandy Alexander

1¹/₂ oz brandy
1 oz dark creme de cacao
1 oz half-and-half
¹/₄ tsp grated nutmeg

In a shaker half-filled with ice cubes, combine the brandy, creme de cacao, and half-and-half. Shake well. Strain into a cocktail glass and garnish with the nutmeg.

Brandy Crusta

2 oz brandy

1 tsp Orange Curacao liqueur

$^1/_2$ tsp fresh lemon juice

1 dash Angostura bitters

Slice a lemon in half. Rub the rim of a collins glass with the lemon and dip into sugar to coat the edge. Pare the circumference of each lemon half's peel and add to the glass. Shake brandy, lemon juice, orange curacao and bitters in a shaker with crushed ice and strain into the glass.

Hot Brandy Toddy

2 oz brandy

1 cube/tsp sugar

Hot water or black tea

Lemon slice

Put sugar in the bottom of an Irish
coffee glass and fill ²/₃ full with hot
water or tea. Add brandy and stir.
Garnish with lemon slice.

Jack Rose

1 1/2 oz applejack

3/4 oz lemon juice

1 oz simple syrup

2 dashes of grenadine syrup

Orange peel

Cherry

Combine all ingredients but fruit and shake well with ice. Strain into a sour glass and garnish with orange peel and cherry.

Metropolitan

2 oz brandy
1/2 oz sweet vermouth
1 dash bitters
1 tsp superfine sugar

In a shaker half-filled
with crushed ice,
combine all of the
ingredients. Shake
well and strain into a
cocktail glass.

Pisco Sour

2 oz pisco brandy
³/₄ oz lemon juice
1 oz simple syrup
Orange slice

Combine all ingredients but orange slice
and shake well with ice. Strain into a sour
glass and garnish with orange slice.

Porto Flip

¹/₄ oz brandy
1¹/₂ oz ruby port
³/₄ oz cream
¹/₂ tsp powdered sugar
1 egg yolk
1 pinch nutmeg

Shake well over ice
cubes in a shaker, and
strain into a cocktail
glass. Sprinkle with
nutmeg, and serve.

Sazerac

2 oz cognac

Splash of Ricard or Herbsaint

$1/2$ oz simple syrup

2 dashes of Peychaud's bitters

2 dashes of Angostura bitters

Lemon peel

Coat the inside of a rocks glass with the Ricard or Herbsaint and discard the remainder. Add the cognac, syrup, and bitters and stir with ice cubes to chill. Strain into a chilled rocks glass and garnish with lemon peel.

Sidecar

1 oz brandy

1 oz Cointreau

³/₄ oz lemon juice

Orange peel

Combine the brandy,
Cointreau, and lemon
juice and shake with ice.
Strain into an iced old-
fashioned glass. Garnish
with orange peel.

Stinger

1 ^{1}/$_2$ oz brandy
^{1}/$_2$ oz white creme de menthe

Shake ingredients with ice, strain into a cocktail glass, and serve.

CHAMPAGNE

Agua de Valencia

1 cup orange juice

2 oz gin

2 oz vodka

700 ml cava spanish
sparkling wine or 700 ml
champagne

Sugar

Lemons or lime wedge

Ice cube

Add orange juice, gin,
vodka and cava or
champagne to a pitcher.
Add the sugar, a pinch
at a time. Stir and taste
until desired sweetness
is reached. Refrigerate
until chilled.

Aperol Spritz

4.5 oz Brut prosecco
2.5 oz Aperol
1 oz orange juice
1 lime wheel
1 oz club soda
Ice

Pour the prosecco into a glass filled with ice. Add the Aperol, orange juice and lime wheel, and top with club soda. Garnish with orange.

Bellini

1 medium ripe, peeled and
pureed peach

4–6 oz champagne

Pour peach puree into
glass and slowly add
champagne. Stir gently.
Garnish with a peach slice.

Black Velvet

5 oz chilled stout
5 oz chilled champagne

Pour stout into a
champagne flute. Add
champagne carefully,
so it does not mix with
stout, and serve.

Buck's Fizz

4 oz champagne
2 oz orange juice
1 tsp grenadine syrup

Add to a frosted
champagne flute.

Champagne Cocktail

Champagne
Sugar cube soaked in Angostura bitters
Lemon peel

Place the sugar cube in the bottom of a
champagne flute. Slowly fill with the champagne.
Garnish with lemon peel if desired.

Kir

6 oz dry white wine
1 tbsp creme de cassis
2 – 3 ice cubes
1 twist lemon peel

Combine ingredients
in a champagne flute.
Twist the lemon peel to
release the oil and drop
it into the glass.

Mimosa

1 oz sparkling wine, cava, prosecco or champagne

2 oz orange juice

Triple sec (optional)

Fill half of a champagne flute with chilled sparkling wine or champagne (about an ounce) and top off with chilled orange juice (again about 2 ounces), gently stir. Add a splash or two of triple sec.

GIN

Tom Collins

1¹/₂ oz gin
³/₄ oz lemon juice
1 oz simple syrup
Club soda
Orange slice
Cherry

Combine gin, syrup, and
lemon juice and shake
with ice. Strain into an
ice-filled Collins glass. Fill
with club soda, stir, and
garnish with cherry and
orange slice.

Twentieth Century Cocktail

2 oz gin
$^1/_4$ oz white crème de cacao
$^1/_2$ oz Lillet Blonde
$^1/_4$ oz lemon juice

Shake ingredients with ice and strain into a chilled cocktail glass.

Alabama Slammer

1 oz amaretto
1 oz Tennessee whiskey
1/2 oz sloe gin
Splash of lemon juice

Pour above ingredients
into a stainless steel
shaker over ice and
shake until completely
cold. Strain into an old-
fashioned glass and serve.

Bramble

1¹/₂ oz gin
³/₄ oz fresh lime juice
³/₄ oz simple syrup
³/₄ oz creme de mure

Shake the gin, lime juice and syrup well with ice,
and strain into a highball glass filled with crushed
ice. Dribble the creme de mure down through the
ice, and garnish with a lime slice and blackberries.

Broux

1 oz dry vermouth
1 oz gin
Juice of ¼ orange
1 slice orange

Shake all ingredients (except orange
slice) with ice and strain into a goblet
glass. Add orange slice and serve.

Dirty Martini

3 oz gin
$^1/_4$ oz olive brine
Dash of dry vermouth
2 olives

Stir together gin, olive brine, and vermouth with ice and strain into a chilled cocktail glass. Garnish with two olives.

Extra Dry Martini

3 oz gin

Three drops of dry vermouth

Olive

Shake gin and vermouth with ice and strain into a chilled cocktail glass. Garnish with olive.

Gibson

1 1/2 oz gin
3/4 oz vermouth
2 cocktail onions

Stir gin and vermouth
over ice cubes in a
mixing glass. Strain
into a cocktail glass.
Add the cocktail onions
and serve.

Gimlet

2 ¹/₂ oz gin
¹/₂ oz preserved lime
juice
Lime wedge

Shake the gin and
juice with ice and
strain into a chilled
cocktail glass. Garnish
with lime wedge.

Gin and Tonic

2 oz gin
Tonic water
Lime wedge

Pour gin over ice in
a highball glass and
top with tonic water.
Squeeze in lime wedge.

Gin Fizz

2 oz gin
Juice of ½ lemon
1 tsp powdered sugar
Carbonated water

Shake gin, juice of
lemon, and powdered
sugar with ice and strain
into a highball glass over
two ice cubes. Fill with
carbonated water, stir,
garnish with a slice of
lemon and serve.

Gin Sling

2 oz gin
1 oz lemon juice
$^{1}/_{4}$ oz water
$^{1}/_{2}$ oz simple syrup
Lemon peel

Combine the gin, water, lemon juice, and syrup
and shake with ice. Strain into an ice-filled Collins
or highball glass. Garnish with lemon peel.

Greyhound

1 1/2 oz gin

5 oz grapefruit juice

Pour ingredients into an old fashioned glass
over ice cubes. Stir well and serve. (Vodka
may be substituted for gin, if preferred.)

Jasmine

1 1/2 oz gin
1/4 oz Cointreau orange
liqueur
1/4 oz Campari bitters
3/4 oz lemon juice
cracked ice

Stir with cracked ice
and strain into a chilled
cocktail glass. Garnish
with a twist of lemon peel.

Kyoto

3 oz gin

1 oz melon liqueur

$^1/_2$ oz dry vermouth

$^1/_4$ tsp fresh lemon juice

Pour all ingredients into a mixing glass half-filled with ice cubes. Stir well. Strain into a chilled cocktail glass. Garnish with a melon ball, and serve.

Martini

1 1/2 oz gin
1/2 oz dry vermouth

Stir with ice cubes,
and strain into a
chilled cocktail glass.
Garnish with an olive
or a twist of lemon.

Negroni

1 oz gin
1 oz sweet vermouth
1 oz bitters

Stir with ice and strain into a chilled
cocktail glass 3/4 filled with cracked ice.
Add a splash of soda water if desired.
Garnish with a half slice of orange.

Pink Gin

2 oz gin

3 dashes of Angostura
bitters

Lemon peel

Shake gin and bitters
with ice and strain into
a chilled cocktail glass.
Garnish with lemon peel.

Pink Lady

1 1/2 oz gin
1/4 oz grenadine
3/4 oz simple syrup
1 oz heavy cream

Shake ingredients with
ice and strain into a
chilled cocktail glass.

Ramos Gin Fizz

1 1/2 oz gin

1/2 oz lemon juice

1/2 oz lime juice

1 1/4 oz simple syrup

2 oz milk

1 egg white

2 drops orange-flower water

Club soda

Combine the gin, juices, milk, egg white, orange-flower water, and syrup and shake with ice. Strain into a chilled Collins glass. Fill with club soda and stir.

Salty Dog

1 1/2 oz vodka
1/4 oz Kahlúa
3/4 oz Godiva liqueur

Shake ingredients with ice and strain into a chilled cocktail glass.

The Darb

1 oz gin
³/₄ oz apricot brandy
³/₄ oz dry vermouth
³/₄ oz gin
1 tsp lemon juice

Pour all ingredients
into a cocktail shaker
half-filled with ice cubes.
Shake well. Strain into a
cocktail glass, garnish
with a twist of lemon,
and serve.

The Last Word

³/₄ oz gin
³/₄ oz green Chartreuse
³/₄ oz maraschino
liqueur
³/₄ oz fresh lime juice

Shake ingredients with
ice and strain into a
chilled martini glass.

Vesper

3 oz gin
1 oz vodka
$^1/_2$ oz lillet

Shake well until ice cold,
strain into a martini
glass. Add a twist of
lemon peel.

LIQUEURS &
SCHNAPPS

Amaretto Sour

1 1/2 oz Amaretto liqueur

1 oz simple syrup
(dissolve an equal
amount of sugar in water)

3/4 oz fresh lemon juice

1 orange slice

1 maraschino cherry

Pour the Amaretto, simple
syrup, and lemon juice
into a cocktail shaker
with ice. Shake and strain
into a glass filled with ice.
Garnish with an orange
slice and a cherry

Americano

1 oz Campari

1 oz sweet vermouth

Club soda

Lemon twist or orange slice for garnish

Fill an old-fashioned glass with ice cubes. Add the
Campari and vermouth. Top off with club soda.
Garnish with the lemon twist or orange slice.

$\mathcal{B}$-52

$^1/_2$ oz Kahlúa

$^1/_2$ oz Bailey's Irish Cream

$^1/_2$ oz Mandarine Napoléon

Layer the ingredients in a cordial glass in the order listed, from the bottom up.

Blue Bay

1 part Blue Curacao
liqueur

2 parts bitter lemon
soda

ice cubes

Mix in a highball glass.
Stir. Garnish with a slice
of lemon.

Chrysanthemum

2 oz dry vermouth

1¹/₂ oz benedictine herbal liqueur

1/4 tsp Pernod licorice liqueur

Pour the vermouth and benedictine into a mixing glass half-filled with cracked ice. Stir well. Strain into a cocktail glass. Add the Pernod, garnish with an orange twist, and serve.

Fuzzy Navel

1 part peach schnapps
1 part orange juice
1 part lemonade

Mix equal parts of each
ingredient in a martini
glass, top with ice,
garnish with an orange
slice and serve.

Golden Cadillac

1 oz herbal liquer
2 oz white creme de cacao
1 oz light cream

Combine all ingredients with 1/2 cup crushed ice in an electric blender. Blend at low speed for ten seconds. Strain into a martini glass and serve.

Golden Dream

2 oz Galliano herbal liqueur

1 oz white creme de cacao

¹/₂ oz triple sec

3 oz orange juice

3 oz light cream

ice cubes

Fill shaker glass one third full of ice cubes. Add galliano, cream de cacao, triple sec, orange juice (non pulp), and light cream. Shake vigorously until creamy and strain into a cocktail glass and garnish with slice of orange.

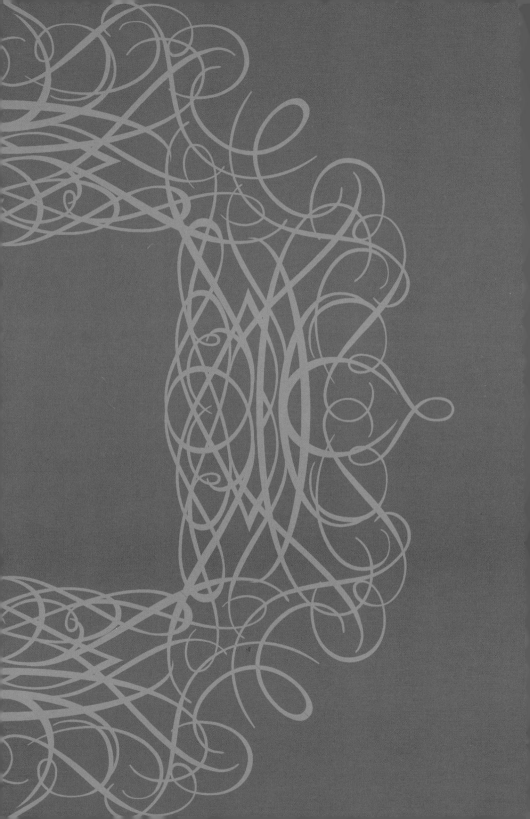

RUM

Bahama Mama

¹/₂ fluid oz rum

¹/₂ fluid oz coconut-
flavored rum

¹/₂ fluid oz grenadine
syrup

1 fluid oz orange juice

1 fluid oz pineapple juice

1 cup crushed ice

Combine regular rum,
flavored rum, grenadine,
orange juice, pineapple
juice and crushed ice
in an electric blender.
Blend until slushy.

Bella Donna

1 oz dark rum
1 oz light rum
1 oz cranberry juice
1 oz orange juice
1 oz pineapple juice

Shake ingredients in a
cocktail shaker with ice.
Strain into a glass full of
ice cubes.

Caipiriuha

2 tsp granulated sugar
8 lime wedges
2¹/₂ oz cachaca

Muddle the sugar into
the lime wedges in an
old-fashioned glass. Fill
the glass with ice cubes.
Pour the cachaca into
the glass. Stir well.

Dark and Stormy

2 oz rum

8 oz ginger beer

Pour rum over ice, add ginger beer, and stir.

Egg Nog

6 eggs, separated

$^3/_4$ cup sugar

1 quart milk

1 pint cream

5 oz bourbon

7 oz spiced rum

Nutmeg

Beat the egg yolks well, adding $^1/_2$ cup of the sugar while doing so. Add the milk, cream, and liquor. Then beat the egg whites with the remaining sugar until they peak. Fold the egg whites into the mixture. Sprinkle with fresh nutmeg.

Mojito

1¹/₂ oz light rum

1 oz simple syrup

³/₄ oz lime juice

2 sprigs fresh mint

Club soda

Muddle one mint sprig with the syrup and lime juice in
the bottom of a mixing glass. Add the rum and bitters
and shake with ice. Strain into an ice-filled highball
glass, top with soda, and garnish with mint sprig.

Painkiller

2 oz Mozart White
chocolate liqueur

1 oz Bacardi black rum

1 dash coconut syrup

1 dash orange liqueur

Mix well in a shaker
with three or four ice
cubes. Strain into an old-
fashioned glass, garnish
with a pineapple piece,
and serve.

Piña Colada

1 1/2 oz light rum

1 oz dark rum

2 oz Coco Lopez

1 oz heavy cream

4 oz pineapple juice

Dash of Angostura bitters

1 cup crushed ice

Pineapple wedge

Maraschino cherry

Combine rums, Coco Lopez, cream, pineapple juice, bitters, and ice in a blender and blend for about 15 seconds. Pour into a specialty glass and garnish with the pineapple and cherry.

Rum Swizzle

2 oz rum
Carbonated water
Juice of 1 lime
1 tsp powdered sugar
2 dashes bitters

Dissolve powdered
sugar in a mixture of
carbonated water and
juice of lime in a collins
glass. Fill with ice, stir,
and add bitters and rum.
Fill with carbonated
water, stir, and serve
with a swizzle stick.

Swimming Pool

1 scoop crushed ice

$1/4$ oz sweet cream

$3/4$ oz cream of coconut

2 oz pineapple juice

$3/4$ oz vodka

$1^1/2$ oz light rum

$1/4$ oz Blue Curacao liqueur

Mix ingredients well, pour into an exotic glass and float the blue curacao on top.

Ti Punch

2 oz Rhum Agricole
Lime(s)
Cane syrup

Mix rhum agricole, a good squeeze of lime,
and cane syrup to taste in an Old-Fashioned
glass. Stir until the syrup is dissolved and add
1 or 2 ice cubes. Garnish with lime wedges.

Tom and Jerry Punch

24 eggs

$^1/_2$ jigger rum

2 lb powdered sugar

$^1/_2$ jigger brandy

2 tsp cinnamon

$^1/_2$ cup boiling water

$^1/_2$ tsp nutmeg

$^1/_2$ oz vanilla

To make the base drink: beat egg whites stiff with an electric whisk. Add the sugar gradually, whisking as you go. Add the cinnamon, nutmeg and vanilla. Add in half of the eggs yolks, and blend until smooth.

For each serving half fill a glass with the base mix, add 2 shots of [60 percent rum and 40 percent brandy]. Balance with boiling hot water. Stir well and sprinkle with nutmeg.

TEQUILA

Classic Margarita

1 1/2 oz tequila

1 oz Cointreau

3/4 oz lime juice

Combine all ingredients in a mixer with ice
and shake well. Strain into a chilled margarita
or cocktail glass with a salted rim (to salt the
rim, moisten it with a piece of lime and dip
the outside of the rim in coarse salt).

El Diablo

2 oz tequila
³/₄ oz creme de cassis
1 lime wedge
Ginger ale

Stir tequila and creme de
cassis over ice in a chilled
collins glass. Fill with
ginger ale, squeeze in the
lime wedge's juice and
drop in the spent shell.

Frozen Margarita

1¹/₂ oz tequila
¹/₂ oz triple sec
1 oz lime juice
Lime slice

Combine ingredients
except lime slice in
a blender with 1 cup
crushed ice and blend
until smooth. Pour into
a cocktail glass and
garnish with lime slice.

Matador

1 oz Jose Cuervo Especial gold tequila

1 oz Red Bull energy drink

$^1/_3$ oz triple sec

1 oz frozen limeade concentrate

1 pinch salt

Combine all ingredients in a blender with half a cup
of crushed ice. Blend until slushy, adding more ice if
required. Pour into a cocktail glass, and serve.

Tequila Slammer

1 oz tequila
1 oz lemon-lime soda

Combine the
ingredients in a shot
glass. The drinker
should cover the glass
with a napkin and the
palm of one hand,
slam the glass on the
bar or table to agitate
the ingredients, and
drink immediately.

Tequila Sunrise

1 1/2 oz white tequila

4 oz lemon juice

Simple syrup

Grenadine syrup

Using the syrup, sweeten the lemon juice
to taste. Then pour tequila and then the
lemon juice over ice in a highball glass.
Top with a float of grenadine.

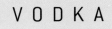

VODKA

Appletini

1 ¹/₂ oz vodka

1 oz green apple schnapps

¹/₄ oz lemon juice

Pour the ingredients into a cocktail shaker with ice cubes. Shake well. Strain into a chilled cocktail glass.

Black Russian

1 oz vodka
1 oz Kahlúa

Combine over ice in an old-fashioned
glass. No garnish.

Bloody Mary

1 1/2 oz vodka

2 dashes of Worcestershire sauce

4 dashes of Tabasco sauce

4 oz tomato juice

1/4 oz lemon juice

Pinch of salt and pepper

Lemon slice

Combine vodka, juices, sauces, and salt and pepper in a mixing glass with ice and roll to mix. Strain into a large goblet or pint glass nearly filled with ice. Garnish with lemon slice.

Blue Hawaii

1 oz Blue Curacao liqueur
1 oz vodka
1 oz sweet and sour mix
2 oz pineapple juice

Pour all ingredients into a shaker and shake thoroughly. Pour over crushed ice in a martini or highball glass, and serve.

Blue Lagoon

1 oz vodka

1 oz Blue Curacao
liqueur

Lemonade

1 cherry

Pour vodka and
curacao over ice in a
highball glass. Fill with
lemonade, top with the
cherry, and serve.

Blue Shark

¾ oz vodka

½ oz tequila

Blue Curacao liqueur

Combine vodka and rum in a cocktail
shaker with cracked ice. Add several
dashes of Blue Curacao, and shake well.
Strain into a chilled old-fashioned glass,
gardish with an orange slice, and serve.

Caesar Cocktail

1 1/2 oz vodka

clamato juice

3 dashes Tabasco sauce

3 dashes Worcestershire
sauce

Line the rim of a glass
with salt and pepper.
Over ice, add vodka,
fill with clamato juice,
then add the remaining
ingredients. Garnish with
a celery stick. Add more
tabasco sauce if desired.

Cape Cod

1 $\frac{1}{2}$ oz vodka
4 oz cranberry juice

Combine in a highball
glass with ice. Garnish
with a wedge of lime,
and serve.

Chi-Chi

1 1/2 oz vodka
4 oz pineapple juice
1 oz cream of coconut
1 slice pineapple
1 cherry

Blend vodka, pineapple juice, and cream of coconut with one cup ice in an electric blender at a high speed. Pour into a goblet or red wine glass, decorate with the slice of pineapple and the cherry, and serve.

Chocolate Martini

2 oz vodka
$1/2$ oz creme de cacao

Pour ingredients into
shaker filled with ice,
shake gently, then pour
into a martini glass.

Cosmopolitan

1 1/2 oz citron vodka
1/2 oz Cointreau
1/4 oz lime juice
1 oz cranberry juice
Orange peel

Shake all ingredients but orange peel with ice and strain into a chilled cocktail glass. Garnish with orange peel.

Harvey Wallbanger

1 1/2 oz vodka
4 oz orange juice
Galliano

Combine vodka and
orange juice over ice in a
highball glass. Top with a
float of Galliano.

Jungle Juice

1 shot Vodka

1 shot Rum

$^{1}/_{2}$ shot Cointreau triple sec

1 shot Cranberry juice

1 shot Freshly squeezed orange juice

1 shot Fresh pressed pineapple juice

$^{3}/_{4}$ shot Freshly squeezed lime juice

$^{1}/_{4}$ shot Sugar syrup (1 water : 2 sugar)

Shake all ingredients with ice and strain into ice-filled glass.

Lemon Drop

$^1/_2$ oz vodka

$^1/_2$ oz lemon juice

1 sugar cube

Add sugar to the rim of an old-fashioned glass, and drop a cube or packet of sugar into the bottom of the glass. Pour vodka and lemon juice into a stainless steel shaker over ice, and shake until completely cold. Pour into the prepared old-fashioned glass, and serve.

Long Island Iced Tea

$^1/_2$ oz vodka

$^1/_2$ oz gin

$^1/_2$ oz rum

$^1/_2$ oz tequila

$^1/_2$ oz triple sec

$^3/_4$ oz lemon juice

$^1/_2$ oz simple syrup

4 oz cola

Lemon wedge

Combine all liquids except cola and shake with ice. Strain into an ice-filled Collins glass, top with cola, and stir. Garnish with lemon wedge.

Madras

1 1/2 oz vodka
4 oz cranberry juice
1 oz orange juice
1 lime wedge

Pour all ingredients
(except lime wedge)
into a highball glass
over ice. Add the lime
wedge and serve.

Moscow Mule

1 $^1/_2$ oz vodka
5 oz ginger beer
Lime wedge

Combine vodka and
ginger beer over ice in a
highball glass. Garnish
with lime wedge.

Orgasm

$^1/_2$ oz white creme de cacao

$^1/_2$ oz amaretto almond liqueur

$^1/_2$ oz triple sec

$^1/_2$ oz vodka

1 oz light cream

Shake all ingredients with ice, strain into a chilled cocktail glass, and serve.

Screwdriver

1 1/2 oz Vodka
6 oz orange juice

Add vodka in an ice-filled glass
and top with orange juice.

Sea Breeze

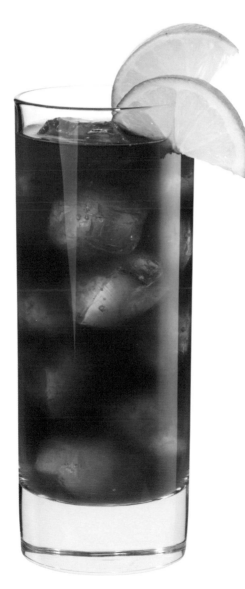

1 1/2 oz vodka

4 oz fresh grapefruit
juice

1 1/2 oz cranberry juice

Pour vodka into an
iced highball glass.
Fill partially with
grapefruit juice and top
with cranberry juice.
Garnish with a lime
wedge, and serve.

Sex On The Beach

1 1/2 oz vodka
1/2 oz peach schnapps
1/4 oz Chambord
2 oz cranberry juice
2 oz pineapple juice

Combine all ingredients
and shake with ice.
Strain into a highball
glass over ice.

White Russian

1 oz vodka

1 oz Kahlúa

1 oz heavy cream

Shake ingredients with ice and strain
into an old-fashioned glass.

WHISKEY

BMW

1 shot Bailey's Irish
cream

1 shot Malibu coconut
rum

1 shot whisky

Pour carefully in the
order listed.

Highball

1 1/2 oz whiskey
Fill with ginger ale

Fill a highball glass most of the way with
4 – 5 ice cubes. Add the whiskey, and fill
the rest up of the way with ginger ale.

Hot Whiskey Toddy

1 oz whiskey of choice
1 tbsp honey
1 cinnamon stick
1 pinch ground nutmeg
¼ lemon
1 cup hot tea

Pour the honey in an
Irish coffee glass. Add
the whiskey, spices and
the squeezed juice of
the lemon quarter and
top with the tea.

Manhattan

2 oz rye or bourbon
whiskey

1 oz sweet vermouth

2 dashes of Angostura
bitters

Cherry

Stir the whiskey,
vermouth, and bitters
with ice in a mixing
glass and strain into a
chilled cocktail glass.
Garnish with cherry.

Milk Punch

3 oz bourbon whiskey
3 oz milk
$^1/_2$ tsp dark rum
1 tbsp sugar syrup
Nutmeg

Shake liquors and milk
with cracked ice and
sugar syrup and strain
into a chilled highball
glass. Sprinkle nutmeg
on top and serve.

Millionaire

1 1/2 oz Canadian whisky
1/2 oz triple sec
1/3 oz grenadine syrup
1/2 oz egg white
1 tsp pastis liqueur

Shake well and strain into
a double-cocktail glass
filled with broken ice.

Old Fashioned

2 oz bourbon

1 tsp superfine sugar

2 dashes of Angostura bitters

2 orange slices

2 maraschino cherries

Club soda (or plain water)

In the bottom of an old-fashioned glass, muddle one
each of the orange slices and cherries with the sugar,
the bitters, and a splash of soda. Remove the muddled
orange and add the bourbon, some ice, and soda.
Garnish with remaining orange slice and cherry.

Robert Burns

2 oz Scotch
$3/4$ oz sweet vermouth
Dash of orange bitters
Dash of absinthe

Pour the ingredients
into a cocktail shaker
filled with ice. Stir well.
Strain into a chilled
cocktail glass.

Rusty Nail

1¹/₂ oz Scotch whisky

¹/₂ oz Drambuie Scotch whisky

1 twist lemon peel

Pour the scotch and drambuie into an old-fashioned glass almost filled with ice cubes. Stir well. Garnish with the lemon twist.

Washington Apple

¹/₃ oz whiskey

¹/₃ oz Sour Apple schnapps

¹/₃ oz cranberry juice

Mix all ingredients in shaker with ice. Strain into shot glass, or pour over ice in a rocks glass.

Whiskey Smash

2 pieces lemons

2 – 3 mint leaves

³/₄ oz simple syrup

1¹/₂ oz Maker's Mark bourbon whiskey

1 oz water

Muddle the lemon, mint, water and simply syrup in the bottom of a mixing glass. Add bourbon, shake, and strain into an old-fashioned glass filled with crushed ice. Garnish with a sprig of mint, and serve.

Whiskey Sour

2 oz whiskey of choice
³/₄ oz lemon juice
1 oz simple syrup
Orange slice

Combine all ingredients
but orange slice and
shake well with ice.
Strain into a sour
glass and garnish with
orange slice.